DELICATE FRIENDS

by Oscar Revelins

1

In hindsight, it never could have worked out. Something told me even back then, a subtle itch of wrongness that crept in while staring at the living room wall with a cold beer pressed against my cheek. I was studying the various black marks and scratches that tarnished the eggshell white, imagining that the imperfections told stories from before I'd moved in. I liked to search for meaning in things where there probably was none. Perhaps a drunken stumble had occurred; dirty fingers reaching across the plaster to keep someone upright, or a late-night kiss pushed up against it, back-pocket-keys carving thin lines. The possibilities were numerous.

The glass bottle soothed my flushed skin, a sure way to escape the punishing heat without using the air conditioning unit, which Juliana refused to turn on because the bills were too expensive. I thought about offering to cover them in full, just to establish a sense of control over our apartment, but I decided it might make her feel cheap. I was the recent addition, the fresh expat. It was far too early for demands, and I didn't want to worsen my situation by saying something out of line. For all I knew, it was only the East-to-West temperature adjustment causing my apprehension, but instincts are a powerful thing, and mine were alert with the idea that this was all a misguided decision with far-reaching consequences. Only time would tell.

'Are you gonna drink that or just use it as an ice pack?' Alé asked while sipping on an identical beer, breaking my staring contest with the wall. He'd been relegated to the floor at the risk of ruining the couch with his wet board shorts. Salt flakes crusted to his dark hair and eyebrows.

'Doesn't everyone prefer warm beer?' I joked.

'You Aussies will drink anything.'

'Nah,' Juliana called from the kitchen. 'Austin's classy. I can tell.'

I turned my head to catch her eyes before her attention dropped back to the salad bowl. She splashed some lettuce leaves with balsamic and set them off to the side.

'I'll take that as a compliment,' I said.

'It is.' She turned away to face the stove.

There was a particular unease found in reaching out to a stranger on social media and agreeing to move in with her, and I knew Juliana felt it too. We were still in the process of sussing each other out, trying to determine if this was going to work out. It didn't matter that we were cousins, we had no history. No Christmas cards or birthday wishes, no extended family vacations – though it was nice to have an invisible thread to anyone, despite that thread lacking strength. Even our features betrayed relatability. I was pale where she was tan, I was thin where she was curved. No one would've made an association through blood.

'Baby, can we do anything to help?' Alé cooed at her.

'No, no, I'm nearly done.'

She was insistent on doing everything herself and I wondered if it was out of compensation. After two weeks of living together, it was our first meal as a household, and Alé was the only person I'd been introduced to. I hadn't expected her to roll out the Welcome Wagon or anything, but our lack of interaction was obvious, and I had spent the last two weeks in Perth mostly alone, meandering about in an attempt to outrun loneliness. I slept around a bit (three different men I'd all met through hookup apps) but sex was an inconsistent and fleeting distraction. Getting a job at the café down the road was more effective – despite the staff being less than friendly. I probably deserved it because of how useless I was, but I just needed something to keep me occupied, no matter how banal or degrading.

Alé set his beer down and leaned back on his hands. 'Liking the place?'

'Yeah, absolutely,' I nodded unconvincingly. 'Great location.'

Ours was a two-bedroom unit nestled amongst a row of red-bricked mid-century apartments, a few blocks away from the beach. At this time of year, the water was dead-still and turquoise, folding passively against smooth bleached sand. Even though I didn't have a direct view of the sea, I could taste the lingering salt in the air. It was everywhere, thickened by the heat.

'Sure…' he said, his voice laced with sarcasm. 'Everyone wants to live in the *GT* apparently.'

Juliana had taught me that the Golden Triangle was another name for the western suburbs of Perth. Their radius changed depending on who you asked; some claimed the triangle stretched up to Nedlands, but most Perth elites resided between Dalkeith, Cottesloe, and Mosman Park, with Peppermint Grove between the three points. A single train line divided the ocean-view mansions from the cliffside estates. There were golf courses, brunch spots, and overpriced grocery stores. Lush pine trees dotted every block. We were on the outskirts, in the old apartments that begged to be knocked down for newer, glossier complexes. Juliana said you could tell who'd grown up there, who'd gone to the private schools, who'd decided that their postcode was a way of life.

'Were you GT born and raised?' I asked Alé.

He laughed loudly. 'I'm Brazilian, if you couldn't tell.'

I *could*, but it seemed rude to assume.

'Like Juliana,' he continued. 'But I moved a few years later, for university. That's where we first met.'

'Did you know my Mum and Dad were never together?' Juliana threw over her shoulder. The steaks sizzling in the cast iron skillet had filled the room with a heavy cajun-tinged smoke.

'I didn't, no.'

Details had always been scarce. We were the wealthy side of the family, the side that had had nothing to do with Juliana and her father since he'd begged to borrow money and was promptly denied. It was only mentioned a handful of times but with enough conviction to make an impression. I knew it was part of the reason why our families weren't close.

'I was an accident. A one-night stand while Dad was travelling through Salvador,' she said casually.

I had to respect her bluntness.

'Mum decided to keep me, raise me on her own, and they stayed on platonic terms. Hardly knew him until I was about ten.' The steaks were done. Juliana turned off the stove and wiped her hands on a balled-up tea towel. 'We visited Australia a few times, and then I moved to Perth permanently for boarding school.'

'Shit.' I blinked. 'Huge move at such a young age.'

'It wasn't easy. Mum was heartbroken, she missed me like crazy. And Dad was doing FIFO up in Broome, so he wasn't always around. But the quality of education was worth it.'

'FIFO? Like–'

'Fly in, fly out,' she explained. 'It's big over here in WA. Lots of people travelling to mine sites, oil rigs…'

'We're teaching him so much,' Alé said. 'Reminds me of when we first moved.' His expression quickly turned serious.

'There's a huge Brazilian population in Perth and yet we still get these looks. Like we shouldn't be here. You know what I mean?' Then he lowered his voice and said, 'Dunno how she stomachs this area in particular. The *caucacity*…'

'That's just Perth in general,' Juliana said, having heard him perfectly.

'Yeah, but the worst ones are here.'

Juliana transferred the steaks to a plate and carried it with the salad bowl to the dining table. We joined her, taking our beers with us. I finally cracked mine with the bottle opener and drank it, my face having cooled down enough.

'Looks amazing. Thank you,' I said.

Alé agreed, and we took turns dispersing the food onto our plates.

'When you say the worst ones…' I said between scoops of salad. 'Like…?'

'White, wealthy,' Juliana answered simply.

I tried not to cringe. I knew it wasn't a personal attack, but I couldn't deny the description applied to me.

'It's a bit of a who-knows-who. Perth is already so small, and the GT is even smaller. Just be prepared for people to ask you your last name and what school you attended.'

'Seriously?'

'It's how they know if you're one of them,' Alé added with a smirk. 'Everyone's expected to have some sort of connection to each other. The same alma mater, or family ties… Otherwise, you've got nothing to offer.'

'I went to PLC, and still I was never one of them,' Juliana said. Realising I wouldn't know what PLC meant, she tacked on, '*Presbyterian Ladies College*,' in her best high-brow Australian accent. It sounded closer to British. 'It doesn't even matter who you are and what you've done if you don't look the part.'

'And now she's their neighbour,' Alé sighed. 'As if she didn't get enough of those stuck-up bitches living as a boarder.'

'That's such a gross word for a guy to use.'

'*Boarder?*'

'*Bitches,*' she snapped, unamused. He blushed beside her, but he didn't apologise. 'Besides, Sierra went to PLC. They weren't all like that. Lots of great girls, and some were on scholarships like me.'

Alé shook his head. 'Sierra can be a piece of work. And even the ones on scholarships were a bit fucking racist now and then. The institutions—'

'The institutions? Please.'

'You know what I mean. All the private schools.'

'This is the most political I've ever heard him, by the way,' Juliana directed at me with a smile, clearly trying to defuse the rising tension. 'I think he's just showing off for you because he knows you're an intellectual.'

'I am?' I tried to ignore the nagging feeling of being backed into a corner, at risk of saying the wrong thing.

'Man, you said you studied English Lit and read books for fun,' Alé said. 'That's *so* intellectual. You'll straight up be a teacher one day, right?'

'Absolutely not,' I said quickly. 'I just like reading. But I hate kids.'

Juliana cocked her head. 'So what do you want to do with an English degree?'

'Honestly? I have no idea.'

It wasn't like I was putting my studies to much use at the café. It was a sad little thing; faded brick and linoleum floors, counting the days before it was torn down and gentrified into a soulless sparkling white cube that only used alternative milk. Leslie, the other barista, was forced to take on the role of my mentor. I wasn't allowed to touch the milk steamer for a week, allocated only to 'dispensing shots': the joyous task of packing the coffee grounds into the group heads, pressing a single button, and waiting for the water to drip through. The girl working the floor was Daisy, barely passing eighteen, but I was a petulant child in her eyes. She tutted and sighed alongside Leslie at every mistake I made, and there were many. I wanted to quit immediately after I'd clocked off, but being unemployed would poke holes in the charade I was trying very hard to establish in Perth, a charade which involved being down-to-Earth, approachable, and effortlessly happy.

'Well,' Alé muttered, 'The locals are entitled as fuck. You'd agree with me if you knew them.'

'Austin would probably fit right in,' Juliana said. 'He's just… *Melbourne-ised.*' She turned her head to me and added, 'No offence.'

'Offence taken!' I said, pained. 'I'm not–'

'God, sorry. I know,' she clarified quickly. 'I just mean… You're a white Australian. You come from money, a private school education.'

I blushed and looked down at my plate, confronted by how much more information she knew than she'd originally let on.

Juliana let out an exasperated sigh. 'You don't need to be embarrassed. It's just the way it is. It doesn't make you a bad person, it just means you have to work harder to be a decent one.'

'Is it okay if you don't… mention that to people? The whole wealthy thing?'

Juliana blinked at me. 'Why?'

'It just makes me uncomfortable is all.'

It looked like she was going to protest, or bring up the

elephant in the room – the unspoken grief she knew existed – but perhaps out of respect or because we weren't close enough to address it, she just smiled and nodded her head slowly. 'Sure. I get it.' Then she turned to Alé and said, 'And I choose to live here because it's an amazing price for the area and I love the ocean. I know you love it too, since you swim in it every other evening, so the bloody gatekeepers can fuck right off. We make our own space to belong.'

'You're right, I'm sorry,' Alé said, taking her hand and kissing it. He said something in Portuguese, and she visibly relaxed. The inflections and sounds in their language were like rushing water. 'God knows I'd hate being stuck out north full time. We're very lucky you have this place.' Then he directed at me, 'Even if we don't fit the demographic,' in a way that acknowledged how I, on the other hand, did.

I noticed it too, working at the café, how many customers looked eerily similar to the one before, with only a discrepancy in gender and generation, a blend of carelessness and impatience, and a routine that was not to be disturbed by an unfamiliar face. They needed their coffees extra-hot and there was always too much chocolate powder on the top. A wait of five minutes was slow. The coffee was better yesterday. I struggled to shrug it off. It was my first job in hospitality, my first job ever. The world looked very different being the server, rather than the one served. I had gone through life rarely hearing 'No' or 'Wait' before, or knowing what it meant to work hard, all on my own, finding despair in a nine-to-five, feeling like an outsider begging for social scraps in the form of housemate dinners.

Throwing twenty years of sheltered Melbourne privilege to the wolves and starting anew in one of the most isolated cities in the world was far more difficult than I had anticipated. All I knew was that it would've been impossible to be happy (or even pretend at happiness) if I'd stayed in Melbourne. So I moved as far away as I could without leaving the country and ended up seated at a Kmart dining table in Mosman Park, struggling to find commonality over steaks and salad. Perhaps one day Juliana and Alé would both become my close friends, but for now, they were a springboard for me to bounce into adjacent social groups normally inaccessible. I simply needed to find one to insert myself into, cementing this clean slate, this new-and-improved Austin.

2

After several turns, Juliana and I were on the highway towards the CBD, parallel to the bay. The water was dark and choppy, catching dapples of gold and silver from streetlights, skyscraper windows, and moonlight. I found it unexpectedly beautiful. It was certainly superior to the route coming from the airport, south of the river, with its warehouses and outlet shopping centres, drive-throughs and petrol stations. We passed a university made up of stone arches and clock towers (this was UWA, where Juliana and Alé had met), and further along, a jetty with a little blue boathouse at the end, and a brewery on the water's edge. Closer to the city, the few skyscrapers that dared to reach for the clouds were no architectural achievement, but their height and cluster gave the appearance of a bustling downtown, despite the emptiness of the streets below. It was like an apocalypse had come and gone without our knowledge. According to Juliana, this was how Perth had always been.

'I meant to do this ages ago,' she said. 'Take you out, I mean. It's just been—'

'No, of course. Don't stress. I really appreciate it.'

'You'll love Sierra.'

'I'm sure I will.' I smiled at the windscreen. After that, she turned the music up so we didn't have to continue engaging in conversation for the rest of the drive.

We parked in one of the free lots and walked the rest of the way to the cocktail bar. The inside buzzed with indistinct chatter and industrial light fixtures. Steel beams lined the ceiling and little black round tables lingered in the shadows. A girl with auburn hair close to Juliana's age sat at the bar, her elbows resting on the counter, an empty wine glass to her left. She gazed around the room absent-mindedly, before lighting up at the sight of Juliana striding towards her. The fabric of her dress may have restricted her movement because she made no effort to climb off the barstool. Juliana came to her instead and buried her face into her neck.

'Hi,' came Juliana's muffled greeting.

'*Jules!*' She locked her arms around Juliana's lower back. 'God, I've missed you. You're working too much.'

'I know.'

'And with Alé too much.'

'I know.'

I hung back, not wanting to interrupt their reunion.

'Sierra, this is my cousin, Austin,' she said, pulling herself from the embrace and presenting me. Sierra's eyes flickered unhappily from my shoes up to my hair, taking me in. Juliana clearly hadn't told her I was coming. I deepened in colour.

'Lovely to meet you!' I managed.

'And you as well!' Sierra said, regaining her composure. She opened her arms wide and awaited my embrace. I obliged with a bear hug and felt the exposed skin on her back, smooth to the touch.

'Is here okay, or should we grab a table? I wasn't aware we needed space for three.'

'Here's great,' Juliana said, sliding onto one of the barstools. She left the spot between her and Sierra vacant, so I ended up between the two girls.

Sierra's fingers twinkled to flag down the bartender, and she ordered us three martinis. He made a show of it, pouring from great heights and stirring loudly, before dragging a lemon peel along the rim of each glass. I wasn't sure it would make much of a difference to the flavour. We clinked glasses and sipped. My nose immediately wrinkled in disgust. I hated to admit how painful I found the taste of gin – as if disliking the liquor attested my immaturity.

'So. Austin. How have I never heard of you?' Sierra murmured, studying me intently.

'Juliana keeps me humble.'

'What school did you go to?'

I could see Juliana smothering a laugh into her drink.

'I'm from Melbourne, actually,' I said, sitting up straighter on the barstool.

'Huh.'

'We were never in contact until a few weeks ago. I just reached out on Facebook and ended up moving into her spare room like an absolute psycho.'

'That *is* kind of nuts.'

'It runs in the family,' I shrugged.

'I've missed a lot, haven't I?' Sierra was shaking her head as if it was all too much to process. Sitting between them made everything more uncomfortable. 'I guess we need to have a proper catch-up soon,' she directed to my cousin.

'Aren't we catching up now?' Juliana frowned.

Sierra pursed her lips briefly before smoothing them out into a smile. 'Of course we are. Tell me everything.'

There was something effortless about the way she held herself. Maybe this was just a natural skill that beautiful people had. Her hair was coloured too meticulously to be a box dye job and the fabric of her dress had a luxurious shine to it. I decided she must be wealthy. She had an ease and gen-erosity in the way most of us with money did. The cost of things had little to no value, so buying a round of drinks or shouting lunch was never a big deal. It was a shrug, a smile, and a flash of the Amex.

The girls mostly talked around me as if I were a pillar separating them. Mentions of names I'd never heard and places I'd never been, though sometimes Sierra would ask me specific questions, like, 'Why did you move to *Perth*? Everyone seems to be leaving here to go to Melbourne, not the other way round.'

'I've lived there my whole life. I just felt like a change,' came my over-rehearsed reply. It was succinct and satisfied most people's curiosity – but not Sierra's.

'Why not go to Sydney? Or like… anywhere else?'

'You're making Perth sound like a last resort,' Juliana said.

'It is. This place is stifling.' Her nose wrinkled. 'I can't wait to move away.'

'Do you know where you'll head next?' I asked.

'Not sure. But somewhere at some point over the next few years,' she replied, as if this was a comprehensive answer. I started to wonder how many times she had made this statement over the course of her life and never followed through.

I asked Sierra what she did for work as she downed her last sip. In between ordering another round, she told me about her father's firm and how deeply she hated the world of corporate law. She had an arts degree after all, and receptionist duties were apparently beneath her. I didn't think she'd meant to sound pretentious, but entitlement oozed from her dissatisfaction. Juliana said she was jealous – that stockbroking was basically just moving money around. They considered doing a *Freaky Friday* and swapping jobs.

The bartender placed fresh drinks in front of us, directing a flirtatious grin at Sierra. She returned it, but only briefly. Those few seconds must've thrilled him. Meanwhile, Sierra looked immediately bored by the attention.

'I'm working at a café around the corner from the apartment,' I told her when she asked me in return. 'The one next to the bookstore?'

'Yeah, I've been there. It's cute.'

'It's a job,' I shrugged.

I could've mentioned the inheritance that was sitting in my bank account and I knew Sierra wouldn't have batted an eye. But I said nothing, not to her or to Juliana. I figured it would've put more pressure on an already tentative dynamic, and she probably thought I'd be crazy for working an eight-to-four in a café and living in the Mosman Park apartment when I could've easily afforded my own place. How could I explain I just wanted to act out a different kind of life for a while? All I desired was surface-level companionship and distraction, which sounded relatively problematic when admitted out loud.

'And you're enjoying the area? I'm in the next neighbourhood from you guys. Still living at home but… Why not, right?'

I couldn't help but feel like I was being interviewed.

'For sure, I mean, the GT–'

'The *GT!* He learns so quickly, it's adorable,' she beamed to Juliana, clearly warming up to me now. 'I'm sure it'll never be as trendy as what you're used to in *Melbourne*, but we try our best.'

The inflection on *Melbourne* had a weight to it. I guessed she was insinuating I was part of the majority that saw Melbourne as a cultural hub of arts and design, whereas Perth was a retirement village for mining dynasties, absent of life and culture. Beneath us in every way. She was pleased to hear me report that I was happy with what I'd seen so far, even if it wasn't entirely true.

'Have you taken him for a dance yet?' This was directed at

Juliana.

'This is our first night out, actually,' Juliana confessed.

'He's been here for two weeks, and you haven't had a night out?'

'We've both been busy,' I said, trying to save Juliana from Sierra's glower. 'Perth, you know. Moves so fast.'

She either didn't catch my sarcasm or ignored it. 'Well, we should all go! Tonight! Marion's at The Court.'

'Marion? God, I haven't seen her in ages.'

'Then…?'

'But The Court is full of eighteen year olds. And they only play bad remixes of pop songs.'

'What, you're too cool for pop music now?'

'I'd be keen to check it out,' I offered. I wanted to dance, to flirt, to solidify a new friendship, all the things a normal twenty-year-old in a new city was supposed to be doing.

'Come on, Jules.'

'I drove my car,' Juliana said, her final defence.

'Oh.' Sierra's energy subdued like a deflated balloon, then perked up with, 'Do you want some coke? It'll sober you up.'

Juliana couldn't find the words to deny her, so after the last of our martinis had been downed, we piled into the disabled cubicle and took turns snorting the white powder off her car keys. It singed the inside of my nose and slowly trickled to the back of my throat. Not as pure as the stuff we'd get in Melbourne, but I bit my tongue at the risk of sounding like those elitist pricks Juliana hated so much.

'Do you do other drugs, Austin?' Sierra asked.

'I try to avoid any major psychedelics,' I replied with nonchalance. 'I'm worried it'll kick off some kind of psychological break.'

Sierra stared at me. 'Really?'

The moment was suddenly grave and I quickly shook my

head, abandoning the idea. 'That was a joke. Don't take anything I say seriously.'

'Noted.'

'That's me with ketamine though,' Juliana said. 'Sends me into a bad spiral.'

'Probably because it has meth in it,' I offered.

'All the drugs in Perth probably have meth in them.'

Someone pounded on the door with impatience. We giggled like caught schoolchildren and wiped our nostrils clean.

'Shall we?' Sierra pushed the door open.

The woman waiting for the toilet shot us a dirty look as we piled out and beelined for the exit.

Out on the street, the girls stormed ahead, wobbling and clinging to each other to stay upright. They were much drunker than I was, which was to be expected considering our height difference. I might've sobered up from the bump, but I was fairly certain it hadn't had much of an effect, aside from that quick thrill of doing something illegal. The air smelled of vomit and cigarette smoke. The city was dirtier deeper into Northbridge, with neon signs advertising kebab shops, Wilson car parking lots, and karaoke bars. A girl in fishnets and a spiked choker exhaled mint-flavoured clouds from her vape. A group of teenagers threw a glass bottle against a curb. A large man in an AFL guernsey urinated into a corner. All around us, the streets vibrated with the sounds of nearby clubs and the blaring of car horns.

We slotted into the queue for The Court and pulled out our IDs. Sierra peered down at the prepubescent face on my driver's licence and tapped on the date of birth.

'You're only twenty?' She exclaimed. 'God, I had no idea. You seem so mature.'

'I get that a lot.' I looked down at the photo of that freshly eighteen-year-old boy I didn't recognise anymore, with his chocolate ringlets and doe eyes – the boy who seemed utterly incapable of fending for himself. Life hadn't completely hardened him up yet. It hadn't taken his joy.

The line pushed forward. Our IDs were scanned on big black machines – Perth hadn't fully transitioned to using iPads yet – and photos of our faces were taken before we paid the twenty-dollar entry fee. Juliana complained it was steep, but Sierra promised to buy our first round. No one reminded her she'd paid for the last one too.

She led us past the front bar, hooked a right down a concrete ramp, and out to the back amphitheater. As we drew deeper into the building – much larger than its facade gave away – the thudding base from a Dua Lipa remix grew more persistent. Green lasers flashed over our heads, and the dance floor bled out like a punctured artery, bodies flooding into any open space. There wasn't a second that went by without brushing up against another person. I could feel the coke too, like a switch had been flipped. A buzzing deep in my chest, tension in my jaw. The music, the lights, and the people amplified it all.

'You know this used to be a gay bar?' Juliana said to me over the music.

I blinked at her. We'd never discussed my sexuality before, and I wondered if this was her subtle way of saying *I know what you are*. Perhaps she didn't care, or this was just a statement with no deeper meaning.

'No, I didn't know that,' was all I said.

'All the *eshays* showed up a few years ago and ruined the vibe. But they left the pride flags on the wall and do a few drag shows as if it makes up for it.'

'Now there's really only Connections,' Sierra added. 'One of the last gay bars left in the city.'

I couldn't decide if the girls were testing me or simply making conversation. I wasn't intentionally hiding my identity; I just didn't feel any desire to have my sexuality oversaturate any early impressions. Sometimes I felt there was an expectation that came with being homosexual. An awaited performance. *Be funny. Be witty.* Surely I could be all of those things completely separately from who I slept with.

Juliana glanced down at something on her phone while Sierra scanned the crowd, eyes wide and determined in search of this Marion person.

'Should I get us some drinks?' I said, straining to carry my voice over the noise.

'Take my card.' Sierra reached for her wallet.

'No, no. On me.'

'Soda water, please,' Juliana said.

'And I'll have something strong,' Sierra smiled. I left them behind on the outskirts of the mosh pit, braving the crowd in pursuit of the bar.

In hindsight, I should've walked around. The throng was so dense, it was almost impenetrable. Bodies pressed down from all sides. I could smell their sweat, and feel their hot liquor-stained breath on my face and neck. There were tangles of arms, legs, and loose hair tossed about. With the strobing lights, I was quickly losing direction to the bar. I did my best to slip through the gaps of people, but like a revolving maze, doorways opened and shut every few steps. I was able to see over most of the bobbing heads. Some refused to move, and I was forced to push around them. It was suffocating. *A few more steps. A few more people to push past.* The crowd thinned; the bar just ahead.

And there he was.

3

He stood alone at the edge of the bar, fingers wrapped tightly around a cold glass. My eyes followed his broad back, down strong arms, over tight denim jeans, and finished at the crisp white Nikes. He was angled to the side, so I could see his front too; golden hair sculpted, clipped sides connecting to a thick blonde stubble, thin lips above a square jaw. Fair skin, far too pale to make any sense in Perth when juxtaposed against everyone else's sun-kissed colouring. English heritage perhaps, or he might've been nocturnal. He focused lazily on a section of the dance floor as if waiting for something interesting to emerge from it. He wasn't strikingly unique or particularly breathtaking, but when he looked at me, I wanted nothing more than to feel the entire weight of him on top of me. It was like I'd been punched. My groin swelled and my mouth watered. Our eyes met for a moment longer than they should have. Something hummed, unspoken and fleeting. I wasn't sure who looked away first. I liked to think it happened at the same time, though it was probably him.

That was it. Brief but visceral. Perhaps it was the horniness, the loneliness, the cocaine, or a combination of the three, but it had been a long time since I'd yearned for a complete stranger in such a way. It was childish and over-romanticised, and somehow the most real thing I'd felt since arriving in Perth. I ordered two Long Islands and a soda water for Juliana. While the bartender began to pour, I sneaked a glance back in his direction, but he had withdrawn into the crowd somewhere. I didn't want to admit I was disappointed. There were pretty people everywhere. What was I going to do, walk up to him and introduce myself? Perhaps if we were at the gay club and I was feeling braver from stronger substances.

I gathered up the three drinks in search of Juliana and Sierra. They wobbled in my hands and dripped onto my fingers. I didn't make it far before the girls found me with a third trailing behind. This was Marion, clad in black shorts and white Converse. Her eyebrows were pencil thin, and her brown hair fell flat and dry by her rounded cheeks. When she said, 'Nice to meet you,' in greeting, her voice was gruff and deep like a smoker's. Shouldered by the two girls with dolled-up hair and tight outfits, she looked plain and brawny by comparison.

'Did you bring Ezra with you?' Sierra asked Marion. Her breasts looked pushed up, and the fingers she twirled in her hair moved with an agenda.

'He's getting me another drink,' she said.

'And Matteo and Nadia? Are they here too?'

'Nah, just us tonight.'

I couldn't put my finger on the shift that had occurred. Juliana was impassive, Sierra, unsettled, and Marion might've been bored. I wondered if they'd gotten into a row or if they just didn't like each other that much.

'How did you guys all meet?' I asked, digging for conversations.

'Marion and I went to uni together,' Sierra said. 'I met Ezra through her, and Juliana met Marion and Ezra through me.' She looked fairly proud of herself for being the glue holding this trio together.

'Are you from Perth?' Marion asked me.

'Melbourne.'

'Oh.' One word, one syllable, but the tone said everything it needed to. 'Visiting?'

'I just moved here.'

'Oh. Why?' I took a moment to acknowledge she wasn't being intentionally abrasive – it was just the cadence of her voice. I was also quick to realise how repetitive my introductions had become; questions, assumptions, and judgements. There always had to be an explanation.

'Um–'

Juliana came to my rescue. 'Austin's taking a little break from the depressing east coast. If we're nice to him, maybe he'll stick around.'

'I doubt it,' Marion said with a half smile. 'I hope you like it so far.'

'Yeah, thanks. Still settling in.'

'What's it like living with Juliana?'

'Lonely,' I said, an attempt at a joke, but the delivery was flat. Sierra and Marion laughed but Juliana shot me a glance somewhere between surprise and betrayal. I bit the inside of my lip and stared down at my drink.

'That's probably because she's chained to Alé,' Sierra egged on. 'I never even see her anymore.' It could've been light teasing if it hadn't sounded so venomous.

Juliana sipped her drink, refusing to respond.

'I'll take some loneliness if you've got extra,' Marion said. 'Can't remember the last time Ezra gave me a moment to myself.'

'And what exactly would you do without me?'

I turned and found him there. He still held the same glass from earlier, untouched. It seemed to function as an accessory, a prop to hold and gesture with, rather than something consumable. In his other hand was a fresh cocktail that he passed to Marion.

'I'd leave all the cupboards open and watch that trashy reality TV you hate so much,' Marion said, taking the drink. He pretended to look horrified.

'There he is!' Sierra cried, drunkenly tossing her arms around his shoulders and nearly spilling half of her drink down his back. 'It's been a minute.'

He returned the embrace and gave Juliana one next before studying me. His eyes reflected no thought or opinion. Whatever intimacy I thought occurred between us in those seconds we locked eyes by the bar drowned in his passive acknowledgment.

'Ezra.' He extended his hand and we shook loosely. No electricity, not even a spark.

'Austin.' Our arms returned to our sides and I immediately felt like an idiot for thinking we'd shared some kind of special moment.

Marion glued herself by his side and leaned her head against his shoulder. Of course he was straight, though the two of them made an aesthetically odd couple. She was stout and masculine where he was manicured and graceful. If it was true what they said about opposites and attraction, they must've been magnets. I wondered what he saw in Marion and I hated that I cared so much.

The DJ played *Untouched* by The Veronicas and Sierra demanded we hit the dance floor. I downed my Long Island, plastered on a smile and pretended to be enjoying myself. Truthfully, I wanted to sneak off and find someone else to hook up with out of sheer jealousy, but I'd been biding my time for invites and cutting the night prematurely would've been a sure way to never receive another one. The ground was covered with broken glass but we danced on top of it anyway. The crowd didn't provide much choice, a pocket had opened up and there we remained, a circle of five facing into each other. Ezra was directly across from me. A vulnerability emerged being watched unawares, and when I looked at him, I saw his guard drop. He was jumping up and down with his eyes closed. Shoulders loose. Smiling. Carefree. I started to jump as well, right as his eyes opened again, and we made eye contact a few centimetres off the ground in perfect synchronicity, suddenly grinning ear to ear despite ourselves.

I imagined pressing up against him, holding his hips, losing ourselves in the music, in the liquor, in the sweat. Rhythmic grinding, swaying, bouncing. How his body would feel against mine. I thought about prying him away from Marion and pulling him into a bathroom stall, getting down on my knees and proving to him how skilled I was with my hands and mouth. I'd done it before, in stalls, with people I shouldn't have. There had been friends back in Melbourne, bi-curious or closeted, some of them with girlfriends. I did it anyway. I loved the feeling it gave me, the control of their orgasm, the intimacy of a shared secret, of a promise not to tell. Lies and secrets were potent drugs. Addictive too.

I thought we'd be dancing for hours, but by midnight, Ezra and Marion were saying their goodbyes. Sierra was wasted and begged them to stay through slurred words. Marion shook her head, holding firm. 'We've got an early start tomorrow. But I'll see you girls and Alé down south for my birthday?' She was polite but final, and Sierra's pleas were pacified. She held her wrist and bowed her head like a muzzled dog. I thought Sierra was the type that answered to no master, but Marion had an unexpected control over her.

'Of course. We can't wait,' Juliana said.

I felt another frivolous pang of jealousy, this time over the mention of plans I wasn't a part of.

'It was nice to meet you,' I said, desperate to have the final word.

'We'll see you around,' Marion promised, touching my shoulder. Ezra smiled and tilted his head, and that was it. I followed their outlines until the crowd obscured them both from view.

Whatever energy I'd been clinging to receded in Ezra's absence. I'd sweated out the drinks and coke long ago. My body felt heavy, and I stifled a yawn. Sierra noticed immediately.

'Someone needs another bump!' She poked my shoulder playfully.

'I'm nearly ready to call it a night too,' Juliana announced.

'You always do this.'

'I didn't realise we were in for a big one.'

'You would've cancelled if you knew.' They were locked in a stand-off. Sierra swung her attention to me. 'Austin? Do you wanna stay out?'

'We're *all* going home.' Juliana sounded like a bossy older sister I didn't ask for, but her eyes were unrelenting and eventually, Sierra huffed and agreed we could all walk back to the car. I wished I'd fought against it. Sierra probably would've let us do the rest of her drugs and check out Connections, though it seemed poor form to abandon my cousin.

Juliana led us out, and we were mostly quiet for the walk back to the lot aside from Sierra babbling about a boy she was hooking up with, but I was only half listening. I'd been obsessed with the idea of expanding my social circle, only to squander any potential by not making enough of an effort with Ezra and Marion. Missed opportunities. I could've asked for their Instagrams, casually set up a next meeting. Perhaps that would've been pushy, though I decided it was better than another month of nothing.

'Did you have fun?' Juliana asked me once we were back

on the road.

'I did,' I said, and I meant it. It wasn't a life-changing night by any means, but the previous lack of socialisation made it feel more special, and there was safety in strangers. No familiar faces approached me with vacant condolences. *I heard the news, I'm so sorry.* In Perth, I was an unknown.

'Thanks for letting me tag along.'

Juliana stole a glance in the rear-view mirror at Sierra, whose head was lolling against the headrest, eyes closed.

'I really needed someone else there,' she said quietly.

I was slow to realise Juliana had only invited me as a buffer between her and Sierra. She eventually told me she still loved her, as one loves another they've known since their youth, but time had propelled them into different stages of life. Sierra was single, and Juliana wasn't. Going out didn't appeal to them in the same way anymore, especially with the cost of entrance fees and drinks. Juliana couldn't keep up. A third party was required to offset the pressure. I didn't mind being used in this way – it was better than a pity invite.

Somewhere in Dalkeith along the rows of mansions that overlooked Freshwater Bay was Sierra's family home. We dropped her alongside a low stone wall covered in moss that housed a tennis court above it.

'This is me,' she said. I gazed at the slick white columns and three stories of glass doors and windows and thought *yes, this is you.* It was built like a beautiful fishbowl.

Juliana got out of the car to hug her while I stayed in my seat, pretending not to eavesdrop as they said their goodbyes.

'I'm sorry I didn't tell you Austin was coming.'

I wasn't watching, but I could imagine Sierra there on the pavement, arms wrapped around herself and avoiding direct eye contact like she was in trouble. She'd been waiting all night for someone to ask her what was wrong so she could finally spill it out.

'I just thought it was supposed to be us tonight.'

'I know.'

'You always invite people along. It's like you hate being alone with me.'

'It just all gets a bit much sometimes. Not all of us can afford a big night out.'

'*Big?* This was nothing. And I offered to pay.'

'It's embarrassing for me when you do.'

Their moment of quiet had no resolution. Perhaps Sierra shook it off and decided it wasn't worth the effort, because her face appeared in the window, and she blew me a kiss. I caught it with a tepid smile.

'See you around, Austin,' she said and retreated up to the mansion, touching Juliana's arm as she passed.

4

The room I woke up in had the fundamentally depressing quality of mismatched furniture and half-unpacked suitcases. I'd bought a king bed and a small bedside table where my books rested in two large stacks, but the tallboy in the corner had been left behind from the girl who had lived here before. The wood had an amber shine to it, clashing with the royal blue bed sheets and the sand washed side table. Perhaps if I made an effort, a nice rug or a few plants might tie it all together, but I couldn't bring myself to make the house a home. There was a stubbornness in it, a deep refusal to get too comfortable in case this had indeed turned out to be a mistake, and I could depart at any time without a second thought.

The house itself was empty. I assumed Juliana had gone out for breakfast. She was one of those, *let's go for breakfast*, or, *let's have a walk* people. It was noncommittal, an hour at the most, reserved for those she felt obligated to see but didn't want to give up an entire evening for. I was currently avoiding the designation of that particular class, at least for the meantime.

I made myself an instant coffee and drank it while inspecting the kitchen; the white paint peeling off the cupboards, the lingering smell of grease permeating the air, the drying rack covered in dishes from the night before. Juliana's cleanliness left much to be desired, but it felt snobbish to admit aloud how I'd taken dishwashers for granted, so I bit my tongue, and smiled, and appreciated all that I'd stumbled upon, even if it was the slightest culture shock compared to past comforts. It was fine. It was all just fine. I added my washed mug to the pileup, changed into my board shorts, and ventured outside.

The morning burned. Heat licked the asphalt and hovered, so anything in the distance looked trapped behind a glossy barrier. I walked briskly with feet bare and a towel around my shoulders, wincing at the searing pain of hot pavement. Shade from the occasional gum tree provided momentary relief, but as soon as I was back out in the direct sun, I sweltered away. Dampness clung beneath my armpits and across my back. The general consensus was to wake up at the crack of dawn to take advantage of the day before the wind picked up and ravaged the coastline. Perth wasn't just one of the most isolated cities in the world, but also one of the windiest, yet thus far, the mornings through to the evenings had been balmy and suffocating. Flies tapped at windows, foreheads glistened, reddening shoulders were exposed in pubs and cafés. Wind would've been a reprieve.

Despite the harsh climate, life had well-emerged around me: a young couple on a jog with their headphones in, a family walking a dog, older ladies with takeaway coffees in hand, a dad pushing a baby in a pram. Lives I felt far removed from.

I took the side streets behind the Ampol and crossed the train tracks. The apartment was far enough from the train station that the screech of metal couldn't penetrate our walls. The next cul-de-sac sloped downwards and ended at the shoreline. Over the grass patch and below the embankment was a scene from a painting: ethereal, shining ocean. Whitewash tousled the shore and retracted back out into the blue. I took the wooden steps down through the dunes, flung my towel and phone to the sand, and wasted no time submerging myself. The water was crisp and completely transparent, like swimming through melted glass. Everything was quiet out here. Different from before, a peaceful quiet. One I welcomed.

On my back and floating, I looked up at the cloudless sky and breathed. If I had nothing else in Perth, at least I had this. An ocean was a safe haven, capable of washing sins, clearing the mind. I'd had an affinity for water since I was a child. I'd kick and scream when pool time was over and spent hours battling swells on the coast of our old beach house along the Great Ocean Road. I once believed there was nothing that couldn't be fixed with a long shower, or a bath, but I now found that notion to be a fallacy.

When I got back to my towel, a missed call and a text message waited on my phone. I groaned at the sight of the notifications.

Are you going to talk to me at some point?

I dried myself and called back. Sabrina answered on the fourth ring.

'Hi,' she said stiffly.

'Hey.' I hoped I sounded chipper.

'I haven't heard anything from you since you left.'

'Busy boy over here.'

'I'm sure.'

I shielded the sun from my eyes and watched the container ships moving slowly along the horizon. Beyond them, you could see Rottnest Island. On a day like today, the GT elite would be taking their speed boats or yachts out across the short expanse of sea, anchoring up somewhere along the reef with their music at full blast, drinking straight from the neck of a liquor bottle. Were those the kind of friends I should've been gunning for? Perhaps we'd have more in common.

'So, how's Perth?'

'I'm sitting on a beach in the sun. You'd hate it.'

'Did you put on sunscreen?'

'No.'

'That's a great way to get skin cancer. Are you wearing a hat?'

She loved mothering me. It was a space she'd constantly tried to fill even before it had become vacant.

'Yes,' I said, though my exposed scalp disagreed.

'Good.'

I wondered what she'd been doing, but I didn't ask. If it was morning for me, it would be close to lunchtime in Melbourne. She was probably sitting in the Botanical Gardens, clad in a fabulous coat with a dismal salad in her lap, glaring at pigeons that begged for scraps by her feet.

'Is everything okay?' I asked.

'Does something have to be wrong for us to have a conversation?'

'You haven't called me on a whim in a long time.'

'Just making sure you're alive,' she said. 'Dad asked about you.'

'Liar.'

'Yeah. He didn't.'

I couldn't help but laugh at that, even if the laugh sounded hollow and disingenuous. 'We're a whole family of liars.'

My father must've had an image of what his son would be like – hoisted up upon his shoulders, clad in football team merchandise, kicking a ball back and forth in the yard, waiting until a certain age to drink and talk lecherously about women, swapping stories of conquests. It once pained me that I couldn't give him those things, until I realised I was glad to be nothing like him. I found him repugnant, with his revolving door of women and appetite for breaking dishes; his raised voice chasing us down the hallway when something wasn't good enough. There used to be holes in the wall where his fist connected. Thankfully, there was never a mark made on our bodies, though the threat of it lingered like a rancid smell. We never uttered the phrase 'verbally abusive' out loud, but looking back it was obvious. Any attempts to impress him were abandoned out of self-preservation.

I was never the son my father wanted, but I was exactly the son my mother needed, especially after the divorce. I filled that mother-daughter bond she never properly had with Sabrina. Mum got under her skin in ways I never understood.

'She picked you as her favourite,' Sabrina had said long ago. 'That's why you get along.'

'Parents don't pick favourites,' I protested.

'Yes, they do. Dad told me I'm his.'

Dad and Sabrina weren't similar, but they both hated Mum, and that seemed to bond them together. Besides, he was historically softer on her, his *princess*. His anger was dedicated to his ex-wife and his son. The territories were drawn up with Sabrina and my father on one side, and my mother and I on the other. Switzerland was the middle ground where Sabrina and I kept the peace and caught up occasionally, avoiding the topic of our parents. It wasn't easy, but it was stable. For a time.

'I'm good too, by the way,' Sabrina said, irritation radiating through the phone.

'Right, sorry. How are you?'

'Fine. Everything's fine. I check on the house every week or two to make sure it hasn't burned down. If you were wondering.'

Sometimes I wished it *would* burn so it was no longer our problem. Sabrina wanted to sell it, but I couldn't bring myself to do so. It remained abandoned, preserved like a crime scene.

'And Graham?' I said, shifting focus.

'He's got an injury, so he can't play at the moment.'

'What will the AFL do without him?' He'd been benched for the whole season, so my sarcasm was glaring.

'He actually works very hard.'

'I never said he didn't.'

I could imagine being an athlete was hard work, but with the way others treated them, it was as if they were solving world hunger or curing rare diseases. Sabrina was an enabler of the highest grade, feeding Graham's vices and cushioning his flaws. Of which he had many: infidelity, spouts of anger, gambling – to name a few. He was an asshole, but so was our father. It was natural she would cling to what she knew best.

'You seem annoyed with me.'

'Yeah, well.'

'Have I done something?'

'You up and disappeared to Perth to live in a shitty two-bedroom with a cousin we never knew for some reason. I guess that's something.'

She'd made her disdain clear the second I'd told her. Her face frozen in a contorted shape somewhere between disbelief and fury had made a lasting impression.

'It's not shitty. It's a decent apartment.'

'That's not the point.'

'What *is* the point?'

'You're avoiding what happened. You're bottling it up and it's all going to explode.'

I sighed weightily, but it sounded more like a grunt.

'Things are better now. Why can't you accept that?'

'Not when I know it's all bullshit. You do this every time something bad happens. It's borderline psychopathic.'

My mouth twisted into a snarl. 'Just because you and Mum were mentally ill, doesn't mean I am. Stop trying to pass it on to me.'

A painful pause. Then she said, 'Fuck off, Austin,' and promptly ended the call.

*

Days before they were due to leave for Marion's birthday, Juliana and Alé came down with the flu. Juliana's happened in stages; first a pounding headache (which she blamed on stress and dehydration) followed by sore muscles and extreme fatigue, and then her body completely shut down, rendering her immobile. Alé toppled like a domino soon after, his symptoms hitting him all at once.

'Just ask her to change the dates,' Alé groaned.

'It's her birthday. And the Airbnb is non-refundable this late.' The walls were paper-thin between our bedrooms, and I could easily hear them bickering between noses emptied into tissues and fits of coughing.

'So we just lost hundreds of dollars. Like that.'

'People get sick.'

'It's not fair.' His whine was childish.

'Ben is gonna pay one of our shares.'

'And what about the rest of it?'

'I don't know. Marion can't think of anyone else who's free.'

'What about Austin?'

Surely she wouldn't bother. I'd met them once. I was nowhere near close enough to be offered a spot at such an intimate gathering.

As if suddenly aware of how easily sound travelled between the walls, Juliana lowered her voice to the point I could no longer hear the conversation. I shrugged the thought away and finished getting dressed for work.

It wasn't very busy at the café, and I had my fifteen-minute break outside on the picnic table with Daisy, who offered me a freshly rolled dart. I shook my head at the offer.

'You don't smoke, *Melbourne*?'

'I used to vape. In uni.'

'That's so gay.'

I snorted. 'Yeah, it is, isn't it?'

She lit the end of the dart and suckled on it. Her legs sprawled out under the table and the flimsy cotton shirt she wore rose up to expose her belly button piercing.

'How long have you worked here?' I asked her.

'About a year,' she said.

'What do you want to do after?'

'Fucked if I know.'

It was our longest uninterrupted conversation since we'd met. She seemed uneager to stretch it out, so I found myself digging for points of discussion.

'Does Leslie like me?' was what I settled on. 'She's always giving me a hard time.'

Daisy stared at the sky, contemplative. 'She's an old cunt with bad knees and no husband. She doesn't like anyone.'

For some reason, her answer satisfied me.

I swung by the bookshop on the way back to the apartment. I had a bad habit of buying three and reading one, so my unread pile was growing larger as the weeks went on. I would have preferred to work here instead of the café, but only one of the two venues had a sign in the window looking for staff. I'd have felt quite at home amongst the pinewood shelves and ladders, the smell of paper. But perhaps it was better to leave it as a pipedream, a fantasy, a total romanticisation of what a retail job encompassed. Besides, there would have been too many quiet hours, too much time spent in my own head.

I bought a debut novel from a young Irish author and two classics I hadn't gotten around to. I loved the feeling of holding books, displaying them like they were for a cosmetic purpose and not internal. I read them too, but there would always be the scepticism in the back of my brain that questioned the dominant motivation. Perhaps I only read for the ego of it, performing as an intellectual rather than truly being one.

Juliana's bedroom door was ajar when I passed it. I knocked softly and pushed on the wood. The blinds were pulled shut and light spilled in from the hallway. Balled up tissues were abandoned on the carpet. The bed sheets were pulled up tight around her and Alé.

'Hey,' came her meek greeting.

'Surviving?'

'Not really. I'm pretty devastated.' Her eyes were hollowed, and her complexion had a grey hue. Alé was all but inanimate beside her, curled into a ball against her side.

'I'm sorry,' I murmured. 'I know how excited you were to get out of Perth.'

'I actually wanted to talk to you about that,' she said, and Alé mustered whatever life he had left in him to meet her eyes. His chin tilted as if to say, *go on*. She cleared her throat and smiled. 'Did you have any plans this weekend?'

5

Behind the wheel of Sierra's bright red Audi, I sped down Bussell Highway and the city slipped away. The engine was alive and purring under the ball of my foot. The windows were down and the music was up, a song by Rüfüs Dü Sol thumping around us. Beyond the edges of the asphalt, farmland and endless rows of acacias and eucalyptus trees swallowed any sign of industrialisation. The highway was empty – we had the road to ourselves. Sierra looked content in the passenger seat. Her sandals were abandoned on the floor, slender feet up on the dash. Large cat-eye Prada sunglasses rested over her tired eyes, and her bright red hair whipped about like an open flame. She'd asked me to drive, as she still needed to do her makeup. I was happy to oblige, revelling in the rush of power from driving a fast car. As soon as I relaxed into the sensitivity of the pedals, and the traffic out of Perth dwindled, I began to take liberties with the speedometer. I liked watching it jump and fall.

'I'm glad you're coming instead of Jules and Alé,' Sierra said over the music. The makeup bag lay abandoned under her chair now that she'd painted a natural glow upon her face.

'Really?'

'It's just…' She turned down the volume a fraction and combed a hand through her freshly brushed hair. The wind was already starting to mess it all over again. 'I'm sure you've noticed how *in your face* they are about being a couple. Right?'

'I don't know. Not really.'

'Alé's a decent guy, of course, but the relationship is so codependent. Everyone else becomes background noise.'

I didn't want to speak ill of my cousin and her boyfriend without them present, but I wasn't going to shut Sierra down when she'd chosen me to air her grievances. It was a step closer to friendship – though she gave the impression she would have said this to anyone who allowed her the opportunity.

'Isn't that how it is when you're in love?'

'Speaking from personal experience?'

'Just an observer.' I drummed my fingers on the wheel.

'So, you've never been in love?'

It was like we were in homeroom, gossiping at the back tables. Women often seemed eager to do this with me. Perhaps it was instinctual, some unspoken bond over shared sexual preferences.

'I've never been in a relationship,' I found myself admitting.

'It could be unrequited. It still counts as love.'

'Speaking from personal experience?' I echoed.

She rolled her eyes. 'I've been in – and witnessed – many relationships begin and end, and I can firmly say that people turn into the most selfish monsters when they couple up.'

'I can't argue with you there.' I'd seen it enough times with Sabrina and her various boyfriends over the years. With Dad and his far-too-young girlfriends.

'And when it all ends, it's everyone else's problem.'

The highway thinned into a single lane, and the trees grew tighter and taller, hanging over the road like an archway of leaves.

'Maybe that's normal? Getting caught up in someone?'

'Just because it's normalised doesn't mean it's right,' she said with an arched eyebrow.

'So you hate love?'

'No, not really,' she sighed. 'Just when other people are in it.' That made me laugh, and she cracked a smile. Her feet receded back under the dash, and she straightened up. 'Apparently you're the one who hates love if you've never been in it.'

'I just haven't found the right person I guess,' I said flatly, though truthfully I had no intention of finding the right person. Once I realised how easy sex was, *love*, in the clichéd sense of the word, was a chore. I preferred the thrill of attraction with no longevity, a game I'd been playing since the age of fourteen, and one I'd become fairly good at. If it became difficult in any way, I'd cut it out like cancer, push on and never look back. Love forced you to give parts of yourself away and I refused to make any more sacrifices.

*

The Airbnb was an old farmhouse overlooking a pond, with outer walls made up of dark wooden slats and grey stone, and a veranda that wrapped all the way around. The driveway ran alongside a vineyard stretching for acres, with a faded wooden sign that read *private property* and rolling hills with sheep and horses in the distance. We were the only building in the vicinity, isolated and rustic. I parked under a low-hanging tree between a white Volkswagen and a dark grey Ford Focus. Sierra's flashy red car stuck out like a sore thumb. She pulled her sandals back on, and we both climbed out into the dry mid-morning air.

'Cute,' she said, unimpressed, and I withheld a chuckle.

We unloaded the car, a suitcase for Sierra and a duffle bag for me, which I slung over my shoulder. Our shoes crunched in unison across the gravel footpath. Sierra pushed the doors wide open to announce our arrival into the foyer.

'Finally!' I heard Marion's gruff voice from deeper in the house. I readied a choral of *happy birthdays* but someone else met us at the door. She was shorter than Marion, with unyieldingly straight black hair and piercing cobalt eyes that I found confronting. She gave Sierra a tight hug, and me a jaded handshake, introducing herself as Nadia.

'You and Juliana don't look related,' she said, crossing her arms over her purple blouse. It had big billowing sleeves that crumpled in on themselves.

'I didn't inherit the Brazilian glow,' I smiled.

'Clearly.' Her blinks were apathetic. 'Everyone's in the back.'

We abandoned our bags in the entryway and followed her further through the house. The living room had a worn grey sofa and a rusted fireplace. Windows stained with streaks of water lined the back wall where we could look out onto the patio and down to the pond below. A bouquet of golden balloons sat floating in the corner behind the dining table. Marion was leaning against the kitchen counter with a large glass in her hand that contained some sort of combination of vodka and fruit juice. She set it down and rushed to embrace us both.

'So glad you guys made it.' It was certainly a warmer reception than Nadia's – though perhaps this was only because I wasn't a complete stranger to her anymore. 'Isn't the place amazing? It was so cheap, I couldn't believe it.'

'Even cheaper when you split it between seven people,' Nadia added.

'Drink?' Marion gestured to the bottles on the counter.

'Anything strong,' Sierra said.

'Make it two?'

We were given a brief tour of the upstairs bedrooms before heading outside to congregate with the rest of the group on the patio. Ezra was there, a large open space beside him which I couldn't help but occupy. He was leaning back against the couch pillows, legs spread out wide, lazily erotic. He wore the same white Nikes and his hair was sculpted perfectly again. Blood-red wine swished in the glass between his fingers. His lips kissed the rim as he drank from it slowly, and I was rendered immune to the introductions of people named Ben and Matteo, as well as the various conversations occurring around me. How could I focus on anything else besides those lips? Pink and plump on the top, thin and straight on the bottom, faintly stained by wine, and very soft, I'd bet. He was looking at me while he drank. I imagined myself splitting like an overripe grape, squeezed out for him to taste.

'It's not a nude,' Marion said on the other side of me, staring down at Sierra's phone.

'It is,' Sierra insisted.

'But you're covering it.'

'Any picture without clothes on–'

'You have to show your tits, at least,' Nadia said, 'but you're holding them and covering it.' She was perched precariously on her boyfriend's lap – this was Ben. He was busy angling himself around her to attack the charcuterie board.

'I don't know how we got here,' Ezra said, shaking his head in bafflement.

'We got here because Sierra's an attention whore and needs everyone to know that she looks good naked,' Marion said teasingly.

Sierra rolled her eyes and slipped her phone beneath her dress. 'I'm getting advice.'

'From these eunuchs?' Nadia said. 'Please.'

'*I* have sex,' Matteo retorted. He was sitting opposite me, legs crossed and vape in hand. His salmon shirt patterned with palm fronds was somehow familiar, bright against his olive skin. I noticed a silver chain around his wrist and quickly realised where I'd seen him before. He was wearing the same outfit in his profile picture on Grindr. We hadn't spoken, but I'd scrolled past him. I knew he wouldn't recognise me because I'd left my profile blank.

'How could we forget? *Dom Daddy 69*?' Nadia teased, rendering Matteo sheepish.

With his mouth full of prosciutto, Ben said, 'Should we give the photo another look? Just to settle the debate?'

Nadia punched him on the shoulder. Ben hollered dramatically, feigning agony. His face was a handsome square; shaved head, shoulders well built. He and Nadia made an attractive couple.

'Are we going to address the elephant in the room?' Matteo said.

'We're outside,' Sierra said.

'Why isn't he Brazilian?'

'Fairly small elephant…'

'He's right here, Matteo. You can ask him.' Marion nudged me playfully.

Matteo angled his body to face me head-on, businesslike. 'You're supposed to be Juliana's cousin, so–'

Sierra replied for me. 'He's on her Dad's side. The Australians.'

'I was expecting a male version of her.'

'Sorry to disappoint you,' I said.

'He speaks!'

'He does.' I forced a smile. 'When given the opportunity.'

Matteo blinked at my sudden directness.

'Ignore him,' Marion said quickly. 'He fetishises brown boys, so he was probably wanting to bone you.'

'Still would,' Matteo sighed to himself, and I felt my cheeks fill with blood non-consensually. The group responded with scattered chuckles. I couldn't help but toss a glance to Ezra, curious at his reaction. His eyes had darkened, as if the ghost of a glare was haunting around the irises, but it quickly evaporated.

'But we're so happy you're here. And Ben too,' Marion continued.

Ben raised his glass of wine as a toast. 'I may not have been the first choice, but I am the right choice.'

'You were always invited, you just had work.'

'Work I've called in sick for.' He saluted the birthday girl. 'And we're not here to fuck spiders, so drink up.'

We all raised our glasses at the same time, though mine had been finished minutes prior. Ezra leaned in close and said, 'It's bad luck to cheers with an empty glass.'

I could feel his warm breath on my ear. He reached for the bottle, holding it up tantalisingly.

'Thanks,' I said. He poured steadily, without a drop spilled. Our fingers brushed on the hand-off; electricity sparked, or I was imagining things again.

'Been a while,' he added.

'Has it?' I said, overly conscious of Marion to my right.

'Maybe not. But good to see you anyway.'

A half-inflated erection prodded the fly of my jeans. It was difficult to ignore and I couldn't blame the cocaine this time. I was undeniably lusting after him. Was he flirting? It seemed indistinguishable from platonic friendliness when a person was attractive.

'Austin, darl,' Matteo said loudly, ruining our brief moment. 'You're a Melbournian?'

'Until about a month ago,' I nodded.

'All back to normal over there *post-Covid*?' Ben asked. 'You guys had a rough go of it.'

'Can we not use the C-word?' Sierra grimaced as if she'd caught a whiff of warm garbage. 'I'm so sick of talking about it.'

Marion smirked at her drink. 'You know there's no such thing as post-Covid? It's still around.'

'Oh, please,' was Matteo's response.

'I kind of miss it. The pandemic,' Ben said. 'Got so much done, working from home. No traffic. Cheap rentals all over WA 'cause no one was flying.'

'People were dying, babe,' Nadia said. Her black skirt spilled over them like hot tar. One of Ben's hands was lost somewhere in the folds of the fabric.

'Not here. It basically didn't exist.'

How lucky Perth was, flitting through the beginning of the decade with ease, while the rest of the world suffered. If Perth was an island, the pandemic had merely lapped at the shores.

'Were you totally depressed the whole time?' Sierra asked me. The group's eyes were spotlights on me.

'I was fine,' I said quickly.

'Really?'

'I've never had a bad day in my life.'

Sierra laughed loudly and tucked a loose strand of hair behind her ear. 'The first night we met, you said not to take anything you say seriously.'

'I mean it,' I nodded earnestly. 'I've never had a bad day. Maybe I'm just a perpetual optimist.' The group was staring at me like I was crazy, and I knew I sounded it too, but this was a test, an opportunity to present who I wanted to be, and I wanted to be the person that nothing terrible had ever happened to. I was determined to make it so.

'That's impossible,' Ezra said simply.

'I disagree,' I shrugged. 'It's all about mindset.'

'Sounds like something a person who grew up rich would say,' Nadia added, causing me to stiffen further. Did she know? Had Juliana let slip my financial status?

'Not necessarily,' I said vaguely and with a false sense of confidence.

It was convincing enough because Ezra visibly relaxed beside me. 'Well, good,' he said. 'I've had enough of rich assholes.'

'Is that a euphemism?' Matteo said with mirth. Ezra chose to ignore the comment, or he didn't catch it.

'The two things aren't always mutually exclusive. Sierra's rich, but not an asshole,' Nadia reached over and poked her on the shoulder. 'Our *PLC Princess*.'

'I hate that nickname. You're just jealous because you were on Centrelink for years,' she volleyed back.

'And I'd do it again. Fuck the government for raising cost of living.'

'Fuck the government for taking away our bodily autonomy during Covid,' Matteo added grudgingly.

'I thought we'd moved on from this.'

Ignoring Sierra, Nadia narrowed her eyes at Matteo and said, 'I suppose certain things needed to be enforced, considering some of us refused to get vaccinated until it was required by law.'

'I'm a naturopath.'

'You're a selfish conspiracy theorist.'

'I don't like putting anything in my body that isn't FDA-approved.'

'The vaccine *was* FDA-approved. Unlike the caps we took on Australia Day.'

My head was snapping back and forth between them like it was a tennis match.

'I thought we weren't supposed to celebrate that holiday anymore. Isn't it offensive or something?' Sierra piped up again, trying to sound intelligent.

Ezra shook his head and said, 'It's offensive to me that you guys still do caps.'

'It's not a common occurrence,' Matteo said.

'Well, I'd appreciate it if we keep it that way throughout the weekend.'

'Ezra hates drugs,' Marion whispered to me.

I kept waiting to see some semblance of chemistry ignite between her and Ezra, one that I'd been stifling with my choice of sitting between them, but it never came. Not even a cheeky glance or a flirtatious comment. The circuit was simply dead.

'Ah, come on mate,' Ben said. 'They're good fun in the right environment.'

'Not for me.' Ezra's assertiveness was arousing, even if his attitude was in direct opposition to my personal tastes, though I was willing to sacrifice a moral or two for a good impression. I could be whatever he wanted. Meanwhile, he probably didn't give me a second thought. It was all a fantasy in my head, this quiet flirtation, completely delusional and one-sided. The age-old straight-chasing I liked to believe I was above – though I knew my ego was derived from feeling special, from being an exception. I was not above it in the slightest. Any attention was delicious.

Matteo threw his hands up. 'No drugs! Just booze! We got it.' But he, Ben, and Nadia all exchanged an unspoken glance that said *yeah-fucking-right*.

'And as the birthday girl, I'll be enforcing that rule,' Marion cemented with her glass raised high above her head.

There were grumbles of reluctant agreement and then Sierra bent her head inward to Marion's ear and said, 'Look who put her pants on today.' Her vocal fry was seductive, crackling underneath the side chatter.

'One of us had to,' Marion murmured back, matching her tone. It felt private, not meant for anyone else, and especially not me. I glanced over at Ezra, but he was looking elsewhere, across the pond that rippled in conversation with the wind.

'Is Perth really as small as everyone says?' I asked, steering the conversation further away from drugs. 'Geographically, it feels very spread out.'

'It's all social,' Ezra replied. I was still caught off guard when he would speak to me directly. 'You sort of… know *of* people. Always one degree of separation from someone else. That's how we all fell into a group.'

'Ezra and I have known each other the longest though,' Marion said.

'Everyone always thought we'd get married,' he chuckled.

'We even dated in high school!'

My brow furrowed. 'You're not… together anymore?'

'No.' Marion exchanged a look of amusement with Ezra. 'We broke up when we realised we were both gay.'

I blinked slowly. They were all looking at me, but I met Ezra's eyes and found a glimmer of triumph awaiting me.

'Oh!' I said.

The group burst out laughing and I could feel myself deepening in colour, wanting to sink into the couch.

'I'm guessing you didn't pick that up?'

I saw Marion then — properly this time — husky-voiced and broad, rejecting commercial femininity since the night I met her. That didn't necessarily constitute queerness, but it was certainly an oversight.

'No, I didn't.'

'Shocking,' Matteo snorted. 'She's so butch.'

'Says the flaming homo,' came Marion's retort.

'This is a gay group,' Nadia said. 'We're all a bit queer.'

'I'm not,' Ben said.

'Only because you're too insecure to try it.'

'I'm insecure because I don't want to fuck a dude?'

'Exactly.' She squeezed his shoulder to soften the blow.

'Remind me how many girls you've slept with?' Sierra asked her, lips pursed in accusation.

'None yet. But I *want* to.'

'Thanks for that,' Ben huffed, clearly wounded, but Nadia ignored him.

'I can still identify as bi.'

'Thinking a girl is hot doesn't make you bi,' Sierra argued. 'Even *sleeping* with a girl doesn't make you bi. It's normal, you know? An experiment.'

'Like when you were with Marion?'

Sierra winced and Marion sucked her lips around her teeth, staring down at the slats of wood on the ground. Ezra and I shared another exchange. This time, his eyes said something along the lines of *don't ask.*

'What about you, Austin?' Matteo added in a not-so-obvious attempt to save the conversation. Of course, it came at the expense of my privacy. 'Have you ever experimented with guys?'

'I suppose it's not an experiment anymore after a couple years of exclusively sleeping with them,' I said nonchalantly. 'But I'll kiss a girl if I'm drunk.'

It was my turn to sit triumphantly and enjoy the looks of surprise over crumbling perceptions. I was usually tentative about revealing myself so adamantly, but this was merely opportunistic. I wanted Ezra to know where I stood, on the slight chance he'd come to the wrong conclusions about me, just as I had with him. It was a declaration of availability, a green light. In my peripheral vision, I saw the hint of a smile cross Ezra's face before he glanced at the ground.

'Huh. I suppose that checks out,' Nadia said, seemingly pleased with the outcome and swishing the wine around her glass like a sommelier.

'I knew it as soon as I met you,' Sierra said.

'That's just what every gay guy loves to hear,' Ezra sighed. 'How painfully *not-straight* he is.'

I was elated by how quickly he'd rushed to my defence.

'There's nothing wrong with that!'

'It's only the basis for why we got picked on through school. "You talk gay. You act gay." Nothing wrong.'

'Not to mention the obsession with masculinity in the gay community,' Matteo added. 'You'd think because we're all queer it would be different, and yet everyone wants to act like the straight boys we had crushes on in high school.'

'If I get called "Bro" one more time, I'm going to start dating women,' Ezra laughed.

'We are better,' Marion grinned. 'Despite what Sierra might say.' She flipped her hair over her shoulder, performatively feminine.

'Okay, very funny,' Sierra scowled. 'You guys can stop ganging up on me now.'

'But it's so easy when Juliana isn't here to defend you.'

I decided that they weren't exactly nice, not to each other at least. I wasn't sure what was supposed to be funny, and what was intentionally picking at a half-healed wound, testing to see if it was still inflamed. Though considering my lack of social options, I was in no position to be picky. I could simply use them for a time, another springboard, eventually branch off to other groups, or situate myself closer to Ezra until we slept together, an event which had skyrocketed from unlikely to inevitable. I only needed to bide my time and say the right things, and I'd get what I wanted.

6

We were divided into two cars, and to my dismay, Ezra drove the white Volkswagen with Marion, Nadia, and Matteo. Sierra and I ended up in Ben's Ford Focus which he drove smoothly through the thin winding roads. The bush was dense, hardly anything could be made out beyond the trees and brambles except for the occasional flash of houses and estates.

'Of course, the *core four* have to go together,' Sierra mumbled from the backseat. I turned from my spot on the passenger's side to examine her sour expression. She'd been sulking since the comments out on the patio.

'The core four?'

'The group within the group,' Ben answered for her, twiddling a loose thread on the leather steering wheel. 'I wasn't planning on coming because they can be cliquey when they're all together… but I was doing a favour for Alé and Juliana. Plus Nadia's happy I'm here.'

'I didn't even notice,' I lied. 'If anything, I just thought they were at each other's throats.'

'Yeah. That tends to happen.'

'Nadia especially,' Sierra huffed. Ben said nothing, but the lack of defence for his girlfriend seemed to agree. 'It's so fucking high school,' she continued. 'And they pretend I was never a part of it.'

'What happened?'

'Aside from the *core five* not having the same ring to it?' She gazed out the window, watching the vineyards, groves, and thickets hurtle past. I wondered how she wasn't getting nauseous. With every sharp turn, I could feel the wine and vodka sloshing in my stomach.

'You guys used to hook up?'

She sighed heavily as if the very act of recollection was a tribulation, though she launched into it immediately after. 'Marion and I met in a psychology class. Second year. I was doing it as a broadening unit and needed someone to copy notes off. We started going for coffee after class and somehow became friends, even though we had nothing in common. She was this northern suburbs girl, determined and hard-working, and I… spilt tequila on my homework.'

She was a natural storyteller. Or the retreading was well-rehearsed. Both could be true.

'We both learned a lot from each other. Jules and I took her out and got her to loosen up. Marion taught me how to care about my studies. I think Ezra was a little jealous of all the time we were spending together. It had been the two of them against the world since, like, birth. They were each other's number one, and I was threatening that. But then he met Callum.'

Just his name was a lashing against exposed flesh. I felt a sudden heaviness, like an anchor had been tied to my ankles.

Sierra continued. 'GT raised, Scotch College, the mansion in Dalkeith, party animal. Our families knew each other from some gala events and fundraisers over the years. To be honest, I thought he was a bit of a dickhead – but that's beside the point.' She took a long pause, perhaps to procure dramatic effect. 'Callum was Ezra's first love. Suddenly he didn't care how much time Marion was spending with me. He hardly even went to uni anymore. Callum became all that mattered. I think he was just swept up by the money. I mean,

Callum's family is filthy rich, and that's me saying that. Ezra went from feeling abandoned to doing the abandoning. I'd always had Jules, but Marion was supposed to be his go-to for everything. Then through Callum, he met Matteo, then through Matteo, Nadia… No time for Marion, so she came running to me.'

'Things developed?' I prodded, not that she needed coaxing.

'I was curious, I guess. We kissed while I was drunk, so I can't tell you exactly what was going through my head, but it happened, and it felt good in the moment. I think I wanted to try something different after all the pieces of shit I'd been with. It was like starting over or being a virgin again. Thrilling, in a way. But Marion fell hard for me, that was pretty obvious. I tried really hard to want the same things. Maybe I loved her, but in a way my body couldn't follow along with. Everything else was great. Hanging out, and kissing… It was just the sex I couldn't wrap my head around.

'Eventually, Ezra and Callum broke up and a group formed between me and Marion, Ezra, Matteo, and Nadia. For a while, it was okay, but I still felt like a plus one. Never fully a part of things. Jules told me I was being unfair to Marion, confusing her, and when she started putting on pressure, wanting me to commit, I knew I couldn't keep going along with it. So I told her I was pretty sure I was straight – thinking she'd understand. All I did was make her absolutely fucked off. The group banded together and shut me out.'

I could feel the colour leaving my cheeks, and I wasn't sure if it was from motion sickness or the realisation that the people I'd chosen to spend the weekend with were more complicated than they appeared. I rubbed my chin in a forced show of contemplation. 'That sounds abrupt.'

'I was already on the outskirts, so it wasn't very hard for them.' She leaned back in the car seat and looked down at her fingernails, picking at one of them. 'Roots go so deep here in Perth, and nothing wins against that kind of history.'

'That's not completely true,' Ben protested. 'Matteo and Nadia didn't have as much history as you and Marion.'

'It's different when there's feelings involved. Matteo and Nadia were there for Ezra after his heartbreak, and the three of them were there for Marion after hers. They thrive off of needing each other. If there was no drama happening, they'd have nothing left to talk about.'

I could see Ben's jaw stiffen as if he was biting down on a thought. 'Why'd you come then?'

She raised her chin in a kind of defensiveness and said, 'Because I was invited.'

Ben shook his head and let out a breathy laugh. 'You're something else.'

She rolled her eyes in self-importance.

'How did you stay friends?' I asked, my curiosity getting the better of me once more.

'Space. Timing,' she shrugged. 'We gave it a few months and the feelings died down. Reconnected over this girl in our psych class getting engaged. I saw it online and just *had* to text Marion. Maybe it was only an excuse to be back in each other's lives.' She stared directly through the windscreen. The motion sickness might have been coming on at last. 'It's still weird sometimes, as you've probably picked up. I can't exactly say we're close friends anymore. The core four was established and that's how it's been for a while now.'

*

We were hit with the smell of freshly mowed grass and

crushed grapes as we piled out of the car. The winery was fashioned with exposed brick and wooden archways, thickets of hydrangeas and clipped hedges, large oak barrels, stone fireplaces, and leather couches. We claimed a circular table beneath a low-hanging chandelier fashioned from antlers. A tasting flight was set up and each one went down like a bowling pin. There was a debate over the best vintage – I preferred the 2023 chardonnay – but Marion chose the cheaper sav blanc and that was the end of it. Besides, we were a group of young Australians. Anything would be drunk regardless.

Whatever animosity that had ignited throughout the day was snuffed with each cork popped. It was easy to forget frivolous things like malicious teasing while getting drunk together. Sierra was seated between Matteo and Nadia, and their olive branch came in the form of a constant top up of the golden liquid. Matteo began to tell a story that required the use of his hands. Nadia grinned, and Sierra listened intently. Watching them, you couldn't see any hint of the resentment that lingered behind their smiling exteriors. Beside them, Marion and Ben were locked into a *deep-n-meaningful* with low voices and precise nods. Ben gripped the stem of his wine glass like it was a microphone. Their attentions were contained inward, so it was safe to assume the conversation didn't pertain to the rest of us.

Somehow, Ezra and I ended up next to each other again. I was starting to think he'd been puppeteering the seating arrangements and there was something thrilling about that. I waited for him to engage me, but instead, he seemed bored and distracted. As one of the designated drivers for the day, he'd reached the legal limit back at the Airbnb, and sat indignantly as everyone enjoyed what he could not. His phone was out and the screen lit up the whites of his eyes. I couldn't tell if he was actually looking at something or just trying to appear busy. In turn, my glass functioned as an excuse for not speaking and was subsequently drained with speed. He noticed me glancing in his peripherals and turned his head to meet me straight on. I felt caught, but I didn't break the gaze. I wanted to be acknowledged. It was a stand-off, excruciatingly long. He caved first by sheathing his phone into his pocket.

'Would you like to go for a walk?'

My eyebrows shot up in surprise, but I managed a casual smile. 'Yeah, why not?'

We abandoned the table without an explanation, vigilantes called to action. The only person that noticed our departure was Nadia. Her penetrating gaze followed us all the way to the exit until we disappeared from sight.

Out in the daylight, the lawn was bright and well-washed. A blanket of baby blue sky arched overhead and the rows of vineyards stretched out along the hills like hallways. He walked ahead without checking to see if I was keeping up, a spring in his step. My legs were longer than his however, and I needed only a few forceful strides to catch up with him.

'Sorry,' Ezra said cheerfully, an aggressive shift in mood. 'Needed to do something besides just sitting there.'

We walked together in unison between the grapes and brambles.

'Forced into being the designated driver?'

'I volunteered. A huge mistake in hindsight.'

'You don't need to drink to have fun.'

'At a wine tour?' He shot me a tortured glance with an underlying grin. It quickly melted and was replaced with a sigh. 'We should've just hired a bus from Perth and gone to the Swan Valley instead. Would've saved us a lot of money and effort.'

'Not impressed with the views?'

'I'm always impressed with the views. We passed Eagle Bay on the drive in, which is probably my favourite place in the world. But I suppose I see it in a very different light these days.' I knew immediately he was referring to Callum. His voice changed slightly when he tried to talk around him, sounding almost suffocated. Anyone who wasn't paying the closest amount of attention would've missed it. 'Sorry, I'm sounding a bit spoilt.'

'Not at all,' I said. 'I'm sure it loses its charm after a while.'

'It's always pretty though. And rare to have everyone together.'

'Not everyone. Juliana and Alé…'

He looked at me with all the delicacy of a first kiss, and said, 'I think you're an adequate substitute.'

My lips curled together to suppress a grin. The hill inclined slightly and we followed it up further, towards the lookout.

'Are you enjoying Perth?' he asked.

'I'm not sure yet.' I surprised myself with my own honesty. I hoped it made me sound enigmatic. 'Still getting to know the city, still making friends.'

He nodded. 'I would imagine it hasn't been easy. People don't really move here. They move away, to bigger, better places.'

'I have heard that once or twice,' I said sardonically.

'You seem better suited to Melbourne anyway.'

'Do I?'

'That's a compliment, I promise. I think Perth will bore you.'

'And you've come to that conclusion after… half of a conversation?'

His hands slotted into his pockets which made me

immediately conscious of how stiffly mine were swinging. 'Perth would bore most people.'

'I'm not most people,' I shrugged, choosing to ignore how self-indulgent I sounded.

'I can see that,' he chuckled, corroborating the flirtation.

The vines thinned and the leaves grew bare where the grapes had been picked for production. They probably harvested the ones closest to the estate last in an attempt to keep the landscape looking lush and full from the windows.

'I think there's something intimate about a smaller city,' I said, adamant to keep the conversation alive and kicking. 'More community.'

'If you're after intimacy and community, you won't find it with the other gays here.'

I spotted an opening and lunged. 'After coming for Sierra's neck, I'm surprised by the internalised homophobia.'

This was the game everyone played, wasn't it? Finding any opportunity to riffle through words spoken, and critique them in an attempt to prove how intellectual and witty we actually were? Little more than an exercise in morality.

'Someone paid attention in their gender studies unit.'

'I actually studied English.'

'Hmm. Reading,' he said in a way that sounded neither impressed nor disappointed.

'Reading,' I agreed.

'Well, it's not internalised homophobia. We honestly just have a piss-poor queer community here in Perth.'

'I assumed as much, considering there's hardly any gay clubs left.'

'There used to be more. The Court was one until it was infiltrated by straights a few years ago. And maybe if you count Steam Works — but that's basically just a sex dungeon.'

I pictured dark rooms with red lighting and wooden

crosses bolted to black walls; the very air coated with the smell of sweat and semen.

'The clubs aren't even the worst of it,' he continued. 'It's the people. We've got this tiny pool of the same guys to pick from, that all know each other and are either related, best friends, exes, have slept together, or are already in an open relationship. And for me, most of them are people I've grown up with. We went to the same schools or crossed over at the same formals. We'd match on dating apps a hundred times but never make the effort to meet up. We'd have a bit of a dance at Connections, and then never speak again. The lucky ones found a boyfriend quickly and stuck to them, while the rest of us… accepted our fate.'

'Which is?'

His hands slipped out of his pockets. 'Growing old and dying alone.'

I laughed loudly. He didn't join in.

We'd reached the top of the hill. Behind us, the estate was just a speck of bricks jutting out from the manicured wilderness. There was a river that ran alongside the property and stretched far into the hills with no end we could see.

'You're quite the pessimist.'

'Or just a realist,' he said with a squint.

Up here, with no relief from the sun's rays, the heat was merciless, but the panoramic view of the valley subdued these detriments. The rolling hills were unbelievably green, with lines of red dirt zigzagging between the vineyards. A small gazebo on the edge of the river was surely a hotspot for wedding backdrops, and though the water looked more brown than blue, I imagined with some colour-grading it would be indisputably picturesque in post-production. Two kangaroos took shelter in the tree line, nearly camouflaged against the pale tangle of tree trunks.

I felt sticky, my shirt hugging my armpits, moisture on my collar. I hoped it was a dewy glistening sort of sweat and not a disheveled oily one.

'Should I start packing my bags and go back to where I came from?' I joked.

'You'll be fine.' He shielded his eyes with the flat of his hand so he could watch me. 'You're fresh meat – everyone will be all over you.'

'Really?'

'You're disconnected from all the history. Yeah. You'll get some attention.' He dropped his hand.

'I don't think I'm prepared for that.'

'I find that hard to believe.' A smile crept back across his face, as if he had no control over it. 'Just be careful, okay? You're nice, and you're cute. People will take advantage of that.'

I flushed. 'You'll have to tell me the ones to avoid.'

'There's a list, believe me. I'll guide you.' That felt sincere.

We made our way back down the hill. While he trotted ahead, I got to check out the shape of his ass through his jeans.

'God knows I need it,' I called after him.

'You seem to be doing just fine.' He threw this comment over his shoulder with a lazy smirk.

'Aside from not having any friends yet?'

His pace slowed deliberately and I was right beside him again. 'We're friends, aren't we?'

'We hardly know each other.'

He thought on this for a moment and then waved it away. 'We'll work on it. We've got the whole weekend.'

'We've got a lot longer than that,' I said, feeling bolder.

'Who's to say you won't go running back to Melbourne?'

'Maybe you'll come with me. I'm a pretty good tour guide.'

His mouth made the shape of a smile, though his eyes didn't match the effort. 'I don't know. My whole life is here.' He stared ahead, towards the estate. 'I'm actually looking at buying a house and settling down in the next year or so.'

My head cocked. 'Jesus Christ. Next year?'

'Blink and we'll be thirty.'

'In another decade,' I laughed and he stopped walking altogether.

'Hang on. How old are you?' His face went slack.

'Twenty,' I replied. 'And you're…?'

'Twenty-nine.'

Something died quickly. It was a decision made in seconds, somewhere in those vacant eyes: I was too young for him. Whatever conviction had begun to initialise during our short walk withered and fell away, usurped by an unspoken mutual disappointment. I found it all ridiculous. It was just going to be sex anyway, what did a nine-year age gap matter? I'd slept with people twice my age and they didn't seem to care. He, however, did. I kicked myself for being truthful, or at least not predicting this would be an obstacle. Perhaps if I'd said twenty-five… but Sierra had seen my ID weeks ago. I needed to limit the possibility of getting tripped up in my own fabrications.

After a time, Ezra said, 'You act older than twenty.'

'Yeah,' was all I could think to reply.

Reflected in his eyes, I saw myself: a naive child sustaining themself on blind hope and expectancy. I felt stupid, and it seemed he did too.

7

The sun dipped behind the horizon and from our spot on the patio, we could see the pink slashes across the sky slowly opening up like a wound. The colours bounced off the surface of the water below and washed everything in a dreamy feminine glow. I was lethargic and dizzy from the day-drinking, but my salvation came in the form of a greasy slice of pizza. I was licking my fingers clean and watching the others by the fire pit. Nadia, Ben, and Matteo were giggling, wide-eyed, staring into the flames as if they were a film. I was sure they'd taken something. Marion and Sierra were tucked into a corner on the couch, conversing intensely. Sierra had a hand placed on her sternum and Marion's arms were crossed. Ezra was somewhere else in the house. I watched them all like I'd watched most of the weekend; merely an observer of things happening to other people. From this positioning, they were no longer performing for me, the newcomer. Marion was more emotional than I expected, Nadia more joyful, Matteo more carefree. I wondered how they perceived me. Did they believe that I was happy?

I collected the empty pizza boxes and carried them inside, placing them down on the counter beside the stacks of dirty plates.

'Idiots,' Ezra tutted from behind me. I turned, finding him staring at the trio by the fire. He played with an empty beer bottle, moving it back and forth between his palms, tracing the head and neck of the glass with deft fingers. It felt intentionally phallic. I turned the water to warm and began to scrub the grease marks from the plates.

'You don't need to—'

'It's all good,' I said. 'I don't mind cleaning.'

'My ex avoided it like the plague,' he laughed hollowly. 'Hated getting his hands dirty. Rich people things.'

I didn't know how to reply to that, so for a time, the only sound in the kitchen was running water. I imagined he was watching me.

'Are they high?' I asked at last.

'Yep.'

'On?'

'Caps, probably. I remember distinctly asking them not to.'

I would have partaken if he hadn't expressed his disdain for it, or if I was offered in the first place, but I'd been kept out of the loop.

'Why do you hate it so much?'

'I think drugs bring out the worst in people,' he said placidly.

Each plate moved in a conveyer-belt formation; rinsed, scrubbed, placed on the rack to dry.

'Let them have fun. You should try to relax.'

'This is me relaxed,' he replied. 'I'm finally drunk, at least.'

'I've been drunk the whole day.'

'I know. I've watched you.'

I abandoned the plate in the sink and turned to face him, wiping my wet hands on my thighs. 'You have?'

'Yeah. And I think you've been watching me too,' he said, gazing down at the bottle and picking at the label. It began to peel under his nail.

'I didn't mean to—'

'No. I... I like it.' He flushed red, all serious and confessional.

'Do you?'

'I know I'm not supposed to.'

'That's of your own construction. You made it weird.'

'You made it difficult.' There was the clink of the bottle as he set it down on the counter. His hands folded together.

'I didn't do anything besides telling you how old I was.'

'Ah.'

'Not that it should matter. We're all adults here.'

'You? Barely.'

I moved closer towards him and he caught me by the hips. I had an inch or two on him, I could see it in the way his eyes angled slightly up at me. It gave me an unexpected sense of agency. I prayed he wouldn't notice the tent rising in my jeans, but his gaze was firmly intertwined with mine.

'I don't date younger guys.' His hands were still on my hips. I was warm all over and we were standing so close.

'Who said anything about dating?'

He smirked at that and I took it as a green light to lean forward and kiss him, my mouth latching around his top lip. Blood pumped in my ears and the kitchen spun, but my hands found the nape of his neck to steady myself. I opened my mouth wider and our tongues met with the taste of wheat from the beers we'd been drinking. I could feel he was hesitant – his lips were tight around his teeth, and it took some slow coaxing to get them to relax against me. There was something endearing about him being a bad kisser, humanising, and the feeling of his stubble against me reached an itch I'd been desperate to relieve. We were growing messy, pressed up against the counter, hips to hips, chest to chest. I no longer cared if he felt my erection. I bucked against him, determined for him to know how hard he'd made me.

'Austin,' he warned, breaking away suddenly. The space between us felt kilometres wide. 'We shouldn't.'

'Why?' I sounded petulant, stepping forward to claim him again. We couldn't just stop. This was what we both wanted – yet his hand went to my chest, cutting down the notion.

'Because… we shouldn't.' He backed away, breathing hard. I forced myself to swallow but the lump stayed there. I wasn't sure what I'd done wrong. It pained me to think I'd crossed some invisible line, but then why had he touched me? I was certain that his hands on my hips were an indication of interest.

I inhaled sharply, smothering my embarrassment. 'It's totally fine if you're not attracted to me.' My voice sounded alien when echoed back at me. 'You could've just said that.'

He was at a loss for words, so I shrugged, pretending to be unbothered, and headed back out to the fire pit. He wouldn't follow me there, not while they were in this state.

'Austin!' Nadia seemed pleased by my presence, but I knew it was a result of the high. 'We were wondering where you'd gotten to.'

I took a seat amongst them and warmed my hands before the crackling fire.

'Do you want some?' Ben whispered.

'Of?'

'Acid. It's just a microdose. You'll barely feel it.'

I almost accepted, but my rule against psychedelics gave me pause. I was fearful of a bad reaction, not only for my mental stability, but for how they would treat me if I couldn't handle it. That, and Ezra's disapproval. I had enough strikes against me thus far.

'I'm okay, thank you.'

'Don't let him hold you back,' Nadia said as if reading my mind. 'You like him, right?'

I shot a glance over my shoulder, conscious of Ezra being in the vicinity, but he'd joined Sierra and Marion on the patio couch and was out of earshot.

'I think he's attractive, but I don't know if I'm his type.'

Matteo groaned. 'Why do all the cute ones always go for Ezra? It's not fair.'

'You think I'm cute?' I could feel my face reddening.

'Are you joking? Come on, Austin.' Matteo's compliments were already reviving my decimated ego. Even if he was high, I decided it still counted. 'I'd be all over you if Ezra hadn't said you were off limits.'

Nadia elbowed him in the ribs, and Matteo yelped.

'What?' I blinked, awaiting elaboration.

Nadia squinted up at her eyebrows as if the words she was trying to formulate were written above them. 'Ezra is very possessive,' she said slowly. 'He wouldn't have said anything unless he liked you too.'

'But—'

'Just don't force it. It'll turn him off.' She was curt, indicating it was all I was going to get out of her.

I frowned at the fire, more confused than before. Patience was a certain kind of torture I wasn't often capable of dealing with.

*

I found the shape of the bed, undressed in silence, and slipped between the covers. Another few hours had written everyone off, and though I wasn't tired, I didn't want to be lingering on the patio alone. Ezra had gone to bed hours ago. When I first passed his door, I was tempted to knock, but in an effort to save myself from further embarrassment, I'd kept my hands by my sides. An hour went by. I heard movement in the house and a door opened and shut, but the source was anyone's guess. I rubbed my eyes and rolled over to the other side of the bed, but the pillow was still warm. I was about to adjust again when there was a light knock on the door that had me sitting upright. I waited for a few moments, not entirely sure it wasn't just a figment of my imagination, but then it came again, even more decisive.

I slipped out of bed and opened the door. Ezra and I met face-to-face. He was in a dark t-shirt and joggers, avoiding eye contact, flushed under the single iridescent bulb in the hallway.

'Hi.' I crossed my arms over my bare chest, feeling exposed in my briefs.

'I just wanted to apologise. And…' He trailed off, glancing at my half-naked body before shifting focus to the carpet. 'I don't know.'

I waited. I wasn't going to initiate, not again. It was his turn.

He licked his lips, some kind of nervous tick, and I watched him blundering around his words. 'I just… You know. I don't remember how to do this kind of thing.' His eyes squeezed shut, as if the admission was too embarrassing to deliver directly. 'It's been ages since I've even kissed some-one, let alone hooked up. I'm not… I'm not that kind of person… But I want to… What I'm *trying* to say is.' He huffed in frustration, expelling the effort. 'I'd love to go for a drink when we're back in Perth if you're keen.'

It was so endearing, so innocent. It made me want to fuck him all the more.

My spine stood erect and I put on my mask of batting eyes and shy smiles. The performance. I said quietly, 'I'm not that kind of person either. I'd definitely rather get to know someone first.'

This was a lie us gay men were often guilty of: that we were willing to put in some form of emotional effort to secure a physical reward. It was all a front to make the game more exciting.

Ezra smiled with relief, believing we were on the same wavelength. I decided I was going to miss him, because once we had sex, we would probably never see each other again.

8

Juliana took a leisurely sip of her iced long black before inspecting me in her peripheral. 'Were they nice to you?' she asked casually.

She'd recovered from the flu, though the colour was still returning to her face. After being bedridden for so many days, she was in desperate need of sunlight and Perth over-delivered. There was an intensity to the rays, more so than with Melbourne – something to do with the ozone layer they'd tried to warn us about in school. The pessimist in me knew that every year we drew closer to a *Mad Max* red-dirt dystopia, but I'd hopefully be dead by then, and I was certain I'd never have any children to pass those horrors onto.

'They were okay,' I said.

She laughed, almost bitterly. 'Yeah. I was shocked that Alé and I were even invited.'

'I think I held my own.'

'I'm sure you did.'

We walked parallel to the coast, the sounds of the tide like a lullaby. Joggers overtook our slow walking pace with ease. I loved this route, hardly any breeze until the afternoon, just salt-tinged air and sunshine. Morning swims had become part of the regular routine, and my skin was already turning bronze. Juliana had joked we were finally looking related.

'I can't decide if I want to be part of their group or if I'm just desperate for friends right now.'

Julianna blinked at me. 'That's the most honest thing I've

heard from you.'

'I didn't mean to be secretive,' I said. 'I'm usually a bit more of an open book.'

'Really?' She fiddled with her paper straw, inspecting the lack of liquid left. The ice rattled against the sides of the cup. 'I'd say you're a bit of a chameleon.'

'How so?'

'At home, you're pretty quiet, reading, doing your own thing. But then we go out, and you can adapt to get along with anyone.'

'Isn't that a good thing?'

She shrugged in response.

I took a cautious sip of my cappuccino and then said, 'I guess I'm just determined to make a good impression with all the new people I've met.'

'Is that why you don't want anyone to know you have money?' She said it so offhandedly, it didn't sound like an interrogation, but I instinctively flinched.

'It's because people get weird about it,' I said. 'It's like a nasty label that you can only get away from when you're around other rich people. And other rich people are wankers.' It was a direct echo of Alé's sentiments, though I wanted to believe them too. I liked to think that I was different, that the stereotypes didn't apply to me.

'So, you're… pretending to be poor?'

'I'm just not throwing my financial status in everyone's faces.'

'But the café job is just for show? You're only there twice a week. I don't see how that would cover your rent.' She tossed her empty cup into a nearby recycling bin.

'Are you angry at me?'

Juliana looked earnestly apologetic. 'Oh my God, no. I'm sorry. I was honestly curious about your situation.'

My coffee was tossed in after hers. We continued up along the coast.

'I feel like I have a unique opportunity to start over in Perth,' I sighed. 'And I'd rather that clean slate be completely based on the person I want to be, rather than my family's money or other things out of my control. People start expecting things, either about how I'll behave or how I'll treat them. Kind of similar to being gay, I just hate having something to prove.'

'See, I didn't even know for sure that you were gay,' she said. 'I had my suspicions, but…'

'What gave it away?'

'Probably all the sneaking out in the middle of the night. It's pretty clear what you're doing.' She stared straight ahead, almost smug. 'And I heard a Grindr notification on your phone.'

My promiscuity was about as prevalent in my brain as mundane tasks like doing laundry or grocery shopping, but there were times I'd be tossing and turning in bed with the knowledge I'd only get some sleep once I ejaculated in someone, or them in me. Porn was a wet blanket, completely unsatisfying. I needed weight on me, I needed the warmth of a body. It wasn't even the climax I necessarily sought out, but everything leading up to it; the flirting, the games, swapping photos, anonymity, the anticipation of what they'd taste like, smell like, feel like. I wished I could be one of those people who played hard to get, who wasn't so easy, but my self-control had been non-existent since year eight. I was constantly held at gunpoint by my own desires.

'I'm not worried – unless I should be? Like… you're being safe?'

'Jesus, of course,' I stammered. 'I didn't realise you noticed.'

'I'd never judge. Have as much sex as you want.'

'I just don't want to get a reputation here. I want to be a certain type; easygoing, uncomplicated–'

'But if that's not who you are, then you're just playing a part.'

'Is that so bad? Maybe I don't like who I am outside of who I play.'

Juliana pondered. 'I think you should be yourself. Otherwise you'll attract the wrong kinds of people, constantly trying to be what they want you to be. Trust me, I've been there. The private school white-washed version of myself; bubbly, ditsy, unoffended. Some of the shit I used to hear… you don't want to know.' She shook the thought away. 'Everyone always counted on me for a good time, but only within their box of expectation. As long as I didn't hammer the reminder that I was different.'

'Do you see them anymore?'

'The PLC girls? Aside from Sierra, not really. But crossovers happen, especially around the GT. It's kind of impossible to avoid people here.' She sighed. 'It takes a while to find your tribe. I'm still not sure if I've found mine.'

'I guess I can't know until I try. And who knows where things will lead.'

It sounded much more suggestive than I'd intended, and Juliana noticed. She stopped in the middle of the sidewalk and cocked her head at me. 'Did something happen down south?'

I was all too eager to talk about him. A schoolgirl with a crush. 'I think I've got a date with Ezra at some point.'

She dissected the sentence. 'What did you like about him?'

'Are you surprised we clicked?'

'He's an acquired taste is all,' she said. 'A bit hard to read. But I suppose I feel that way with all of them.'

'It's just drinks. Nothing serious.'

'Well, good luck with that,' she said, an earnest warning, and turned us back in the direction of the apartment.

*

Hello Austin

I set the book I'd been reading facedown on the bed and stared at the unknown number. There was the capital H with the full hello, followed by my name, which I thought was oddly formal. What person in this day and age said 'Hello' in a text message anymore? It was almost serial-killer-core. Perhaps this was our age disparity actively working against us, or maybe his awkwardness emerged even digitally.

And this would be ?

That guy you made out with a few days ago

Which one ? I've got a few on the roster

Woooooow

I grinned and bit my lip. I might've preferred talking to him over text. It removed so many of the nerves that arose when we were face-to-face and reduced the possibility of blurting out something stupid. My knees folded up tight against my chest.

What's up?

Watching a Marvel movie

Aha lol

What?

Nothing

I just think superheroes are cringe

Excuse me??

Which ones have you watched?

Idk they're the same movie every time

Wow. Okay.

I'm making you watch every single one

And then you can have an opinion

Isn't there like fifty of them ?

Maybe

But you don't have a choice

Can we cuddle at least ?

As soon as I sent that text I wished I hadn't. I was supposed to be playing the game, letting him come to me. But before I could panic, he replied.

Sure haha

There was the proof; it didn't have to be so manipulative and thought-out. I was convinced that a part of him liked my boldness.

How about you? Wyd?

Struggling to get through this book

Of course you read books for fun

English major remember

I remember very well

I'm not much of a reader

That's ok

I like being the smart one

Hahaha

Yeah I'm definitely not intimidated by you at all

I think I'm the one who's intimidated

How is that possible

You being pretty is part of it

I think it's the painfully large age gap
I'm an old man and that is scary
You're not even old omg
I already have back problems Austin

Stupid and giddy, I was chuckling to myself in the silence of the bedroom.

Well

If they let you out of the retirement home this week
Should we go for that drink ?

I nearly gnawed my thumb off waiting for the reply. It was red and wet in my mouth, the nail jagged from where my teeth had torn into it. The new message appeared and I flushed in quiet victory.

Yeah I would like that

A call from Sabrina interrupted the exchange. My excitement melted into ambivalence, and my finger immediately moved over the decline button. Perhaps it was a pang of familial duty or an undercurrent of guilt, but I ended up answering with a forced smile.

'Sabrina,' I said.

'Going alright?' I couldn't detect any aggression in her tone.

'I'm great, actually,' I said slowly. 'I went away for the weekend with some new friends.'

'I'm glad to hear it.'

I waited for the pleasantries to rot and asked, 'How's things with you?' remembering not to directly assume anything was amiss. It was just a catch-up, things that normal siblings did from time to time.

'Yeah, I'm…' I waited for some jaded response about work, Graham, or even our father. Instead, she said, 'I'm having a pretty hard time actually.'

I wasn't sure I'd heard her correctly. 'Huh?'

This was the sister who had been incapable of emotion since she'd finished school and began her antidepressants. Ice-cold, sharp enough to cut yourself on. Most people seemed to have a better handle on their emotions after starting medications, but for Sabrina, it seemed to have switched them off completely. I hadn't seen her smile or show vulnerability in years.

'I'm… I'm finding it hard. To take care of the house.'

'The house?' My brows knitted together in confusion.

'Yes. Mum's house. You just… You just left me to take care of the house, and it's a lot of work.' Her tone was strained. There was only so long she could play nice, especially if she wanted something.

'You offered,' I huffed, already growing defensive. 'When I said I was leaving, you offered to check on it while I was gone.'

'I know, but now I don't want to anymore.'

My fingers prodded the base of my skull, trying to dislodge the strain that had quickly seized up there. 'Okay. Okay, I can find someone else to do it.'

'No!' Her reply was quick and desperate. 'You need to come home and do it yourself.'

'I can't, Sabrina. I'm trying to set up a life here.'

'It's only been a month. What sort of life could you possibly have already?'

'Is there something wrong with the house?' My silent prayers of it burning down and freeing us from its clutches echoed somewhere from the depths of my mind.

'No. It's exactly as you left it.'

'Then what are you going on about?'

She launched into her words with belligerence. 'It's all fine for you to run away and leave all the grown-up stuff to everyone else like Mum would've done. But it's just another responsibility that I felt obligated to do for you.'

'Sabrina, what–?'

'You left me here. Alone.' Her voice splintered into pieces with the hot rush of emotion. 'You never had to worry about anyone but yourself, and I've always been stuck, taking care of the house. Of you. I always took care of you. And who took care of me?' I thought I could hear her crying but it might've just been the rage that made her voice shake. 'I'm here picking up the pieces of our family while you're on a fucking vacation. Hope you enjoyed your *weekend away*, with your *new friends*.' She spat the repeated words and phrases.

'I'm sorry,' I said pathetically after a few moments.

'If you were sorry, you'd come home.'

'I can't.' My voice was faltering. 'You don't know what it was like.'

'For fuck's sake, I'm the only person who knows what it was like. I lost my mum too.'

'Yeah?' I snapped, feeling brave. 'You didn't even cry at the funeral.'

'Because she fucking hated me and she was obsessed with you,' she seethed and I was reduced back to a stammer.

'That's... That's not true.' My heartbeat felt suffocated.

'Of course it was. Every time she fucking looked at me, she saw a body she drank away, a future she wasted on playing housewife. She was jealous and delusional, Austin. I was the only one that saw her for what she was. Meanwhile, she babied you, made you feel special, her *little man* – so Freudian it was actually disturbing. And you wonder why Dad cheated on her?'

'You wanna bring up Dad, as if he didn't shield you from the worst of himself? You're such a fucking hypocrite!'

She ignored this. 'You refuse to accept reality. *You're* the one that can't feel. You're playing make-believe with all this fake happiness and confidence, pretending to be impenetrable. And this isn't a new thing! You've done it since you were a kid. You're a compulsive liar, even to yourself.'

I wanted to throw up over the side of the bed.

'I don't need this family,' I said, my face flushing. 'I can build my own.'

'They won't want you when they realise what a trainwreck you are.'

This time, I was the one who ended the call, throwing the phone across the room with disgust. It ricocheted off the wall and landed facedown on the carpet.

9

We sat outside at a table by the window. Devil's ivy dangled listlessly from the balcony above and swayed in the warm night air. As we said our *hellos* and made small talk, I watched the thin layer of foam on the lager Ezra bought for me diminish until it was a flat line. He had ordered a cider. It still bubbled with enthusiasm from his side of the table. I'd offered to pay but he wouldn't hear of it. I liked his dominance, even if it was fleeting and soon replaced by the same passivity I was used to. Long silences and awkward glances, with warm smiles sprinkled in between.

'Have you been here before?' he asked.

'I haven't. A bit further east than I'm used to.'

Queen's was situated on Beaufort Street, intimately shielded from the outside world by low-hanging ficus trees. It had the rustic charm of an old pub, with faded brick walls and chunks of white plaster still clinging on for dear life, nestled amongst the fresh upgrades of a new bar and sturdy wooden high tables.

'Ah of course.' He bent forward. 'You're a GT boy now.'

I smiled down at my lager. 'I'm starting to think that GT is a slur.'

'Maybe it is.'

'I thought everyone wanted to live by the beach.'

'With the geriatrics and the trust fund wankers? I think I'm alright,' he said with an impertinent smile and then drank from the long glass.

'I'm not like those rich assholes you all despise. I just happen to live there.'

'I never said you were an asshole. In fact, you're painfully sweet. All of the time. It must be a ruse.'

'Like I said, I've never had a bad day in my life.' The line was coming out more naturally now, as confidently as if it were true.

'Yeah, let's interrogate that for a second.' He touched a finger to his lips, surveying me. 'Never lost a friendship?'

'Nope.'

'Never done something that haunts you in the middle of the night?'

'Not that I can remember.'

'Never got your heart broken?'

'I haven't, no.'

'Must be nice,' he murmured gruffly. 'I can't tell if that makes you naive or lucky.'

'Can it be both? Doesn't everyone want to be... untarnished?'

He grinned. 'Your English major jumped out again.'

I rolled my eyes. 'Is untarnished a big word?'

'Either that, or I'm just dumb.'

'Well, you watch Marvel movies, so—'

'Wow,' he laughed. 'So much for being painfully sweet.'

'The ruse is slipping.'

'Indeed.' He paused to take another sip of his beer, then said, 'Seriously though. I can't imagine being so... *untarnished* and still having a personality. I'd argue that the bad parts of my life made me slightly interesting.'

'How so?'

He shook his head. 'There's no way I'm telling you all my fucked-up stuff if you're Mr Perfect.'

'You seem pretty well adjusted to me.'

'You don't know me well enough.'

That comment got my attention. Maybe we were more alike than I dared to admit.

'I never said I was perfect,' I said, actively avoiding his eyes. 'I just refuse to be sad. About anything.'

'I think sadness is cosy,' he said, tucking his hands under his armpits boyishly. 'I love curling up under a blanket with all my clothes on, listening to sad songs and crying my eyes out.'

'Really?'

'Wallowing and feeling sorry for myself is one of my favourite solo activities.'

'That is shocking to me,' I laughed. 'You give off… I don't know… golden retriever energy.'

'Is that how the kids put it these days?' I cringed at the reminder of our age gap, but he didn't seem to notice, too busy thinking it over. 'I guess I could see that. Maybe I used to, but not anymore.'

'Is Callum to blame for that?'

Sudden anger flared in his eyes, a silent roar of *how dare you speak his name*, but it was so brief, he'd surely deny it if I ever called him out. Instead, he rubbed his forehead and said, 'Remember how I told you about the gay scene in Perth? The ones to avoid at all costs?' I nodded, and he stared at me, direct and serious. 'Well, he's at the top of the list, along with anyone connected to him.'

'I think you have to say that,' I challenged. 'If he's your ex.'

'I have some decent things to say about most of my exes. But not him.'

'What made him so awful?' I could assume the wealth disparity, but otherwise, their past relationship was mostly a mystery to me.

'I guess we're doing this now, aren't we?' He smiled to

himself with that same melancholy expression I'd seen between the vineyards.

'What are we doing?'

'Talking about why I don't do hookups or date younger guys.'

I was aware of how warm my face was. I said nothing.

'I don't think you realise how big of a deal this is,' he said quietly. 'How special you are.'

It was a guilty punch to the gut. Here I was, biding my time with the intention of getting him naked, while he blood-let his secrets in front of me.

'You've been celibate since your breakup?'

The question seemed to instil a fresh discomfort and he reached for his glass. 'Yeah.' The drink was raised to his lips and he knocked it back.

'You haven't wanted to—?'

'Not really,' he murmured, setting the glass back down on the table with a soft thud. 'When you lose someone you thought was your soulmate… you kind of abandon all drive to try anything again. That was it, and it won't come back around.'

'I'm surprised you feel that way about someone you hate. Most people end up realising the breakup was for the best.' I don't know where I plucked this wisdom from, but it sounded like the right thing to say.

'I hate how he ended things, and I hate the person he is now. But I loved him when we were together.'

I squirmed between his words.

'I loved him more than I've ever loved anyone, even my own family. People still assume the money drew me in: the parties, the houses, the trips. It's bullshit. If anything, it was one of the hardest parts of the relationship. When a person already has everything, it kind of messes with you. Like you couldn't possibly offer anything of value. But he made me feel irreplaceable. For a while.'

He was surprisingly eager to talk about it. To make me understand.

'When we met, he couldn't even hold a conversation. He was so stiff… awkward. But there were the flowers, the dinners, driving all the way across Perth just to kiss me goodnight. I caved. Fell in love. Not because he was generous, but because he was thoughtful. And so fucking nice. They're always nice in the beginning.'

I was draining my lager quickly. Drinking forced me to listen and held me back from implementing commentary or audible reactions. He didn't notice my silence. In fact, he hardly looked for confirmation that I was still paying attention.

'He started dressing better, went to the gym, made more friends, and gained his confidence. He was partying a lot, actually, got a bit addicted to coke – which really messed him up if you ask me – but mostly he just… thrived. And I struggled to keep up.'

His eye contact was more direct now. 'You have to understand that being in his life was like being abducted by an alien and dropped into a fantasy world. No one ever said no to us. There was no queue we couldn't skip and no table we couldn't sit at. It was just an excess of everything. And, yeah, it was nice.' He muttered that last part bitterly, flushing a light shade of red. 'How could I not enjoy it, after years of busting my ass at shit jobs and never even scratching the surface of the life I always wanted? I was suddenly a part of it. But I fucked it up, I know I did. Trying to launch my own marketing company was stressing me out; I was eating too much, I was grumpy, never in the mood for sex. He wanted to pull me out of my rut. It wasn't something either of us had any control over, but he kept trying anyway. So, for our birthdays, he planned a trip to Europe. Need another drink?'

He was staring at my finished glass as if it were a trespasser.

'It's my round,' I offered, sliding from the stool. He agreed to this with a brief nod, and I walked to the bar alone. The inside was alive with music and conversation, and a fireplace in the corner of the room suffocated the air with heat, but I'd somehow felt more smothered at the table. The mere mention of Callum was a foot on my throat. I was dreading the return, wondering if it was worth trying to pivot the conversation, but we were too far gone by that point. I would have to endure it.

'Alright. Where were we?' he muttered when I sat down with fresh drinks.

'Europe,' I said.

'Europe,' he agreed before another sip. 'I've never been outside of Australia, so I was blown away by the idea.' His eyes had a far-off distance to them as he gazed at an unspecified point somewhere behind me. 'We'd very casually discussed marriage, and at the time, there was no one else I could imagine spending the rest of my life with. We were young, him even younger, but it felt right. Maybe I secretly hoped I'd come back from our trip with a ring. Does that sound insane?'

'No,' I said. 'It sounds honest.'

'I wouldn't let him pay for my ticket, too bloody proud, so we split it. Used up all of my savings because he refused to fly economy. Everything was… Everything was set, the flights, the accommodation, the fucking restaurant bookings, and a week before we left, he just ended it. Out of the blue.'

I blinked at him in silence.

'I never got a definitive answer as to why. He just told me one morning that we should talk and said that it wasn't working anymore.'

'Fuck. Are you serious?' I ran a hand through my hair performatively, emphasising the bewilderment.

'After two years, yeah. Just like that. I thought he was joking at first,' he mumbled. 'When I realised he wasn't, I... I cried, I begged, I pleaded... I told him I'd do anything to fix it. I'd wait as long as it took until he changed his mind. But that was it. He just let me grab my things, and... I drove home alone.' The moisture in his eyes threatened to leak, but he refused to acknowledge it. 'We haven't spoken since.'

I ached for him, but I ached for me too. I was completely out of my depth, and I hadn't properly grasped that until now. I couldn't do this to him. I couldn't use him. He was too fragile.

'You know, Austin, I think heartbreak is one of the most traumatic things to happen to a person.'

My name in his mouth startled me. My body had permanence again. I wasn't just a transparent object to gaze through and talk at.

'It's like someone died. Only it's worse — because they're choosing to live, just without you.'

My jaw set. How could I argue without a forced explanation of my past? It was easier to say nothing, and besides, who was I to tell him he was wrong? I'd never been heartbroken in that way. I didn't know any better.

'And it wasn't just Callum that disappeared, but the entire world I'd built around him. Our friends chose him since I didn't have the money to keep up with their lifestyles, and they already saw me as northern suburbs trash. I was sent back to where I came from. Back to planet Earth, to my boring and difficult life, savouring the taste of how the one percent live.' His Adam's apple pulsed as he tried to swallow the lump that had formed in his throat. 'If it wasn't for Marion, Nadia, Matteo… I say sadness is cosy, but only if you're able to slip in and out of it. For a while, I thought I'd be stuck there.'

'I'm really sorry,' I said. There wasn't much else to do except apologise.

'Don't be sorry.' He shook the emotions away as if they'd gathered in his hair like snowflakes. 'It was fine after I decided to stop caring. About everything. That made it all a bit more bearable.'

I traced the rim of my beer. 'You just… decided?'

'It's like a switch when you hit a point. You just turn it off. It's a lot easier to feel nothing.'

'Isn't that a bit…' I nearly said *dramatic*, but I ruminated on my approach. 'You still care about things, and people. You have emotions. You're not a psychopath.' I laughed nervously, trying to ease the tension. His face had formed into hard marble, adamant not to betray any more emotion than he already had.

'Sure, but not in the same way. I don't let my feelings control me anymore. I don't wait for male attention to boost me up. I don't waste time with younger guys that aren't mature enough to communicate or be honest with what they want. I focus on my life, my friends, and my career.' He touched the side of his pint. 'I don't think I'll ever care about people the way I used to.'

I found myself nodding. 'Actually, I completely get that. I find it really hard to let people in, to rely on them. Especially romantically.' I picked up my beer. 'Divorced parents and all that.'

'I thought nothing bad had ever happened to you,' he said while I was mid-sip. I took longer than I usually would, lowering the glass extra slowly, wiping my upper lip with the back of my wrist, clearing my throat – anything to give me more time to think of a response.

'It was amicable,' I said eventually. 'Nothing particularly traumatic. But it definitely made me question traditional partnerships.'

He was staring right through me.

'How many boyfriends have you had?'

I met his eyes ready with another lie, but something about how vulnerable and forgiving they looked made me blurt out the truth. 'None. I've never been in a relationship.' My mouth was dry. It was going to be the final nail in the coffin, even though I'd already decided to give up on the game moments prior. It wasn't worth the hassle, the cruelty. There were so many other people I could sleep with, ones with far less baggage.

I expected him to look disappointed or pissed off, like this had all been a waste of time, but he was grinning from ear to ear.

'What?'

He played with his hair, sheepish and flirtatious all at once. 'I've decided that your lack of experience might be the sexiest thing ever.'

'I'm confused.'

'I misjudged you, okay?' He was blushing. 'Most twenty-year-olds just wanna fuck around, do drugs, get messed up… As they should. Power to them. I thought you were wanting that too. Meanwhile, I'm on the other side, so boring that I haven't had sex in a year, but maybe I need to find a middle ground somewhere.'

I stared at him in disbelief. The reversal had occurred so unexpectedly. 'So, now you want to have sex? After all that?'

He turned a darker shade of red and began to stammer. 'I

didn't… I mean… Who knows what's going to happen with us. I just want a friend to hang out with, no pressure. Someone smart, someone interesting, someone… *untarnished.* I didn't realise that until now.'

'And I fit that criteria?'

'Well… Yes.'

'So—'

'So, let's go with it? I don't know. I like you, Austin, and I'm getting the sense you like me too.'

'Is that right?' I couldn't help but smile and blush myself.

'But I also don't have the capacity to be a boyfriend to you if that's what you were hoping down the line. Not right now, at least.'

'I wasn't thinking that far ahead,' I soothed him. I couldn't have worded it better myself.

'I know, but I don't want to blindside you, so I'm telling you now.'

'Honestly? That's a relief. Considering I just moved here, I have no intention of diving into a relationship.'

'You're so mature,' he sighed, and those words gave me such a rush, crystallising the feeling of being special, feeding my ego. 'I guess we're on the same page then?'

'We want to keep hanging out?'

'Yes.'

'As friends?'

'Maybe a bit more than that.'

'But no feelings?'

'No feelings,' he affirmed. 'Can you handle that?'

It wasn't *no strings attached*, it wasn't a one-night stand, but it was close enough. The game was back on.

'Yeah. I can handle it.' I replied. 'Can you?' I washed down my triumph with the remainder of the lager.

'I guess we'll see,' he grinned, and then I extended my foot out under the table, stopped against his calf, and slowly dragged it up and down the length of his leg. His eyes were full of longing. I was sure his erection was growing, and I knew I had him where I wanted him.

*

Deep north in Nollamara, there were no pine trees or sea breeze, just half-empty highways tunnelling through suburbia. Perth was the most threadbare here. Streetlights flickered. Cars sat abandoned alongside parks made up of dried grass. Next to the public school was a TattsLotto and a bottle shop. There was something desolate about the dark shopping centres and the copied-and-pasted houses. I couldn't imagine anyone wanting to live around here, much less Ezra, but he'd shrugged and said it was affordable, which made me embarrassed for questioning it in the first place. We pulled into a stone-slabbed driveway shouldered by spiked shrubs and passed two grey townhouses until we reached his at the end of the drive. The garage door opened and he rolled us inside and turned off the engine. The silence and darkness were intimate. I was going to kiss him over the console, but he was already exiting the car and beckoning me into the house.

The kitchen and the living room were divided by a half-wall. Two ceramic mugs sat finished on the edge of the sink with the tea bag string still hanging over the edge. A lit candle flickered, and somewhere further into the house I could hear a toothbrush whirling.

'Marion's getting ready for bed,' he said. 'My room is in here.'

It was right by the front door and lit by a single lamp. The room was spotless, without a single speck of dust or strewn laundry. The headboard was tall and wrapped with grey fabric, and the sheets were navy blue, tucked and pressed like hotel staff had made them up. Alongside the bed was a floor-to-ceiling mirror. I glanced at us in it, standing there awkwardly, each waiting for the other to make the first move.

'I really don't do this,' he said softly.

'I bet you say that to all the boys you bring here.'

'No, seriously. I… I don't even know what I'm doing.'

'Well, it usually starts like this.'

I kissed him. My confidence was unexpected for him – so much for innocence being sexy – but with my prior escapades, I'd always been fairly comfortable with leading. It was natural, the way our lips crashed together like waves against a shoreline. My arms wound around his neck, his around my waist, and we stood there, washing each other in greedy kisses and touches. The bed was right at my legs and I was pulling him back onto it, and on top of me. His hands planted on either side of my ribs and he slid between my thighs, denim and friction and panting. I kissed his neck and he moaned and rolled his growing erection into mine. My hands slipped between us, finding the top of his jeans. He breathed in sharply when I unclasped the rivet.

'Am I moving too fast?'

'No. Keep going.'

I pulled the zipper down and slipped my hand into his cotton briefs. He was groaning and holding me, thrusting softly into my closed grip. Warm and close. I'd tug and he'd buckle, and with that single hand wrapped around his cock, I felt powerful. I motioned to pull the jeans and briefs further down his hips when he grabbed my wrists. His eyes were closed and he was panting as he said, 'Wait, wait. If we're doing this, I need to shower.'

'What?'

'I need to shower. I didn't know this was going to happen.'

'Ezra, you're fine.'

'I'll be really quick, I promise.'

He rolled off the bed and retreated to the ensuite bathroom, tucking himself back into his pants. The door shut behind and I was left alone in immediate silence.

I wrapped my arms around myself and took a miserable breath. It was so cruel, that sudden lack of weight. I didn't know what to do with myself except stare at the wall and listen to the sounds of the shower. This was the second time he'd abandoned me in such a way. Perhaps he wanted to be penetrated but hadn't prepared, and that was why he panicked. It made sense considering how passive he was, and how carefully he tended to each aspect of himself – his hair, his physique, his room. Maybe he wanted everything to be perfect. I only wished he understood how little I cared about those things where sex was concerned. It was supposed to be dirty, natural, spontaneous, savage even. I liked it in bathroom stalls and in alleyways. I liked it on floors with our pants around our thighs. I would take it any way he saw fit – but he might've been far too clinical for that.

Five minutes later, he re-entered the bedroom in a loose towel, backlit against the bathroom light and glistening with moisture. He left the door slightly ajar, and without a word, walked around the bed to turn off the lamp. If not for the slit of light coming from the bathroom, we'd be swimming in the black. I sat up straighter as he crawled onto the bed and over to me.

'Okay,' he mumbled, ready at last.

'Okay.' I moved to take off my pants and underwear, looking to him for permission. He gave it with a swift nod and watched me shuffle the fabric down my legs. My erection sprang free. My shirt came next, up and over my head, and I was all at once completely naked beside him. I grasped my cock, stroking the length of it, and he stared with a nervous longing. Achingly slow, he parted the towel and tossed it to the floor next to my clothes. Our eyes indulged themselves with ferocity. A hand went to his chest. He let me push him onto his back and take him into my mouth. He tasted faintly of eucalyptus body wash with an undercurrent of salt-tinged flesh. His hands made fists in my hair and he was gasping and saying my name, drunk with pleasure. I quickly found all the spots that would make him moan and hitch a breath, keeping them in my memory like a promise. I pulled my mouth back to his and rolled us over so he was on top. A sudden aggression arose in the forcefulness of his kiss. With me writhing beneath him and his hands pinning me to the bed, I was at his mercy.

'Austin,' Ezra whispered in my ear, 'Can I fuck you?'

'Yes, please.'

'Do you want me to use a condom?'

'No.' I didn't want anything keeping us apart, just skin-to-skin contact, as intimate as possible.

'Okay then.' He reached over to the bedside table and pulled out a bottle of lubricant, lathering it along his erection and between my legs before pulling me closer. 'I'll go slow.'

My knees hunched up against my chest. His eyes were downcast at his cock, positioning himself before he pushed in. Pain slashed its way up my abdomen and I sucked in air before a deep exhale, imagining my insides contracting and widening to allow for space. It could take up to several minutes like this, breathing through the tearing of my body, but I found myself responding with ease shockingly fast. There was so little resistance after the initial thrust, an immediate physical surrendering. I wondered if it had to do with trust. So rarely did I know the person I was getting penetrated by, let alone felt safe with them. Instead of having to use breath work to trick my body into this false sense of security, it was doing it all on its own for Ezra.

'Is that okay? Is it too fast?'

'Yes. No, it's...' I gasped. 'You feel great.' It was effortless, perfect even. He was deep, hands holding my thighs, his face scrunched up like he was anticipating a punch.

'Austin, you're so tight.'

My ankles curled around his hips, pulling him even closer. I clung to the bedsheets, and to him, begging him not to stop in jagged whispers, and we were like that for a few minutes until his eyes rolled back and his body tensed up. He couldn't fight it any longer. He finished inside me with a groan of release and collapsed against my chest. He felt rigid in my arms, a frightened bird, and I wondered if his eyes were open.

'Sorry, I didn't mean to—'

'It's okay,' I whispered.

Usually, I felt so hollow after they climaxed. There was something traumatising about it, back to reality, back to pretending I enjoyed my reflection and the world around me, no distractions, no sexual attention that made me feel alive. Yet in the afterglow of sex with Ezra, I was warm and complete. Even when he pulled out, a feeling which often made me want to cry, I was flushed and elated and so... happy. Irrevocably happy.

Was the game still going?

'I want you to come too,' he said with a newfound determination. He kissed down my chest and ended at my hips, mouth eager around me. Within a few minutes, I was touching his hair and crying out, shuddering as I came. He pulled away and let it coat my stomach, face dewy and flushed in the dark. I was sure mine was too. We smelled of semen and sweat and joy. I waited for the comedown, for the suffering of it all. It never arrived.

'Shower?' he offered.

'Another one?'

He shrugged and rose from the bed, making his way back to the bathroom. His cock was limp and wet. I gazed longingly and decided to join him. In my cupped hand, I gathered up the mess I'd made in my navel and rubbed it into my stomach like lotion.

The shower wasn't large but we managed to both squeeze inside it, pressed up close and warm beneath the water. Despite the orgasm, I was still hard. With shy eyes and bodies up against each other, we lathered soap onto our hands and took turns scrubbing each other clean. His ass cheeks felt like clay in my hands and I imagined resculpting the shape of them as I squeezed and caressed.

'That was…'

'The best sex you've ever had?' I smiled, uncaring if it sounded arrogant. He didn't correct me, and I took his silence as agreement. I kissed him again to mark my territory.

*

In the middle of the night, I became conscious of how loud I was breathing. I tried to synchronise my inhales with Ezra's in an attempt to disguise the sound but ended up feeling like I was suffocating myself. He was already sound asleep and probably wouldn't notice. Mouth hung slightly agape, his face was half-hidden in one of the pillows. The other pillow was stuffed between his legs and arms. I was jealous of how intimately he was cuddling it and not me. He'd mentioned something about not being able to sleep if we spooned and then placed a colourless pill in his mouth and washed it down with some water. I refrained from asking what it was, and he passed out thirty minutes later. He didn't stir, not once.

10

Juliana pulled the car up next to a bungalow made of flimsy-looking wooden panels and a terracotta roof – though *bungalow* might've been a generous word. It was more of a beach shack, barely peeking out of the bush that encroached. Stairs led up to a wooden porch and a single light washed the garden in a dreary orange. The place was sagging with fatigue – one gust of wind threatened to topple the structure into the neighbour's yard.

'This is his place?'

'Yeah,' Juliana murmured. 'It's a bit shit, isn't it?'

I chuckled darkly at the floor of the car, glad I wasn't alone in the thought. At my feet was a crushed-up Zambrero bag and there were crumbled receipts in the cup holders. Like the apartment, Juliana didn't clean up after herself often.

'Thank you for agreeing to do this.'

'He's my uncle,' I said, forcing a smile. 'Gotta meet him eventually.'

We got out of the car, climbed the creaking steps, and Juliana pushed open the door without knocking.

'We're here!' she called out.

The house was sparsely decorated except for a few fake indoor plants and a large shelf of records. The spines were too hard to read from far away. I inspected the stains on the carpet with impertinence before privately scolding myself. Our apartment was no palace, we too had marks and scratches and peeling paint, but maybe I held men over fifty to a higher standard. The kitchen radiated with heat. Ray was humming with his back turned as he fried things I couldn't determine on the stovetop, but the smells were familiar from the dishes Juliana would cook up. He looked younger than I expected, tall and thin. Grey hair crept out from his scalp like root rot. He sensed movement behind him and placed the tongs down.

'Look who it is.' He smiled warmly at his daughter.

'Thanks for having us.'

They embraced, and then his eyes met mine over her shoulder.

'Austin,' he said in acknowledgement.

'Ray,' I replied.

He and Juliana broke apart as he said, 'You look just like Mark.'

'You know my dad?'

'Met him once. That was enough,' he said with a laugh. I could've joined in on the joke, but I decided to give him nothing. His eyes were promptly downcast as he scratched his neck. 'Hungry?'

'Starving,' Juliana said as she strode into the kitchen. Her acrylic nails plucked a piece of meat right off the pan and into her open mouth. She smacked her lips together in satisfaction. 'Needs more chilli powder.'

'It's perfect the way it is,' he tutted as he gathered plates. 'Sit down. Please.'

Juliana and I sat opposite each other and watched the plates of spiced rice and meat fill up the open space on the dining table. Ray joined at the head.

'When I decided to move to Perth, Dad was determined to learn how to cook all my favourite Brazilian dishes,' Juliana said, using the serving spoon to disperse the food between us. 'He was always showing off when I stayed over.'

Ray looked pleased by the comment.

'Why did you board at PLC if Ray was right here?' I asked Juliana. 'Too long a drive?'

'It's only a one-bedroom,' Ray answered for her. 'I've owned it for years.'

Juliana's fork scraped against her plate. 'I was on the pull-out couch over the holidays,' she said flatly. 'Or staying in one of Sierra's spare rooms.' She looked uncomfortable with the existence of the memory, or uncomfortable with the fact that I now knew about it.

'You were so little,' Ray murmured, staring at me. 'The last time I saw you.'

I sat up straighter. 'I didn't realise we'd met.'

'I visited you all in Melbourne. When your parents were still together.' He opened a bottle of red. It made a gurgling sound as it emptied itself into our glasses. 'You were four, I think. Too young to remember anything.'

'And how was your time in Melbourne?'

His nostrils flared, but he managed a smile. 'Brief.'

I waited for the few pieces of him I'd been given over the years to fit together into a coherent image, but it remained hazy, inconsistent. *We're a whole family of liars*, I'd joked to Sabrina. Was that more true for him, or for my parents?

'So, you're happy here?'

'Sure,' I nodded.

'He's just started seeing someone,' Juliana mused down at her plate, avoiding the narrowed eyes I shot at her. 'I think it's made Perth a little bit more exciting for him.'

'Oh really? What's her name?' Ray asked.

'*His* name is Ezra,' I replied dryly. 'And we're just friends,' I added, directed at Juliana this time.

'Right. That's... That's fine with me, of course,' Ray stammered.

'Thank you for your permission,' I blinked slowly.

'I just mean–'

'Dad–'

'You don't look gay.'

I sighed. Ray drowned his embarrassment in a sip of wine. Juliana kept a cool disposition, pretended nothing was amiss, and plucked a new topic out of thin air to salvage the conversation. 'He's gotten quite close with Sierra too.'

'Oh really?' Ray exclaimed, aiding the attempt. 'Great girl.'

'She's a riot,' I agreed.

'Yesenia didn't like her. Said she was a brat.'

Juliana shrugged. 'Mum doesn't like lots of people. And Sierra has her moments. But she's been there for me through a lot.'

'Are you and Juliana's mum… *Yesenia*, still friendly?' I asked Ray. I decided it would be easier to follow Juliana's cue, pretending everything was going smoothly, asking tame questions and making small talk as if I didn't feel we were teetering towards a precipice.

'Sort of,' Ray shrugged. 'Although she still blames me for separating them.'

'It was my choice to come to Perth,' Juliana said. 'She just misses me. We were close.'

'But we all agree your coming to Australia was for the best. You were lucky to get an education here. At one of the best private schools in Western Australia, I might add. The connections, the opportunities…' He picked at the space between his teeth to dislodge the debris that had gathered there. Once it was clear, he said, 'Though Yesenia still sends me strongly worded emails now and then.'

'She holds grudges,' Juliana nodded.

'Mel did too.'

Dead silence fell over the table. Even Juliana hadn't found

the bravery to utter her name, let alone discuss her in passing. It had been the first time since leaving Melbourne I'd heard it.

'Sorry,' was all Ray said. It was gasoline to my fire.

'Sorry for mentioning her?' I said. 'Or sorry for not coming to the funeral?'

He opened his mouth but no words fell out. Fury was blurring my vision like a thick fog. I was doing it again, letting my anger and sadness infect me, a virus I couldn't shake. It was what had pushed the few Melbourne friends I had away, forced them to cease calling and messaging. What had kept me isolated in her house. My palms were damp and my heart thudded in my chest.

'Excuse me,' I said, rising from the table to beeline down the hallway we'd entered through. I wasn't one to storm out and cause scenes, but this time felt appropriate.

Outside, after taking a long inhale free from the confines of the dinner table, I surrendered to the porch steps. My focus trained on the static weeds stretching their long fingers across the fence posts. Overgrown into disarray, careless. That's what Ray was, *careless*. The door opened behind me, and I knew it was him who emerged. The crumbling wood moaned under our combined weight as he sat down beside me. He'd brought the smells of the kitchen with him – they lingered in his hair and shirt.

'Do you smoke?' he asked, extracting a pack of cigarettes from his baggy jeans. The box was covered in images of rotting toes and flesh falling from cheeks, a substantial effort to sway the masses from partaking.

'No,' I said, but motioned for one anyway.

He lit the end of mine first, then his, and together we breathed in the taste of ash. Engines rumbled from the next block over. Midges swarmed the porch light. Our shadows painted the pavement.

'I smoked my first with Mel, you know?' he said after a few moments. 'We were friends a long time ago. Until she decided she was ashamed of us and left Perth. She never called. She never visited. Too busy performing another life.' He put the box away.

'It's all her, isn't it?' I took another drag. On the inhale, the embers at the end of the cigarette burned red and bright like a blood moon. 'Everything's her fault.'

'Not at all. I blame the sickness.'

'Even when you were kids?'

Ray shrugged. 'It wasn't obvious right away. It certainly got worse over the years. She was never quite rooted in reality. She had all these big dreams of being famous – singing in a band, being a movie star, modelling, you name it – but no skills or drive to achieve any of it, and it made her resentful. Filled with shame for where she came from, and the lack of opportunities it provided.'

'What, like you were the golden child?'

He laughed heartily, deep from his gut. 'God, no. She was the one that made it out and married rich. And I was spending my time and money at the pokies, just like our old man, and his old man before him.' He played with the cigarette, letting it spin between his fingers. 'But things changed when I found out about Juliana. The daughter I never knew existed… I wanted to give her the best life possible, only I was up to my ears in debt. I didn't know what else to do, except to go to Melbourne and beg my rich sister for a loan. With the mansion and all the holidays… I thought it would be pocket change, but she refused to lift a finger once Mark was in her ear. "The principal of it." Frankly, I didn't want their money after I saw how miserable they were, Mel especially. It proved that there was nothing she could do, no money she could spend to make it all go away. It was chemical depression. Bad wiring in the brain. Unavoidable.'

'Mum never talked about you, or my grandparents,' I said quietly. 'Were they awful?'

He sighed, slow and heavy. 'We have a sadness in our family. A coldness. Death and loss and regret, generations of emotional abuse. I refused to let it infect Juliana, but I refused to abandon her in South America. I had to provide somehow.' He touched his stubble absentmindedly. 'I cleaned up my act and saved whatever I could. I got her citizenship sorted, put her through school. Juliana was brilliant, and the scholarship from PLC was generous. What they didn't cover, I'm still paying off.' He glanced behind us at the crumbling house.

'I'm sorry,' I said out of instinct.

He turned back to me, ignoring the apology. 'Are you close? You and your sister?'

I swallowed hard and shifted back against the stairs, feeling the rotting wood pressing into the small of my back. 'Not anymore. It got too toxic, and I couldn't stick up for Sabrina, not against her, I couldn't...' I squeezed my eyes shut for a moment. 'Mum was so fragile. I had to be her best friend. And I could never say how suffocating it was or that I might struggle with the same things as her. Depression. Emptiness.' It felt wrong saying the words, like I was intertwining myself with a diagnosis.

Ray nodded slowly in understanding. 'It can be taboo for men.'

'I'd never do what she did,' I snapped bitterly. 'You just have to fake it. Pretend until it feels real.'

'It was the only way out she saw,' Ray replied simply. 'It must've been very difficult. I hope you don't blame yourself.'

I gazed at nothing. 'I was supposed to be the one taking care of her. Dad left, Sabrina left, but I stayed. And it wasn't enough.'

We both sat there, stumped.

'I regret not coming to the funeral,' he said after some time had passed and our cigarettes had burned down to the butts. 'I hope you hear me when I say that.'

'Why didn't you?' This time, the question wasn't accusatory. I genuinely wanted to know the answer.

'I believed she wouldn't have wanted me there. I thought I was respecting her wishes.'

'That sounds like a bullshit answer.'

A rustle in the trees above us seemed to agree.

'It's not,' he said. 'She didn't want to know me. I reminded her too much of the life she was trying to forget. We kept drifting further apart until we were strangers.' He was stock-still beside me, and I wondered if he was holding his breath. 'But I should've been there for you and Sabrina. *That's* what Melissa would've truly wanted.' He rose from the steps. 'You should make it right with your sister. You won't get another one.'

He wandered back inside, leaving me in the dark. I hugged my knees.

*

'Does he know?' Juliana asked, more to the windshield than to me. The streets were empty as we passed the threshold of familiarity back into the GT. The train clattered alongside us, a flurry of metal until it slowed at a station and we barreled past it.

'Who?'

'Ezra. Does he know about your mum?'

I gazed out the window and counted pine trees, quietly nursing what felt akin to a hangover. 'No. No one does. Except you.'

Juliana looked at me pointedly and said, 'Maybe you should tell him.'

11

A haze coated the street from a nearby bushfire, creating an almost theatrical atmosphere, like a stage that had been fogged up to amplify light. My eyes were sore from blinking away the traces of ash. The headlights of Ezra's Volkswagen splashed my shadow on the road as I passed the front of the car and slipped into the passenger seat.

'Austin,' he beamed the second the door shut.

'Hi. How've you been?' I moved to clip the seatbelt into place. It always felt intimate inside cars with him, breathing the same air, encased in metal and leather. What might've been a Bleachers song vibrated through the speaker next to my calf.

'I've been good. I missed you.'

'You did?' I blinked. 'I thought you didn't feel anything.'

He laughed dryly and shifted us into drive.

I added, 'I missed you too.'

He reached across the car and let his hand rest on the inside of my thigh. Fingers splayed across my jeans and squeezed the flesh beneath. I melted – until he withdrew his hand to place it back on the steering wheel, and I was solid once more.

We sped through the dark. There was something erotic about the self-assurance he found behind the wheel. Drifting between lanes, revving the engine and overtaking traffic were opportunities to prove his skill and bathe in my admiration. I noticed him glancing over at me throughout the drive, trying to spot the times I was impressed. A kid showing off for his crush. I found myself performing these moments for him, my mouth consciously making small 'o's as he shot through orange lights and drifted around corners.

'You know, I can name the make and model of any car on the road.'

'Prove it,' I challenged.

He pointed them out as we drove, excitement glinting in his eyes when we'd pass a luxury one. For someone who mostly despised the upper class, he had an obvious yearning for the finer things in life; a nice car, a clean house with soft sheets, dinners out. He was a paradox. I tried to compensate for my lack of vehicular knowledge with eager nods of feigned interest. I liked listening to him talk about the things he loved. I liked how happy it made him, even if they were basic or childish. It was endearing, his boyishness.

Into Fremantle, we passed the congregation of multi-coloured shipping containers and cranes poised like steel dinosaurs, each backlit by the moon. We zipped over the bridge and parked along a dimly lit street of heritage buildings and warehouses. I didn't catch the name of the restaurant as we walked in, but we were seated at a table lit by a single candle, some of the only patrons in attendance.

'If you only want to be friends, you're gonna have to stop taking me to romantic restaurants,' I said after our drinks arrived. He had an Aperol spritz and I had a Negroni. The bitterness of the drink was another kind of costume, one of maturity – in the same way that whiskies or martinis aged a person. A performance of evolved, acquired tastes. I sipped on it and found it far less painful than I expected.

'Next time we'll get Maccas,' he joked.

'Probably not the best food to eat before sex.'

He stifled a shy grin. 'Who says we're having sex?'

'Was that only a one-time thing?'

'Maybe. I think there's a general rule against it.'

Our eyes were engaged, taunting and playful. I noticed his arms looking shapely through the cotton button-down as he gripped the flimsy bit of paper that was supposed to be the menu. He brought it closer to his face to read.

'I thought the rule was no feelings,' I said down to the page, pretending to skim it.

'No feelings, but friends primarily.'

'Friends can have sex.'

'I thought it was impossible after a point.'

'Is that right?'

'Too intimate. Haven't you seen the movie?'

I frowned at him. 'The Mila Kunis one?'

'No, the other one. With Natalie Portman.'

'I swear that's the same movie with different actors.'

'Oh,' Ezra realised with a measured nod. 'So it is.'

'Isn't this what you wanted?'

'Yes! Fuck, sorry.' He shook his head from side-to-side in self-imposed frustration. 'I still do. I'm just very inconsistent. It's one of my worst qualities.'

I reached out and placed my hand over his, giving skin and bone a soft squeeze. 'We're having fun. And as soon as we aren't, we can stop. Yeah?'

He sighed with relief. 'Yeah. Great.' He was more of a chronic overthinker than I was.

I moved my hand to my glass and brought the Negroni to my lips.

'I'll admit...' he began, dropping his voice to a near-whisper, despite there being no one around to eavesdrop. 'It was fucking hot that you didn't want to use a condom. But that was a bit reckless.'

'So reckless,' I agreed over-enthusiastically and set down

the glass. I tried not to smirk.

'We haven't even had the chat.'

'Not *the chat*.'

'I'd rather get punched in the face–'

'Well, we're in Freo,' I said. 'It could happen.'

Ezra snorted. 'Stop avoiding–'

'I don't have any STIs if that's what you're panicking over.'

'Incredible work.' He held up his Aperol to toast to it. 'And neither of us are slutty, so we won't get them.'

I clinked his glass, avoiding a verbal agreement. It wasn't a lie if I said nothing, and besides, it wasn't his business – especially if I was getting tested every now and then, which I was. There was no reason to feel guilty, so I actively chose not to.

'You really hate casual sex.'

He took a sip and shook his head. 'Not in the slightest. I just hate having it and having sex with people that have it. It makes me feel–'

'Dirty? Sinful?' I couldn't help myself. 'Is that why you always have a shower before and after?'

Ezra blushed scarlet as if he was mortified I'd noticed. Perhaps he thought I was too polite to ever call attention to it.

'It's fine,' I said quickly. 'I don't care if you–'

'It's mostly Catholic guilt.' Not the most elaborate response, but a surprising one.

'You believe in God?'

'Yeah.' He blinked at me with an expression that was difficult to read. 'Do you?'

'Absolutely not.'

'He's not as popular with your generation.' The age gap mentioned again, like a scab being brushed.

'Huh. So, you shower because it makes you feel… clean

of sin?'

'And I kind of hate the smell.' His nose wrinkled.

'Of sex?'

'It makes me think of locker rooms or puberty.'

'Light a candle,' I suggested simply.

'I do! I have candles everywhere. You've seen them.'

'You need to get over that. It's one of the best parts, lying in each other's arms right after, panting, covered in—'

He was blushing. 'Oh my God, stop.'

'Did you just say the Lord's name in vain?'

'You're a bit fucking funny, aren't you?' That made me blush too, and then he shook his head. 'I know I sound like a prude. It's because I am a bit.' His expression shifted into something more deliberate, more serious. I was starting to think he'd planned this conversation ahead of time, and that made me feel suddenly ill. 'I just... I don't know. Is it conservative to think sex is special?'

There was an awkward pause as the waitress approached the table to take our orders. We both met her with polite smiles, but our sudden silence insinuated she shouldn't linger.

As she departed, Ezra's eyes followed, waiting until she was out of earshot to continue. Clearing his throat, he said, 'Nearly every gay guy treats it like it's nothing. I know we're in this whole wave of sexual empowerment, but there's something really empty about hookup culture. We use each other when we're horny and then toss each other away.'

'Obviously I agree,' I said, touching the sides of my glass that were now dripping with condensation. 'But for some people...' – I hoped *some* implied *absolutely not me* – 'it's better than being alone. It's validating, and sometimes it's even fun. Is that so bad?'

'I'd rather not have sex at all. I just think it says a lot about a person if they do it all the time with strangers. Like... is their self-worth really that low?'

'It's not that simple.'

'I'm not talking about you, of course.' He reached over the table to touch my arm. The brush was brief and pathetic. 'I don't care if you had a few hookups in Melbourne. It's a part of growing up. I'm talking about the guys that do it constantly, who have no respect for themselves.'

'Right.'

'In Perth especially, it's so easy to get a reputation for sleeping around. I don't want something like that to happen to you. I just want you to be safe and smart.'

It was hard to discern if he was being patronising or protective. Perhaps somewhere in between. I simply nodded down at the table, paranoid the truth would start to leak out of me like a rusting pipe.

My silence was met with an attempt from him to fill it. 'Was it normalised in Melbourne? I guess it's easier to be anonymous in a more transient city.'

'Melbourne was…' I thought extremely hard on how to proceed, how candid I could be without shattering an illusion. 'I didn't have many queer friends, so it's hard to compare. I wanted them. But I struggled to find people I fit in with.'

He was hanging onto every word. Precious lore he'd been coaxing me to divulge for some time.

'I wasn't feminine enough for most of the gay guys, I wasn't masculine enough for a lot of the straight guys,' I rambled on, 'And not to say it's a set metric, because queer culture is always evolving, but I kept waiting to find my… What would I even call it? In-betweeners? All the others that didn't fit anywhere? I kept missing out on them somehow.'

Ezra nodded in agreement. 'I used to feel like that for years.'

'There's a million spaces I could've inserted myself into, but nothing felt genuine. I only had a few surface-level friendships through uni that ended after graduation, and from then on… I was mostly alone.'

He paused, thinking of something delicate. 'What about your family? Are you guys close, despite the divorce?'

I felt my stomach tighten. Now was the time, wasn't it? The opportunity to be completely exposed. It would contradict everything that had come before; the cool-headedness, the forced positivity, the ease, the absence of baggage. It could ruin everything, or bring us closer. It was impossible to decipher what I wanted, if it was worth risking, or if I cared enough about him outside of sex to be so vulnerable. I wished we didn't have to talk at all. I wished we could get back in bed together. That was much easier.

Eventually, I said, 'My mum used to be my best friend.' I made a fist under the table, digging my nails into my palm. *Keep going*, I thought, but I wasn't strong enough. I pivoted, like a coward. 'Other than that… We aren't close. Yours?'

'Nah,' he shook his head. 'My parents are just sort of… there. Marion, Nadia, and Matteo are my real family.'

I nodded slowly.

'They really like you, by the way,' he tacked on innocently, which immediately brought a smile to my face.

'It's nice to be liked.'

'It is.'

'Thank you. For letting me in.'

'It's such a fucking rarity,' he chuckled. 'You have no idea.'

'I think I have *some* idea.'

He was studying my face with a fondness. 'If I'm being perfectly honest, I feel like I've known you for ages.'

My cheeks were pink. I could feel them, warm like a sunburn and full of blood. 'Yeah. I feel it too.'

'I'm glad you showed up when you did.'

We ate, ordered more drinks instead of dessert, paid (splitting down the middle), and left the restaurant to make out against a brick wall. Ezra's saliva coated my neck and face, smelling of Aperol. He broke away briefly to check if people were watching. Amongst the drunk hipsters and the homeless tucked into sleeping bags, we were far from an unexpected phenomenon, but he wasn't the biggest fan of public affection, so instead we climbed into his car and drove past the shipping containers to somewhere private along the port. Hills burned in the rear-view mirror, a thin line of orange lighting up the night. The bushfire was far enough to not be a threat, but I could still smell it all around us, that ash, somehow foreboding.

Ezra switched the engine off. I reached over and unbuttoned his jeans quite immediately, and he let me, without protest. It was becoming second nature to us, these transactions, conversations followed by sex. He sought companionship, I sought a warm body. We both won in the end. I gave him head from the passenger's seat with his pants shuffled down his thighs and his shoes still on. It was almost clinical, laborious. I did it anyway. He started pushing on my head, making me gag until my eyes filled up with salt. I just needed to forget any painful moment that had ever left a mark and focus entirely on making him feel good. Losing myself in him. He climaxed in my mouth and my mind was wiped clean.

12

How did it happen? From such a taut dance, using each other for our own agendas, something gentle seeped between the familiarity of Ezra's bedsheets. Each night spent together we drew closer, both physically and emotionally, and with the slow coaxing of fingers along each other's backs, Ezra began to rely on my touch, and me on his. It wasn't supposed to be this way, so tender and comforting, and suddenly I wasn't sure what I wanted anymore. Back scratches led to soft kisses, soft kisses led to cradling each other. If it was too warm, a leg would sneak out of the side of the duvet, or we would shift positions, but our bodies remained locked in conversation. We just wanted to exist in the same space, skin against skin. The sound of his breathing never failed to lull me to sleep.

There was a black toothbrush in the holder for me, and a few of my t-shirts and pairs of underwear lay idle in one of his drawers. I had a special spot on the couch, a designated side of the bed. The showering before sex stopped, only after. I deleted Grindr.

I'd completely underestimated the intimacy of lying beside someone I felt safe with. It was impossible to write Ezra off as just a physical thing when he'd brushed the outlines of my deepest hurts, gazed into me, and even if he might never reach the centre of it all, it seemed he wanted to. Still, I preferred to think of him as my best friend, nothing more, despite knowing this wasn't how friends traditionally behaved. It was dangerous to think too hard about it, to consider where the line was, to ponder what it could mean for us if we continued this way. Instead, we carried on, naive and drunk on each other's company.

He was so charming yet pedantic, frustrating yet easy, unlike anyone I'd known, though what exactly set him apart was difficult to pinpoint. Perhaps it was the way I felt when I was with him, like he'd ironed out the creases in my life, or perhaps it was how I felt in his absences. Rooms widened and time meandered. Silences grew to a deafening roar. He pushed it all down, and for that, I was tethered to him, to his particulars and his hopes, his complaints and misgivings.

He hated the beach (or so he claimed), his pale skin too susceptible to burns. 'How can you live in Perth and hate the beach?' I'd questioned, and he just sighed in amusement. He had winter in his blood but summer in his hair, that halo of gold only more radiant under the sun's spotlight. I persuaded him to join me in the ocean eventually, splashing cold salt against his chest when he was waist deep beside me, and he splashed me right back, surrendering to the moment. Both of us laughed, a child-like playtime kind of sound.

We didn't kiss during the day. Our relationship evolved with the sky, braver and more sexually charged in darkness, easier to pretend it was all accidental. *It's late, I suppose you could crash here*, as if that wasn't the plan the entire time. Or my plan, at least.

We often met up for breakfast or dinner somewhere between us, and then Ezra would drive us the rest of the way back to his. I memorised the pleated leather interior of his Volkswagen and the faces he made as he drove, the way he held the steering wheel, or held my hand. I traced his knuckles, snaked between the calluses on his palm, squeezed his thumb. We frequented Mary Street Bakery for chilli scrambled eggs and Besk for evening wines. We strolled through Hyde Park sharing a pair of headphones, taking turns to show each other our favourite artists.

'For such a happy person, you listen to a lot of sad shit,' he said, examining my rotation of Mitski, The 1975, and Lana Del Rey.

It warmed me that he thought of me as such.

'Coming from you and your breakup pop ballads,' I tutted after catching a glimpse of Adele and Taylor Swift.

Funnily enough, sad songs assisted in subduing my blues. There was something cathartic about hearing devastating things happening to someone else, allowing me to subsequently dissociate or dull whatever was going on in my own head. It was one of the only self-medications that worked, besides completely ignoring it all.

'We should make a combined playlist,' he suggested, and we did, and I listened to it front-to-back several times, hyperfixating on the songs that mirrored our situation – anything that sounded like pining or danger.

He told me I'd love Swift's *Folklore* album, which I did, and it played continuously in the background while I read books with my feet up in his lap. I'd sneak a peek over the tops of pages, watching with amusement as his tongue darted out in concentration, attention stolen by his laptop screen. He often asked me to help edit emails or client inquiries for his one-man marketing company. I felt grown up helping him, like we were more than best friends, we were partners. Equals, despite age, knowledge, class, experience.

Marion would come home from work, and we'd pour three glasses of wine, turn the music up to full blast and dance around like idiots, laughing loud and guttural. She cooked her renowned chicken pasta. We ate in front of the TV nearly every night, like clockwork, as if I'd lived with them for years. Was this what belonging felt like?

As promised, Ezra forced his favourite superhero movies upon me, and I obliged, cringing at the cheesiness of their construction, but slowly learning to love them too. Soon enough and completely against my will, I grew attached to the characters.

'You're crying too?' he implored after one particularly devastating on-screen death. We both wiped tears away and I laughed in spite of myself.

'I can't believe you made me care about a guy who wears spandex.'

He was elated – not because my pain gave him pleasure – but because our mutual tears affirmed yet another point of bonding between us. It was our special thing, those movies. We caught all the midnight showings in the cinemas that month. I bought the tickets, he bought the snacks. We called it even.

*

'We're not together.'

'And yet, you're always together,' Juliana interrogated me one of the few nights I was home. Ezra had never asked to stay at our apartment, and I hadn't offered. Why would I? My books were still in piles, and the decor was as stark as the first week I'd moved in, whereas Ezra's room was oppressively tidy with an ensuite bathroom, and, most importantly, was on the other side of the house from Marion. It was far more ideal than the single wall that divided Juliana and I. Alé was quite a vocal lover, and I was reliant on my headphones to drown out the sound of him and Juliana together. I was certain they'd realise how embarrassingly thin the plaster was if we ever returned the favour, but the opportunity hadn't arisen. I was more than content with the intimate bubble of Ezra's to do as we pleased, where I could bury my face in his armpit and breathe him in, kissing from his collarbone and up again to his lips, where he could lick inside my ear and crush my hair in his hands, where he could nuzzle his face between my legs, parting them, getting me wet before entering me. Our sex improved each time. He said it was all me, making him better. I'd rolled my eyes and said he was just saying that to flatter me, but I knew it was true.

I opened the fridge and found my designated shelf empty, except for an open packet of tortillas and some hummus that had gone off. With a grimace, I let the fridge door swing shut and decided to order food instead. 'We're just friends.'

Alé snorted from the living room and said something loudly in Portuguese. Juliana's mouth curled into a smile.

'What was that?'

In English, he repeated, 'If you're sleeping with him, going on dates, and basically living at his house… you're not just friends.' His eyes were glued to the AFL match on the TV, a chorus of whistles and roars blaring in the background, and his bare feet were up on the coffee table. One of my books suffocated beneath his heel.

I leaned back against the fridge door and crossed my arms. Juliana met my gaze with a probing raise of her eyebrow.

'It's a companionship,' I said. 'Fuck-buddies that actually hang out.'

'I think that's called a *situationship*,' she snorted. 'And it's messy.'

'Who cares about the label? Traditional monogamy is so…' I searched for a word that would make me feel intelligent: '*Archaic*.'

'I feel like you're saying that because it's easier than admitting he can't give you what you truly want.'

'Amen,' Alé said and washed his mouth with beer.

'I don't want a relationship. I never have.' My phone was out now and I was tapping away as I selected the fillings to go inside my burrito. 'If anything, this is a lot more serious than I'm comfortable with.'

'You can't even look me in the eyes when you say that.'

'I'm ordering dinner,' I laughed. 'Do you want anything?'

'I'm okay, thank you. We're trying not to spend too much this month.' She blushed with embarrassment, as if I'd reprimand her for being frugal.

'My treat?'

'A bribe to get us off your back?'

'Exactly.'

She was silently contemplative, probably deciding whether accepting would contradict her morals, before surrendering and calling out to Alé, 'Babe! Austin's ordering us dinner.'

'Sick!'

It seemed ridiculous that they were concerned about Ezra when I was in complete control of the situation, but their care also made me feel loved, so I rewarded it the easiest way I knew how – with gifts of gratitude.

*

Ezra's office was in a tiny backroom in the corner of a car modification warehouse in Osborne Park. The office had no windows, but he was happy enough watching various vehicles roll in and out through the crack in the door. We sat at the desk, he worked, I read my book, and even if it was stuffy and far too warm in that office, I found comfort in his quiet presence. Our half-eaten sandwiches took up the desk space. A few crumbs clung to his stubble. It was a reliable scene, nearly every Thursday afternoon.

He gazed at me over the desktop computer. 'How often

are you at the café?'

'Do you think I have too much free time?'

He shook his head and laughed. 'You can't answer a question with a question.'

'Says who?'

'You just did it again.'

I closed my book and set it down on the table. 'Is this about my new car?'

'It's definitely part of it.'

Tired of taking Ubers everywhere, I had gone out and gotten myself a matte black *few-years-old* Tesla, nothing particularly flashy or ridiculous, but something that was a bit of fun to drive around in. I wasn't going to waste money on a death trap, though I should have opted for something more subtle. Ezra had looked baffled as I'd climbed out of it.

'Like I said, it's just a lease.'

'It's worth more than your rent.'

'How do you know that?'

'Because I remember Juliana bragging about how cheap the place was for Mosman Park, and I know off the top of my head what a 2021 Model Y Tesla costs per month – unless the dealership fumbled so unbelievably hard – but I highly doubt it.'

I picked up my sandwich and took a slow bite. His impatience at my response was amusing; he crossed his arms, glared as I chewed, and the vein in his forehead swelled when I took a second bite.

'Austin.'

I put the sandwich down, swallowed, and wiped my mouth with the napkin. 'Why is it so important to you?'

'It's sketchy.'

'I just had some money saved up before I got to Perth.'

'Would you tell me if your family was rich?'

I blinked and smiled. 'Nope.'

'So they are.'

'Does it matter?'

'I think it's weird if you lied about it.'

'When did I lie?'

'You said you weren't rich.'

'I said I wasn't a rich *asshole.*'

'I'm pretty sure—'

'Ezra,' I groaned, throwing my head back to stare at the ceiling in annoyance. 'Part of the reason I moved to Perth was to get away from all that.'

'Yeah, that's another thing,' he murmured and sat up straighter in his swivel chair. 'Why *did* you move to Perth? All I hear is some robotic excuse about wanting to try something different and it doesn't sound genuine.'

My brain power was operating at full speed, manufacturing the perfect excuse.

'Okay!' I surrendered. 'Yes, my family has money. But it's my *family's* money. I don't have free reign of it. It's also the reason mine and Juliana's sides of the family were never close. Our dads hated each other, mostly over financial stuff.'

Technically, no lies told. He was still scowling, but I could tell I hadn't said the wrong thing. Not yet.

'I'd always wanted to meet Juliana, and after uni, I decided to take a gap year, finding myself and all that… So, I came to Perth. I love the weather, I go for a swim a few times a week, the people are nice. It's literally that simple.'

'Right,' he said slowly.

'And trying to make new friends while they're all hammering on about how much they hate money didn't exactly open the door for honesty.'

When he looked down at his lap in remorse, I knew I'd nailed it. 'We don't hate money. Just the people that act like they own Perth.'

'Callum?'

'And his friends,' he said. 'Trust me, if I had money, I wouldn't be hateful. I'd love to be rich. But some of us have to work really fucking hard for that to happen. We're not just born into it.'

I agreed with a measured nod. 'It's a really gross power trip, one that I've tried to distance myself from.' Then I said quietly, 'I don't want it to affect how you see me.'

He sighed and offered me an apologetic smile. 'If anything, I'm just jealous. Don't take it too personally.' And then, in a very sudden shift, he leaned over the desk and hooked his fingers around my jaw. 'Why am I always thinking about fucking you?'

'Because I have a pretty dick and a nice ass,' I said, and he kissed me in agreement.

I'd never had other gay people as a strong presence in my life. I felt a sudden weightlessness with Ezra and Marion, a deeply submerged commonality that couldn't be found with my heterosexual counterparts. We'd all endured such a singular experience of otherness, of mourning normalcy, of wondering if we were born unlucky or special. What if we were just as banal as everyone else, but with smaller dating pools and certain countries where it was illegal to hold hands? Ezra and Marion understood the nuances of this. I was just Austin, at ease, finally. Although ease was a fragile thing.

'We're gonna have to start charging you rent,' Marion said one night, hardly looking up from her phone. She held dominion over the left side of the couch, knees up against her chest, free hand balancing a glass of wine.

'I pay my rent in alcohol.' I held my own glass high above my head and some of it splashed out of the side and down my arm. We both giggled.

'Austin, be careful please!' Ezra warned from the dining table, bent over the computer. 'If you stain that couch, you're buying us a new one.'

'Someone's in a mood tonight,' Marion tutted. Ezra glared at the screen and brought his elbows up onto the table. Fingers slipped between his golden hair, tugging on it. His wine glass was empty, having drunk it twice as fast as Marion and me.

Is he okay? I mouthed to her.

'He's always like this. "Stop talking so loud, close the cupboards behind you, put your dishes away!"' She spoke loudly enough so Ezra could hear every word.

'Hypocritical, considering how often I do his dishes these days,' I grinned at her, joining in on the teasing.

'Yeah, because you don't have a real job,' Ezra said, perhaps more bitterly than he'd intended. His phone rang before I could retort. 'I have to take this.' He rose from the desk and retreated to his bedroom.

Marion and I were quiet for a few moments. Despite how much time we spent in the same house, even the same room, we were seldom alone together. I hardly knew her outside the filter of her best friend and housemate.

'It's not you,' she said, apologetic.

'I know he's stressed with work.'

Marion nodded but her eyes were avoidant. They jumped back down to her phone and glued themselves there. I sat cross-legged on the couch and sipped on the wine, struggling not to say something painfully insecure.

'How does he feel about me?'

Marion locked the device and abandoned it on the couch. 'Like... Romantically?'

'He's a bit hard to read. I know we're just friends, but–'

She glanced in the direction of his bedroom, anticipating

his re-entry, but the call was ongoing through the wall. She sat up straighter as if her physical positioning changed the context of her words. 'If there's one thing I know about Ezra after all these years, it's that he doesn't know what he needs. He *thinks* he does, but he's always wrong.' We both chuckled and my body contracted in relief as she spoke. 'I think he needs someone like you. And try not to take this on, but he obviously has feelings for you that he can't come to terms with yet.'

It was surprisingly reassuring to hear her say it out loud.

'Just give him time. Emotions are a scary thing for him. Very up and down. Intense.'

'Since Callum, you mean?'

'Nah,' she said. 'Since… always, I guess.'

Ezra's bedroom door creaked open. We covered our discussion of him with overenthusiastic smiles as he rounded the corner. With one quick flourish, he fetched his wine glass and retrieved the bottle from the counter, finding a seat directly between us on the couch. In silence and with careful precision, he topped up all three of us.

'Everything okay?' Marion asked, and we exchanged a tumultuous glance.

'I have a new client,' he announced, and the serious facade evaporated.

'Ezra, congratulations!' I beamed, bounding up closer beside him. Marion squeezed his shoulder.

'I thought they were going with someone else,' he said. 'That's why I was in such a foul mood.'

'A call for celebration.'

'Matteo suggested Sí Paradiso.'

'He knows already?'

'I messaged the group chat.'

This happened often, with plans for the core four being

constructed around me with little-to-no acknowledgement of my existence. I'd grown used to it, though each time stung the tiniest bit, like citrus in a papercut.

'It's gonna be a record-hot day, you know,' Marion said.

'But if we go early, we'll probably get a spot in the shade.'

'I've never been to Sí Paradiso,' I said loudly and pathetically, a bit too desperate to be included.

I cringed when I replayed the moment in my head, but Ezra just smiled and placed his hand on my knee. 'Come with. Unless you have other plans?' He was too pleased with himself to think of shutting me down.

13

Sierra sauntered down the steps of her house, dressed head-to-toe in boutique athleisure. She had a half-consumed green juice in her right hand and a baggie of white powder sticking out from between her long fingers.

'Hey you,' she said when she approached. The glass house loomed in the foreground, reflecting the sunlight so harshly, I was momentarily blinded.

'Thanks for this.' I squinted through the oversaturated light. 'You're the only person I thought to ask.'

'I'm deciding not to take offence,' she said, handing over the baggie. I was surprised by how publicly she'd dealt it, but if she cared about rubbernecking neighbours, her expression didn't reflect it. 'What's it for anyway?'

'Just… uh…' I scratched the back of my neck. 'Heading to Sí Paradiso with Ezra and his friends.'

'Oh,' she said, lips tight. 'Thanks for the invite.'

'I'm sorry—'

'Austin, I'm joking. I really don't care.' A smile was plastered on her face, but her cold eyes betrayed her. We went from friendly to transactional in a matter of seconds. She got out her phone and said, 'It's three-fifty. Perth prices these days… Is bank transfer okay?'

'Yeah, of course. No worries.' I pulled out my phone. Sierra received a little *ding* when the money jumped across.

'I'm shocked Ezra is allowing this.'

'He doesn't know,' I said sheepishly. 'Nadia and Matteo

asked me to get it for them.'

Her long lashes dipped and kissed the top of her cheeks, a slow blink.

'Naughty.'

'Yeah.'

'Don't let them use you. It's kind of their thing.'

'Don't worry,' I laughed. 'I won't.'

She kissed the air right beside my cheek in goodbye — maybe a subtle effort to avoid direct contact – before heading back up to the house.

*

Nadia and Matteo arrived at pre-drinks an hour late. Matteo brought a plastic bottle of margarita mix that tasted like battery acid and Nadia had a six-pack of beers that sat on the countertop untouched. 'None of us drinks beer,' Ezra frowned at the cans.

I did, but I didn't feel the need to correct him. No one thought to bring tequila either, so the mix was shaken vigorously with some leftover gin found in Ezra and Marion's liquor cabinet. Ezra strained them out, managed a taste, and winced in disgust.

'That's foul. Let's stick to mixers.'

'We're all out,' Marion murmured.

Ezra groaned and fetched his keys from the counter. 'Okay. I'll run to the shops.'

'Do you want me to come?' I piped up.

'Nah, I'll be two seconds.' He threw me a wink and disappeared through the garage door. The engine rumbled to life, tires squealed, and he was off.

'Well, at least we can have some coke now,' Nadia grinned. 'Before he gets back.' She planted herself down on the couch and pushed her hair behind her shoulders.

'You brought coke?' Marion was taken aback.

'Austin did,' Matteo said.

Marion threw me an accusatory stare that I attempted to dodge with downcast eyes. 'Well… I'll be… straightening my hair.' She picked up her drink and retreated to the bathroom. Her hair was already dead-flat around her ears but none of us commented on it.

'Don't look so guilty, Austin. She would do it too if he wasn't coming back.'

I latched onto Nadia's reassurance as a scapegoat and joined her and Matteo on the couch. With a debit card in hand, Matteo cut three lines atop his phone screen, hastily, each one a different length and thickness. Nadia went first. She snorted the biggest one through a rolled-up twenty-dollar note, palmed it off to Matteo – who inhaled his – and then it was my turn. I had only just come up for air when we heard Ezra outside.

'Fuck,' I breathed, wiping my nose as the front door was thrown open.

'Forgot my wallet.' Ezra rounded the corner into the kitchen, stopping when he spotted us on the couch. The baggie sat on the coffee table in full view and our guilt was indisputable on our faces. There was nowhere to hide. 'Seriously?' Betrayal flared in his eyes. 'Like, are you actually fucking serious?' He retrieved his wallet from the dining table, gave us one last zealous glare, and exited for the second time. The door slammed behind him, and the walls responded with a resounding shake.

We took two Ubers into Highgate, Ezra and I separated from the rest of the group. Pressed against him in the backseat, he snarled in my ear, 'That's the shit Callum used to do. Sneaking off to get high behind my back. I expected it from Nadia and Matteo, but not from you. Don't ever bring drugs into my house again.'

My cheeks burned hotter than the inside of my nose.

We arrived too late to secure a spot in the shade, and Ezra's angst seemed to simmer under the sun's tyrannical glare. The top of the round table was burning hot, so our hands remained in laps or clutched around our drinks. Everything was harsh and bright, and the surrounding limestone walls seemed to reflect the heat and the sounds of disco-house music back at us with even more intensity. I was shouldered between Ezra and Matteo, all of us with half-finished espresso martinis, courtesy of Matteo. It felt less like a gift, and more like a debt paid after leaving me to front Ezra's blame. Across from us, Nadia and Marion shared a bottle of wine they hated. Each sip was chased with a wince.

'I thought it was a SB,' Marion said.

'Is *skin-contact* code for *fucking atrocious*?'

'Good looking crowd,' Matteo said, eyeing the tanned men in colourful t-shirts and linen button-downs. A handful of them – the ones well-groomed enough to flirt with femininity – eyed us back, though who it was directed at remained unclear. 'I think he's done my pilates class.' I glanced in the general area of the man in question, but he'd already slipped between a throng of women in flimsy summer dresses and disappeared.

'He was definitely looking at you,' Nadia cooed, stoking Matteo's ego.

'He was looking at *Austin*,' Marion said. 'He must like the young ones.'

I laughed and shook my head. 'No way.'

'It's always you two, of course,' Ezra said with a tepid chuckle, perhaps his attempt at a joke, but it sounded too bitter to procure laughter.

'Must be your frown lines scaring them off. Is that a grey

hair?' Nadia stirred further, and the others tacked on a laugh. Ezra glowered and instinctively touched his scalp as if he could feel the grey poking through.

'This was the guy, right?' Matteo said, flipping his phone around to show the girls. 'The one that was making eyes?' They leaned closer to examine the screen and began debating.

I turned my head in towards Ezra and said quietly, 'Are you going to be pissed off all day? I already said I was sorry.'

'I'm not pissed about that.'

'There's something else now?'

He demolished the rest of the espresso martini with a single flick of his wrist. 'Sometimes I feel a bit invisible next to you and Matteo,' he said, brushing the corners of his mouth dry with his thumb and index finger.

I glanced around incredulously, but no one else had caught the statement. 'Invisible? Is that a joke?'

'You guys are very... No one looks at me the way they look at the two of you.'

'I do.' It sounded far more pitiful than I'd intended.

'You don't count.'

'Why don't I count?'

'I don't know Austin,' he said with a sigh. 'Because you're... you.'

'What's that supposed to mean?'

'I need another drink,' Matteo said loudly, looking between the two of us expectantly. It appeared the martini wasn't a debt repaid after all – just a loan awaiting compensation.

'I'll get it,' I said, downing my final sip and eager for an excuse to escape my exchange with Ezra. He and Matteo nodded – I wanted to assume in thanks – and I abandoned the table, but not before I leaned into Ezra's ear and whispered, 'Your insecurity is fucking painful.' I didn't give him time to respond, and I felt sufficiently less irked once I was on my own.

The large veranda hanging over the bar offered some respite, at least in keeping the sun off my neck. My thighs felt itchy under my jeans and my shirt was sticking to my skin in patches. While tugging at the collar, I noticed a man doing a double take of me, before blatantly staring. I stiffly turned my head to meet his gaze and raised my eyebrows.

'You're Austin, right? From Melbourne?' he asked, a veiled smile spreading across a face imbued with so much botox, it hardly moved as he spoke.

'Do I know you?'

'We've never met. I've just heard of you through the Perth grapevine.'

I was nearly two heads taller, and gazed down at him with a certain defensiveness.

'You're dating Ezra,' he continued. It wasn't phrased as a question.

'We're not dating,' I said. 'And you should really mind your own fucking business.'

He paled. I wondered if it was the coke making me aggressive, or if I was just bitter over how the day was unfolding. A spot opened up at the bar and I strode in front of him to order my drinks. The interaction was silly, pedestrian, but something about it made me feel as though whatever anonymity I'd been clinging to had crumbled in an instant. I was *known* in Perth. I hated the idea of it.

Precariously holding the three martinis, I made my way back to the table, set them down, and glanced over my shoulder at the bar.

'Do you guys know him?' I pointed out the stranger.

We followed his trajectory to a smaller crowd of gays in their mid-twenties. One of the drinks he carried was kept for himself, and the other was given to a man with his back to us, tall and broad, with distinct ears that protruded from the sides of his buzzed head. After some words were exchanged, the guy with the buzzcut snapped around to stare directly at us.

Marion bent closer inward to the group, and with a lowered voice said, 'Great. Callum's here.'

Callum was painfully handsome, but his eyes were cold and lifeless. From across the amphitheatre, I could imagine them darkening like a shark catching a trace of blood. He loomed over his friends, taller than me by at least a few centimetres. Beneath the thin line of his moustache, his lips curled into a challenging smile.

'Yeah, I see him,' Ezra said flatly. 'You were talking to Tedd, his minion.'

'His drinks runner, more like,' Nadia snorted.

'They're both cunts,' Matteo said.

I watched Ezra, and Ezra watched Callum. He was staring at him in a trance, zoned out of the conversation. The ship was sinking in front of my eyes and there was nothing I could do, no rescue line to throw. The yapping continued as an overture:

'I don't see his new boyfriend.'

'I'm pretty sure they broke up.'

'Really?'

'Yeah, I saw him on a dating app.'

'Ezra, remember when you glassed him?'

'What?' I was hooked back in, staring at Ezra for clarification, who looked inextricably uncomfortable.

'Um... It was my birthday weekend. We were at Connections,' he began slowly and quietly. The vein in his forehead was already starting to bulge.

'We were *all* there,' Matteo said, making sure I knew his

existence was integral to the narrative.

'These guys dragged me out to try and cheer me up, about three weeks after he dumped me. My first time getting out of bed. I saw him across the dance floor. He waved at me, I waved back, thinking he was trying to be friendly. And then he grabbed the nearest guy and started making out with him. In front of me. So yeah. I threw my glass at his head. It didn't do any major damage, but I was put on a ban from the place for a few months.'

I stared at him, gobsmacked. I'd never thought he was capable of something so violent. Many of us had heard horror stories about Australian nightlife, people getting glassed in the head or stabbed, king hit on the way home, bashed in a back alley. It was mostly antisocial behaviour or bikie activity, though crimes of passion probably took a decent percentage.

'That's why we started going to The Court instead,' Marion said. 'Plus, Connections is rapey.'

'All clubs are rapey if you're good-looking,' Matteo said.

I narrowed my eyes at his irreverent comment, before turning my attention back to Ezra. 'Maybe he deserved it,' I offered, though I didn't agree with the sentiment. It just seemed like the only thing to say, a feeble attempt at vindication in the hopes it might win him back over.

Ezra just shrugged and after a few moments, excused himself to the bathroom. Everyone waited in silence until he was out of earshot.

'Can't believe he still carries on like this,' Nadia said. 'It's actually so draining.'

'He's not doing anything,' Marion defended.

'His mood went sour the second he saw Callum.'

'I thought he was getting better. With…' Her eyes darted to me briefly, blushing when she realised I'd caught the act. 'I dunno. Maybe it'll always be like this.'

'Fucking hope not.'

'It's been eight months. Kind of embarrassing at this point,' Matteo tutted into his drink.

'That's a bit shit to say,' I said. 'Aren't you his best friends?'

'And *as* his best friends,' Nadia shot at me, 'we've had to listen to the Ezra-Callum soap opera for a lot longer than you've been around. I'm happy to pass the torch if you want.'

I eyed Marion, expecting her to back me up, but she avoided my eyes in cowardice.

'No thanks,' I said, glancing back in Callum's general vicinity. He was absent from the huddle of gays and I couldn't spot him by the bar either. Paranoia struck, completely debilitating. I made an excuse to leave as well, heading straight for the bathrooms, ignoring Nadia and Matteo's snide glances. My heartbeat was in my ears. My mouth was bone-dry. I stormed deeper into the venue, rounded a corner, and found Ezra leaning against the wall with Callum beside him. They were talking low and close. Ezra's face was devoid of emotion. He wasn't looking at Callum, instead staring straight ahead, studying the curves in the stone wall. Callum's mouth moved too fast for me to lip read, though I certainly tried. Ezra caught me in his peripheral vision and his expression darkened at the sight of my intrusion. Callum looked at me too, but not with a glare or grimace as I expected – only that sly smile. I was panicking. This was it, it had to be. We were done for.

Ezra said something briefly to Callum and slipped off the wall, storming right past me before hissing, 'Are you spying on me?' He continued on, not waiting for an answer.

I thought about going after him, but Callum was still watching, amused. I met him by the wall and he straightened up at my approach.

'What did you say to him?'

'Well, hi to you too,' he said. His voice was cold, smooth as ice. 'No need to get so worked up. We were just talking.'

'Sure you were.'

'I have nothing against you, Austin. You seem like a lovely guy.'

'Then stay away,' I snapped. I'd never been so territorial before. I was a rabid dog off its leash.

Callum raised his hands in surrender. 'He's all yours,' he said, and meandered back to the amphitheatre.

I couldn't bring myself to face the group again without some more cocaine, so after huffing a substantial bump in the stall and splashing some water on my face, I returned to the table. 'Where's Ezra?' I demanded, staring at his empty chair.

Marion, Matteo, and Nadia gazed at me quizzically. I probably looked wild, eyes bulging, face and hair still wet.

'Isn't he in the bathroom?'

'No, he's…' I trailed off, glancing around, but I couldn't see him anywhere. 'I think he's…'

I couldn't formulate words or thoughts, and being around the group was only eroding what was left of my sanity. I abandoned them, beelining for the venue's exit. It was much quieter out on the street with only the suppressed thud of the music from deep within and the distant sounds of traffic. A few birds cawed overheard. Ezra was sitting on the curb alone, head bent over his knees.

I approached gently and sat down beside him. 'What did he say?'

'It doesn't matter.'

'It matters to me.'

'I've already made a complete ass of myself.'

'But–'

'Are you incapable of giving me a second of privacy, or do

you have to insert yourself into everything?' he spat at the street.

I began to pick at my nails. My tongue felt too large for my mouth. I wanted to kick something. The world around us felt spacey, zoomed out to a bird's-eye view. I pictured what we looked like there on the curb, two hunched bodies angled away, separate planes diverging. I wanted to make it right, I wanted to say the appropriate things that would dig us out of this hole, but my teeth ground themselves together instead. *Just shut up for once*, I thought. My head turned to the right and I gazed up the road, realising Queen's was just a few blocks down, where we'd had our first date. I'd felt so in control back then. The volley of flirtation, the roles we both played, the shy nakedness and candid intimacy. How did it go so wrong? Where was the misstep?

'He said he missed me,' Ezra mumbled.

And then I felt nauseous. I touched my pocket, confirming that the baggie was still there as if it were a talisman.

'I'm gonna go home,' he sighed.

'Because of him?'

'Just go back inside with our friends, it's fine.'

'I don't want to be with *your* friends, I want to be with you.'

Ezra lifted his head weakly and gazed at me with defeat. His eyes glistened with moisture. In a single breath, I decided to lean over and wrap my arms around him. He didn't hug me back, but he absorbed the affection with the slightest tilt of his head against me. It felt like enough of an indication that it would be okay.

'Let's go home,' I said, and he let me order an Uber.

I prayed he would say something on the drive back, but he didn't. I prayed he would say something when we went into his house, but he didn't. He just kicked his shoes off and got on the bed, curled up into a ball on top of the duvet, faced away from me, and said nothing. It was still daylight, so I drew the shades to darken the room. An hour passed. I flitted in and out, set a tea on his dresser – which he ignored – and tried to touch him, but any contact was met with a groan and a roll away from my fingers. His stillness and his silence were disturbing. I'd never seen someone so catatonic.

14

'Phone away, get in.' Juliana was floating on her back beside the boat, her long body making ripples in the water, eel-like. I licked my teeth, frowned at the unanswered text messages one last time, and buried my phone under my t-shirt.

'I'll meet you around the back,' I called down to her before crawling to my feet and diving off the bow. The splash rang in my ears, and then silence. Every part of my body tingled with the rush of cool water, and I pulled myself further down into the depths until the pressure began to build around my skull. I briefly taunted myself to swallow the ocean water and let it flood my insides, fill up my brain, pop my eyes, bloat my stomach. A juvenile idea, but as soon as the thought appeared, my breath dwindled, and I was kicking back up to the surface.

I swam over to Juliana who was already sitting on the stern with her legs dangling in the water. My fingers held the edge while I squinted up at her.

'You're addicted to that thing,' she said.

'I'm waiting for something.'

'Ezra?' There was an obvious distaste in the way she said his name, like expired milk on her tongue. 'What's going on?'

I sighed. 'He's avoiding me.'

I kicked around for the ladder, climbed up and onto the boat, and sat beside her. My board shorts made a wet squelching sound against the leather. We squinted at the other boats anchored up around the reef. Some were nicer than Sierra's, others were merely for fishing. I could hear Spacey Jane blasting from the closest one – a sleek, albeit small yacht, packed with twenty-year-olds drinking from plastic cups.

It was another perfectly still day, scorching sun and cloudless skies. Sierra had called up Juliana and told her we had fifteen minutes to get ourselves ready or we'd be left behind. This was apparently classic Sierra, extravagant excursions made instantaneously. We arrived at the port with two minutes to spare and Sierra drove us across the short stretch of sea to Rottnest Island – she had her boating licence, of course – while Alé played co-captain. The sand was bleached white, the water so turquoise it could've been Grecian. Various reefs of black rock dotted the bay and somewhere over the dunes, quokkas ran amok, coarse brown balls of fur grinning at tourists and scavenging for scraps. The day should've been a perfect distraction from Ezra's silence, but I was already ravenous for his attention again.

'You're in deep, aren't you?' Juliana said.

'I hope not. It's too soon.'

'There's no such thing as too soon. If it's right–'

'It doesn't feel right. And I can't tell if that's just me being all emotionally screwed up and self-sabotaging or if we're fundamentally ill-matched.'

She nodded slowly, thinking, and tucked her wet hair behind her ears. I found her measured calmness so easy to talk to. How quickly we'd evolved from those tentative first weeks of living together, side-stepping awkward conversations around bills and our parents, to now forging a sacred pocket within the mess. She knew about my mum, and she never treated me any differently for it. She was always firm, but not judgmental; opinionated, but not bossy. A rare human being.

'How can you find out unless you give it a proper try?'

'I'm not gonna ruin things by making ultimatums,' I said quietly. 'I'd rather suffer through it, and still have *something*.'

'But you have feelings for him?'

'I think so. Yeah.' All it took was him torturing me with silence to comprehend how much I cared.

Behind us, Alé and Sierra were digging through the esky for more booze. Sierra had promised she was a better driver when she was pissed.

'Well,' Juliana shrugged. 'As long as you know your breaking point.'

'Maybe I don't have one.'

'Everyone has one.'

'—no, no, I wanna open the stuff I brought,' Sierra was saying.

'Such a white girl drink,' Alé laughed loudly. They were immune to us down the back.

I nodded at Alé and said quietly to Juliana, 'How are you guys?'

She chuckled to herself. 'Sometimes he understands things that no one else in Perth does, but other times I feel so separate from him.'

We watched him make his way to the bow of the boat, yelling, 'I'm king of the world!' and then he chugged his White Claw before cannonballing into the ocean. Sierra recorded it on her phone and laughed as she watched it back.

'He's Brazilian through and through, and I'm... something else.'

'Does that make you feel lonely?'

She looked surprised, as though no one had asked her

before. 'Yeah. A lot of the time.'

'You know, you're one of the only people I feel like I can be honest with,' I said.

'That's how family is supposed to be.' She playfully punched my shoulder like a big sister would. 'It's one of the few things in life we don't get to choose.'

'Ezra would disagree.'

'No offence, but I couldn't give less of a fuck about what Ezra thinks. Especially if he's putting my cousin through emotional distress.'

'I'm not distressed, Jules.'

She smiled at the lighthouse on the hill, stout and white-bricked, quietly surveying Pinky Beach. 'You know, Sierra's the only one who calls me that?'

'Oh. Is that okay?'

'Of course. It reminds me of how close we've gotten.'

Before I could reply with something heartfelt, Alé was swimming up to us, paddling happily like a dog with a toy in his mouth. He pulled himself back on the boat and rolled onto his back, stretching in the sunshine. 'This feels right for me. Being on a boat.'

'And yet, you give me shit because my family owns it,' Sierra said from the captain's seat.

'I have no problem with wealth as long as I can enjoy it.'

'And there it is! That's what everyone is too pussy to admit. You *all* want it!'

Juliana shook her head. 'Not me. As long as I can send my kids to a good school and go travelling once a year, I don't need much else.'

'I wouldn't mind a big house and a boat,' Alé huffed. 'Why not, you know? And people treat you differently when you have money. *Better.*'

'I just think it's hypocritical to make fun of me if you get to benefit from it.'

Alé sat up straight and looked at Sierra earnestly. 'I'm very grateful for rich friends such as you. And I thank you with my whole heart for including me.'

She looked amused for a handful of seconds, and then shrugged it away. 'Well, we all know I would struggle without money, but it's not my fault. I'm simply a product of my environment.'

'Right you are, babe,' Juliana laughed.

'The least I can do is be generous… Without being a total pushover.'

'I think you've balanced it pretty well over the years.'

'What about you, Austin?' Sierra blinked at me with a casual expectancy.

'I guess it depends on what I want to do in life,' I said slowly. 'I've never really thought more than a few months ahead.'

'If money wasn't an issue,' she probed. 'What would you do?'

What do you wanna be when you grow up? One of those tedious icebreakers echoed in classrooms while sitting cross-legged on the floor. I never knew the answer. As I grew older, that question grew more urgent, and my lack of an answer became a demonstration of privilege, especially when there were suddenly peers giving their blood, sweat, and tears for things I could have had if I'd only asked for them. If I had every opportunity to be exceptional, and still managed to be ordinary, I only had myself to blame, so I avoided the concept completely. This was still somewhat acceptable at twenty, but soon I'd be operating on borrowed time.

'Travel, maybe?' I said. 'Get lost in Europe? Become a poet or a painter or something else completely unrealistic?'

'Fall in love?' Juliana suggested with a sly smile.

'Sure,' I said. 'That too. Just… live.'
'And what's stopping you from living now?' Alé asked.
I didn't have an answer for that.

15

Ezra and I went to the cinema after all, a spin-off of a reboot that was so uninspired, even the taste of frozen Coke couldn't rinse the dissatisfaction from our mouths. I think Ezra only agreed to it because he knew we wouldn't have much time to talk; he even said he was running late and to text him his ticket. He was never late for anything. He shuffled into our row right as the previews ended, and sat down next to me with nothing but a hollow, 'Hey'. It had been three weeks since that Sunday and only a handful of text messages between us. I would have been convinced he'd died in a freak accident if it wasn't for Marion's updates:

> *He's just in a bad place rn*
> *I'm sure it'll pass*

The panic in my gut was so severe, I was self-medicating with mid-morning bumps of leftover cocaine and more late-night hookups (so much for deleting Grindr). I'd fucked five people since, and each one felt like a twist of the knife in Ezra's back — whether he was aware of its existence or not. I felt powerless, and this was the only retaliation I could think of. I *wanted* to hurt him, but I simultaneously prayed he would never find out. It was all very contradictory.

I watched him from the corner of my eye the entire runtime. His hair was a mess, his eyes dark-ringed. He looked like he hadn't been sleeping, or like he'd been sleeping far too much. The credits rolled after an agonising two hours and we stood up in silence, gathered our rubbish, and shuffled to the exit. We were hardly out of the door when I shot, 'What the hell is going on with you?'

He didn't look surprised that I'd asked. He'd probably been dreading the conversation for days. He took my empty cup from me and tossed it in the bin with his own, as well as the half-eaten box of popcorn.

'We can talk outside.'

I didn't realise how much I'd missed him until we stood opposite each other, leaning against one of the bike racks at the edge of the car park. The sky was littered with stars. He crossed his arms over his chest which made his biceps swell and I recalled the last time we'd had sex, nearly a month ago. He'd kissed me so hard I could taste blood in my mouth, before turning me over and pushing my face into the headboard, a hungry fuck that ended with me ejaculating all over his pillow. He was a different person in the bedroom: someone who made it obvious how badly he wanted me. All that fire had been snuffed out now, and it felt as if we were warming ourselves on smoke.

'Did I do something?'

Ezra looked crestfallen that this was the takeaway. 'What? No. Of course not.'

'Then why–'

'I have bipolar, okay?'

He might as well have slapped me. I blinked at him stupidly and said, 'What?'

'It's type two, which means it's more of the depression and mood swings instead of the week-long manic episodes, but it's manageable if I'm heavily medicated.' His expression looked pained.

'What kind of medication?'

'You haven't noticed I take a pill every morning and night?'

I racked my brain and said, 'I thought they were magnesium tablets, or–'

'*Magnesium tablets?*' He couldn't help but laugh at my naivety. It broke up the seriousness of the moment, if only briefly.

'I don't know! It didn't seem like any of my business.'

'I take Lithium during the day and Trazodone to fall asleep. For some people it can be a bit of a lethal combo – serotonin syndrome and all that – but it's mostly worked for me. Sometimes I lose my temper, or go cold, or cry over dumb stuff, and that's healthy, you know, gets it all out, but if I go numb or lose the drive to exist… That's when it's a big fucking problem.'

I held the bike rack for support. Ezra was staring out across the lot, probably examining cars again.

'Why didn't you tell me?'

'Because it's very personal and difficult to deal with, and only the people closest to me know.'

'I'm not one of those people?'

His eyes flickered back to my face, apologetic. 'You are. Of course you are. It just never came up. I wanted it to be the right moment, but I missed it.'

'Okay,' I breathed and nodded. 'Okay, so–'

'I'm in a down right now. And it's not fun. Sometimes they last a few weeks, but I just need to ride it out, and I need some space.'

'Alright. That's all you had to say.' I crossed my arms against my chest.

Ezra cocked his head, examining me. 'You're hurt.'

'Kind of. Yes.'

'Because I kept this from you?'

'Because you don't want me around during this.'

'I don't want *anyone* around when I'm like this,' he muttered. 'I'm hiding in bed all day with the sheets over my head. Ask Marion, or ask Callum—'

'*Callum*? Why would I ask Callum?'

'I just mean,' he replied slowly, 'he knows from past experiences—'

'Have you been seeing him?'

We stood there in tense silence, a stand-off. I kept my arms where they were, locked over my ribs, protecting my stomach. Instinctual shielding. Ezra was red in the face, and whether it was from embarrassment or guilt, I couldn't discern.

'He came over to check on me. Once. He knows how bad it gets.'

'And how did he know you were in a down?'

'We've been talking a bit since Sí Paradiso.'

Cicadas chirped in the dark. Seconds felt like hours.

'Okay.'

'It's just a comfort thing.'

'Yeah.' I couldn't manage more than one-word answers. I was too afraid of what would spill out.

Ezra glanced around, conscious of the few passersby leaving the cinema. 'Can we talk in the car? I hate...' He huffed out oxygen and straightened up. 'We're in public. It's awkward.'

'Fine.'

He led us to the Volkswagen and I slid into the passenger seat, as I had a hundred times before. I'd never been behind the wheel, not once with him, even in my own car. He was always in control, to steer us straight or drive us off the road.

He closed the door and cleared his throat. 'I know this is—'

'Whatever. I don't care. Do what you want.'

I knew he was gazing at me over the centre console, but I refused to meet him head-on; instead I sat facing forward, glaring at the brick wall he'd parked in front of.

'Clearly you care a bit.'

'We're not dating. I don't get a say on who you talk to.'

'Of course you do. You have no idea how much I care about what you think, and feel, and how you see me–'

'Then why are you leaning on Callum and not me?'

'Because it's cruel to do it to you. Especially if we're supposed to just be–'

'Friends?' I spat it out like it was a vulgar word. 'Well maybe I want more – maybe I want more than just friends.' I hadn't fully comprehended that until I spoke it aloud. 'And since I'm competing with Callum now–'

'No one's *competing*–'

'–I feel like I'm out of time.'

'Please don't do this,' he begged. 'Don't ruin this.'

'I didn't want to.' I felt my jaw tense, mortified by the admission. 'I honestly believed I preferred it the way it was, that it was easy. But I've been lying to myself. I do that a lot.'

He dashed a hand through his hair, agitated, panicking. 'So what do you want? A boyfriend?'

'I don't know. But isn't life too short and fragile to do this to each other?' I couldn't help but think of Melbourne, of how quickly things could disappear in a single instant. 'Aren't you feeling it too? How painful it is sometimes?'

'It's better than the alternative.'

'Which is?'

'Walking away,' he said. 'Because I can't give you what you want. I'm a fucking mess, okay? It might not seem like it, but I'm… crumbling.' He looked ashen, eyes lost in some kind of labyrinth, searching for an escape route. 'I hate being alone, and I love the time we spend together, but I'm not ready to be back in a committed relationship. Frankly, I don't want one. I missed out on so many experiences, and lost so many friends, just by existing in someone else's life.'

'I'm not Callum,' I said. 'I would never ask you to orbit my life.'

'Yeah, because you're orbiting mine. My friends, and my house… and I've wanted it. I've thoroughly enjoyed it, but you can't sit here and say the scales are balanced.'

I wanted to fold into myself.

He continued with the calamity. 'I've done my best to help you set up a life here. I'm lucky I'm a part of it. But this romance thing? It conflicts with any independence you're supposed to be building when you move to a new city.'

'Who cares about what I'm *supposed* to do?' I hurled. 'It's arbitrary.'

'It's really not. Austin, I'm one of the first guys you met in Perth. That doesn't make me the best one, or the right one. I was just… there.'

Perhaps he was right. It could've been anyone. It would've been easier if it was.

'Your insecurity is what's ruining this,' I said quietly.

'Me trying to be a good person is ruining this.'

I scoffed. 'Oh really? How's that?'

'An asshole would keep stringing you along for sex, lying to your face about what they wanted, not giving a single fuck,' he retorted. 'I would never do that because I care about you so much–'

'Just not enough to date me. Not enough to even try.'

He shook his head at the steering wheel, angrily abstaining from eye-contact. 'You're over-simplifying it.'

My gaze remained on his profile. 'Am I?'

'Yeah. You are.' He took a sharp breath, preparing for the killing blow. 'And even if it was about that… Even if I was ready… You're too young. You don't know what you want any more than I do. And you can't sit here and tell me you actually like Perth when I know you only tolerate it. Or that you're ready to get married, buy a house, and have kids all within the next few years.'

I widened my eyes at him, incredulous. 'So you *do* want that.'

'Eventually, of course.'

'Well, I'm sure eventually I will too.'

'Not before twenty-five.'

'If I loved someone and they loved me, I would try.'

'Do you love me?'

My voice faltered. 'I… Well… Would it change anything?'

'You can't answer a question with a question.'

We locked eyes. I searched his irises for the correct response, but I was sure there wasn't one.

'I don't know, okay?' I said, and the response felt heavy, but authentic. 'I've never gotten close enough to it. I don't know how it's supposed to feel.'

He took this in slowly and painfully. It was clearly the wrong answer. With a solemn tone of voice, he said, 'We promised we'd stop when it wasn't fun anymore–'

'It isn't fun anymore,' I said flatly.

'Yeah. I know.'

I examined the dashboard, free from a single scratch or speck of dust. He was so particular about everything in his life; it all had to be sanitised and perfect. All the things I wasn't. They all knew, everyone but me; Marion, Nadia, Matteo, even Juliana. I was the butt of the joke, the so-called *intellectual* who was in fact a complete idiot.

Ezra cleared his throat again. 'Look, I'll get through my down, we can be normal friends that don't have sex–'

'I don't think we can. So maybe we should just…' My jaw

set as I gazed at the wall. I felt putrid saying the words but my pride had been charred to a crisp. I felt angry, cheated somehow, mourning the time and effort I'd relinquished for him.

In the corner of my eye, I watched as his head tilted downwards. The slightest indication of despair. 'If that's what you want.'

I threw coolly at the wall, 'That's what I want.'

We waited in a silence so painful I could barely stand it. What else was there left to say? I pulled on the handle of the car door and let myself out. He didn't stop me.

16

'Austin?'

Juliana waited outside the door for a full five minutes before continuing on. Either she'd decided I was asleep, or she'd given up on waiting for me to respond. I turned the music up louder in my headphones, squeezed my eyes shut, and blindly combed for answers in the songs Ezra and I used to play for each other, but each one was too close, too real to be comforting; musical mirrors held up to remind me of our failure. We'd spent so much time with sad songs, we'd become one.

*

I really miss you

It doesn't make things easier saying that

But I miss you too

*

Two takeaway iced mochas. One latte. Two oat milk lattes. One espresso, one flat white. Three iced lattes, one cappuccino, takeaway. One cappuccino. Two iced long blacks with syrup, takeaway. One milkshake. One latte. One latte. One almond flat white. Work was monotonous, and it was a relief. I didn't want to think about anything else.

'Good work today,' Leslie said gruffly as we went through the motions of closing up. I simply nodded in reply.

I wiped the counters; Leslie polished the coffee machine,

and Daisy mopped the floors. We were a trio of few words.

*

It was all about eye contact. An entire conversation could be had in just eye contact. *You're hot. So are you. Should we fuck? Where? The bathroom? I'll meet you there.* I'd never cruised as a teenager, but I was aware of the language, the foreign tongue spoken around me. I'd never realised I was so adept until I tried. Bars. Dance floors. Shopping malls. But it wasn't just eye contact. There were codes. A foot tapping underneath a stall. Grabbing your crotch. Following or being followed into quiet places. These things might go unnoticed to the unwitting, but for those of us on the hunt, it was how we sniffed each other out. Animals in heat. It was static and transactional, the way I preferred it. The way I needed it. I hardly thought of Ezra. Others were tearing me open and putting me back together. Folding me. Reshaping me. Pulling my hair and arching my back and choking me until black spots dotted my vision.

*

How was it already December? Time was moving around me, but I was stuck in one place.

*

Merry christmas

You too

I kept my phone resting face-up on my thigh for the entirety of the Christmas lunch, praying for it to buzz just one more time. It was sustenance. Feed me one more morsel, just a crumb of attention.

Ray cut the ham. Alé served the potatoes. Juliana poured

the wine. I sat there, stagnant, overly conscious of the fact that no one knew how to engage me. Juliana asked how I was doing more times than I could count, but I was far too disgusted at the vision of myself reflected in her pitying expression to reply with anything candid.

I'd said, *I'm fine*, so many times, the words had become gibberish, meaningless.

'Austin, would you like any more food?' Ray asked.

'I'm fine. Thanks.'

Ray's presence in Juliana's life only reminded me of my lack of familial figures, and I began to quietly resent him.

*

I might unfollow you on insta
Don't take it personally

Okay?

*

I was walking briskly when I passed Daisy outside of the Ocean Beach Hotel. She was smoking a dart and watching over a girl who was throwing up in the street.

'Oi, *Melbourne!*' she said. 'Happy New Year!'

'Hey.' I came to a stop and glanced at the display by our feet. 'Is she okay?'

'Boyfriend dumped her.'

'Oh shit. Were they together long?'

'Who knows. I just met her ten minutes ago.'

The girl retched again and started sobbing.

'Well, enjoy your night,' I nodded, turning to leave.

'Where're you off to?'

'Um...' I briefly contemplated lying, but what was the point anymore? Dryly, I said, 'Some guy I hooked up with a while back invited me over for a threesome with his boyfriend. Literally didn't have anything better to do. Bit sad, isn't it?'

Daisy stared at me in bewilderment before her face spread into a grin. 'Good one!' she gleamed. 'So, no plans then. Come to the beach rave. I need someone to split the Uber to Floreat.'

'Beach rave?'

'You'll love it.'

We didn't know each other well enough for her to have the faintest idea about what I'd love, but I didn't have the energy to say no. I wasn't missing out on much anyway. The men I'd been seeing were just toys – I was only playing with them out of boredom.

We piled into the back of a Toyota Prius with the random girl. Her inability to refuse an invitation was enough of a *yes* to Daisy. All the girl could manage dribbling out was her name: Sara (or it might've been Saphira) but her words were too slurred for us to know for sure. I was paranoid that she was going to throw up again and make the driver give us a bad rating, but we managed to stumble out of the car with a clean backseat.

The carpark was already packed with people, glowsticks around their necks and bodies half-naked in boardies and bikinis. I spotted string lights and strobes attached to a plastic gazebo, a DJ booth situated beneath it and a few hundred people off their faces from various substances, jumping up and down to hard-style techno. There was no security, no queues or fences, just the beachgrass quivering in the evening breeze and the open ocean stretching out to a black horizon. We left our shoes in the dunes and joined the crowd, dancing our way through people of all ages, ethnicities, and gender expressions. I'd never seen Perth so diverse. Sand squished between my toes and my calves ached from treading across uneven ground. Sara (or Saphira) had already disappeared into the crowd. Daisy held firm to my t-shirt so as not to lose me too.

'Do you want some coke?' I asked her when we'd found an opening in the throng.

'Yeah, let's start with that, and then I've got some ket for later.'

We leaned our heads into each other, making a little huddle, and took turns snorting bumps. The bag was getting low again. Sierra had already replenished it for me twice.

Daisy groaned in satisfaction as the coke hit. She took her top off, revealing a salmon-pink lace bralette, and tied her singlet to one of her belt loops. I grinned and did the same with my t-shirt. She giggled, feeling up my chest and abs. 'Wanna make out?'

'Sure,' I shrugged, bending down to collide her mouth with mine. She tasted like ash and saltwater. We danced and kissed and danced again, taking breaks to do more drugs and sit in the dunes and watch the night sky. The stars were vibrant. It was the most fun I'd had in months.

Happy New Year

Thanks

Daisy and I were still kicking on from the beach rave, but we'd ended up at a hostel in Fremantle with three Irish backpackers, cutting lines and huffing bumps. The jokes they told were horrendous and I was convinced they were homophobic, but I was on too much ketamine to unpack it properly. Besides, Daisy made a perfect beard, nuzzled into my neck. My legs were paralysed from the drugs and I hardly felt the sting from Ezra's text.

*

I ate like a pig or nothing at all.

I went almost two days without a solid meal, and then scoffed down $40 worth of McDonalds – fries, nuggets, burgers, a large shake – only to throw it all back up again. *What a cliché*, I thought, retching brown mush into the toilet bowl.

*

This is really tough

I know

But I really think it's for the best right now

There's just a lot going on

Like what?

*

Behind a little blue door, next to a Chinese restaurant, up some stairs with a key-code security system, was Steam Works, the gay sauna. Unlike my assumptions when Ezra had first mentioned the place months ago, I found it less visually threatening.

The walls were beige, not black, and there were leather couches by the lockers, an outdoor patio littered with plants where we could smoke, and a series of corridors leading to private rooms. There were the standard sex sauna adornments too: swings, mirrored rooms, TVs playing gay pornography, and amongst the smell of chlorine and ammonia, I was passed around like a liquor bottle, emptied into a new set of lips, never with the same man twice. I flirted on the steps of the white-tiled hot tub. I had my drinks bought for me at the bar. I widened my legs in the suffocating darkness of the steam room. There were times I never even saw the face of the person who sucked me off. It could've been anyone. This was where I truly belonged, in dark liminal spaces of sweat and musk.

Clouded by that Steam Works haze, it became quite baffling to me how I'd ever imagined wanting the same things as Ezra. Marriage and children? It was an absurd fantasy – toddlers and Christmases and Easter Sundays, matching pyjamas and swimming lessons, pigtails and Scholastic book fairs, bath time and playdates, sunlit rooms with scattered Lego bricks on the floor, bedtime stories and night lights. It wasn't real. It would never be real, because I knew the truth: crying babies, the lingering smell of faeces, Ezra's house in Nollamara that we'd never move out of, Perth inescapable, flights untaken, men untried, a young dad with no idea of what he's doing – who sacrificed everything he'd ever wanted to fulfil someone else's dream.

I saw Ezra and I, and all of his friends, at the same pub every Sunday night, drinking because there was nothing else to do, quietly hating each other and ourselves.

I would've dirtied Ezra's picket fences, and it would've only prolonged my suffering.

*

The bed I slipped into every night was persistently damp and unsatisfactory. I couldn't remember the last time I'd felt the crisp and soothing touch of fresh sheets.

*

Are you seriously ignoring me

*

I was in the ocean nearly every morning. I'd wade out to my shoulders and float on my back in the still silence. Unbreakable blue, stretching infinite. When I sank beneath the surface, a part of me hoped I'd never come up again. I couldn't stay down for long.

I tried, lazily, holding myself under until my lungs screamed for oxygen, until my head went woozy, until the end seemed like a single step, not a jump; but I was always chickening out, breaking free, coughing and spluttering as I inhaled, reclaiming life. I wasn't suicidal necessarily, I was just tired of existing.

*

I'm not ignoring you

I'm just trying to give us both space

Yeah but like

You don't need to wait days to respond

It all feels very intentional

Texting is going to make things harder

Okay

I'm really sorry

It's been hard for me too

Has it?

Of course it has

I want my best friend back

But I know how much it's been hurting you

*

'So what's your story?'

Daisy's dark roots had grown out substantially in the five months we'd worked together. Despite this passage of time (and the amount of drugs we'd consumed within it) we still knew so little about each other. I knew she stank of smoke; she rolled her eyes at customers the second her back was turned, she never missed a shift, she hardly ate solid food, she thought university was a waste of money, and she'd never considered another career. She could also function at full capacity without a wink of sleep. It was a marvel to behold.

'You'll have to be more specific,' I said over the rim of my beer before taking a long sip.

She squinted at me, while behind her, a group of eighteen-year-olds were bent over the worn pool table, sending the coloured balls spinning with a loud *crack*.

'You're one of the most available people I know. What d'you do when we're not getting cooked together?'

I shrugged. 'I read books. I go swimming. I hook up with guys. What else is there to do in Perth?'

Only one of those was a lie. I couldn't remember the last time I'd read a book. The letters seemed to drag themselves around the pages like I was experiencing late-stage dyslexia, and I couldn't stand the sound of my own voice reading silently. I'd never been so aware of my internal monologue until I needed it to shut up.

'Fair,' she nodded. *Crack* went the balls again. I thought that was it, but then she added, 'You're an endless supply of cocaine, so I'm wondering if you're a dealer, or on OnlyFans, or—'

'Fucking hell,' I laughed. 'No. I've just got a bit of family money.'

'Explains the Tesla.'

'It's a lease.'

'Still.' For such a frail body, she chugged at a speed that eclipsed my leisurely sips. When she set her glass down, there was only a few centimetres of liquid left in it.

'Does it bother you? That my family is rich?'

'Why would it?'

'I don't know,' I murmured. 'It bothers some people.'

*

Not to sound crazy

But was Callum in your post last night ?

I thought you unfollowed me

I did

Then why are you checking?

Was he dancing with you guys ?

I don't care if he was btw

Just wish you'd be honest with me

Nothing is going to happen with him

I promise

Promise. What an empty word.

*

Strobe lights. The Connections dance floor. The afterparties at Steam Works. Sweat-stained shadows. Men touching, rubbing, rhythmic. Dark spots in my vision, hands down my back, on my ass, in the front of my pants, nothing tangible or real. *Did I want that?* The music was too loud to say no. Me, too weak to stop it. The silent language, in eyes and in bodies. How do you say *stop* without any words? Bathroom stall bumps. Too much ket and the world melts. His hands on my waist, turning me around, pulling down my pants, slurred words asking him to use a condom. He ignored it or didn't hear, grabbing a fistful of my hair, slamming my head against the wall. Pain. He pushed inside me. More pain. Blinding this time. His hand was over my mouth, his breath on the back of my neck. I didn't fight it. Semi-coherent thoughts swam, things like *I should've gotten on PrEP,* or *this could ruin my life. I could have something by now. He could be the one to give it to me. Don't think about that.* I wanted this. I was having fun. His voice in my ear: *I've heard about you.* So much for anonymity. *I know you like this.* So much for not wanting a reputation. *Yeah, you like that, don't you, slut?* So much for Ezra. Everything was going to shit. *Disgusting faggot.* Don't text him. Don't think about him. Lose yourself. *Why are you doing this?* What would Mum think? All I had to do was keep pretending. *Why didn't you tell him?*

*

I'm feeling really lost right now

Austin I'm sorry

I'm incapable of being a good friend to you rn

I have too much going on in my head

Just talk to me about what's happening

I can help

I can't talk to you about this

It's the one thing

Callum ?

Yes

Are you back together ?

We've been hanging out more

I don't know what's going on

But I know it's going to hurt you

I can handle you and Callum being friends

I can find a way to be okay with it

We'll never just be friends

There's too much love there

So you still love him ?

Of course I do

I'm always going to love him

In some capacity

Please just tell me you haven't had sex

I can handle anything else but not that

I can't tell you that

I'm sorry

I'm so so fucking sorry

Okay

I think I'm done

Please don't say that

I don't know what's going on

I'm fucking terrified and confused

And I just need time to figure things out

You fucking promised

You lied to me

I meant it at the time

I'm still processing everything

I feel like I'm drowning

My down is so fucking bad right now

I'm not coping at all

I'll never understand you

He left you and you're still choosing him

He doesn't love you

And probably never did

You're a fucking idiot frankly

You know what ? Have fun

Not my problem anymore

Enjoy ruining your own life

So immature and hurtful

I really thought you were better than that

You made me behave this way

This is your own fault

Yeah well if you can't take responsibility for yourself

then you're a fucking child

I never want to hear from you again

We finally agree on something

Goodbye Austin

*

'Just breathe,' Juliana was saying over and over. 'Just breathe.

Just breathe.'

'I keep losing people. I can't go through it again. I can't. I can't cope.'

'It's okay. It's gonna be okay.' Circles on my back, soothing, slow.

What had Ezra said all those weeks ago? *It's like a switch when you hit a point. You just turn it off. It's a lot easier to feel nothing.*

What was it like to feel nothing? Anything was better than this.

17

There was an unexpected downpour of rain in early March, and it flooded most of Perth. Streets surged into rivers, cars were waterlogged, ceilings leaked. I pictured myself as a yellow-raincoated-child, kicking my feet in puddles, squealing and laughing. Regrets and pains curtailed, simple pleasures at the forefront. I wasn't sure if the image was a memory or a fabrication. Maybe there was no yellow raincoat. Maybe I wasn't a happy child, and would never be a happy adult.

18

With the pre-roll between her teeth, Daisy twisted her hair up into a ponytail. Smoke escaped from the corners of her mouth as she spoke. 'Why did we start hanging out?'

I was crouched on the pavement, knotting up my grime-covered work shoes as I frowned up at her. 'What do you mean?'

'We went from co-workers that never talked to best friends pretty fast.'

I blinked at her and said, 'I'm your best friend?'

'I'm not yours?'

I straightened up, stole the half-smoked dart right out of her mouth, and took a long draw from it. I didn't wince from the taste anymore. I didn't cough either.

'I never thought about it, I suppose,' I said flatly, exhaling the smoke. 'But sure. We're best friends.'

She looked triumphant as she took the dart back from me, and we began to trudge away from the café and down the road towards Juliana's and my apartment.

There were numerous nice properties along the route; quaint terrace houses and large cottages with character, rather than the monstrous concrete blocks that were supposed to reflect wealth and modernity. For all my parents' failings, I felt they'd at least raised me with decent taste.

'As to why we got so close…' I chewed on my thoughts. 'I suppose we ran into each other at a weird time.'

'Good-weird?'

'No,' I said. 'Very bad-weird.'

She nodded knowingly. 'I wanted to ask. Seemed you had some shit going on.'

We passed the roundabout with the flowers in the centre. The hill was a steep decline, firing up our calves. It was jacket weather now, and we braved the nippy breeze with determination.

'I had a falling out with someone,' I said eventually, realising she'd been waiting for me to elaborate. The dart bounced between us.

'Someone important?'

'I think I loved him.'

'He didn't love you back?'

'Not in the way I needed. And I don't know if I can even call it a breakup because we were never technically together.'

'Those are the worst,' she groaned. 'You feel like you can't even be sad because it didn't count as a real relationship. You're mourning what could've happened.'

'Yeah, that's it exactly.' Her wisdom took me by surprise.

'Sounds like a fuckin' nightmare.'

The street levelled again. I could see the train pulling up to the station at the end of the road.

'It wasn't always,' I said. 'He did a lot for me. Gave me comfort, helped me make friends–'

'And where're those friends now?'

I flinched at the reminder. 'Well. Yeah. I guess they were never really mine. In fact, I sort of despised them.'

'I'd say you're better off. Even if you're a bit colder these days.'

'That's a good thing,' I said. 'It means I'm mentally stable.'

She eyed me in her peripheral vision. 'You're pretty self-aware.'

'No, I just know the right things to say.' I took the last drag of the dart and threw it into a patch of dirt.

She laughed. 'I think that just proved my point, dude.'

Daisy had been over to the apartment a handful of times, mostly for pre-drinks or kick-ons. I'd promised her beers out on the patio as a reward for a hard day's work. We'd been under the pump from open to close, and we'd decided a few beverages were well deserved – though we also rewarded ourselves with beers on quiet days too. There was always an occasion to drink.

We languished on the wicker seats, smelling of burnt coffee grounds and sweat, and cracked open our cans. They were from an Aussie distillery, a red dingo logo on the side that matched the one painted on the flour mill further up along the train line.

'Cheers,' I said. We touched the aluminium together.

''Kay, I have a game.' She straightened up in the seat. The wicker creaked from the movement.

'Yeah?'

'It's pretty obvious that our upbringings couldn't be more different, so…' She took a quick sip and then wiped her top lip. 'We take turns telling a memory from when we were younger, and then the other has to match it with their own version of it.'

'Alright,' I nodded in amusement at the prospect. 'You first.'

'My first time getting drunk,' she grinned, well-prepared. 'Thirteen. Down in Albany. Everyone knew if you wanted to drink, you'd go to the jetty. And there were these meth-heads chugging from a bottle wrapped in a paper bag, so I asked if I could have some. They said they'd give me the whole thing if I flashed my bra. So I did. I went back to my mates, feeling like a champion, and we all got drunk on Fireball.' She was beaming when she took another sip of the beer.

'Jesus.' I scratched my head as if the memory was an itch. 'Okay. I was twelve. My parents were still together, they went out for a fundraiser gala. I had this friend Ryan at the time who was a terrible influence on me, and he suggested we raid the wine cellar. We polished off a couple Italian reds we couldn't pronounce and jumped in the pool with our clothes on. It was the middle of winter and we nearly got hypothermia. I woke up in the bathtub.'

Daisy burst out laughing. 'See? I knew the comparison would be hilarious. Mine's rogue as fuck and yours is all posh. *Pools* and *fundraisers. Italian reds.*' She stressed each repeated word with a drawl, oozing out the syllables like pus.

'I'm not sounding like a wanker?'

'You are, but it's intentional, so it's funny. Your turn next.'

'Fine,' I sighed. I held the beer between my thighs and leaned back on my hands. 'The time I almost got arrested. My Dad was a prick, and the only way I could think to punish him was to steal his AMEX and treat myself to whatever I wanted. I'd done it a few times and he'd never found out. Well, I took out this big group of friends…' I shook my head. '*Friends* is the wrong word. I hardly knew them. But I copped the bill, drummed up about three grand on the card. Dad saw the charge and did some digging. I thought he'd just yell and scream or break something, but instead he got the police to put me in handcuffs. I was shitting myself. And at the last second before they hauled me into the car, he told them to let me off. He just wanted to give me a good scare. It got him off, seeing that fear.'

Daisy's eyes were wide. Lit up by the afternoon sun, they were a brilliant green. 'It's like a TV show.'

'Some dysfunctional family drama, maybe,' I offered. 'Your turn.'

'There's been a few times I almost got arrested.'

Somehow, that didn't surprise me. 'No kidding,' I said with subdued mirth.

'But my favourite might be for starting a bar fight. I broke a bottle over some guy's head. He gave my brother bad ket that nearly sent him into psychosis. And then suddenly half the town was throwing punches. They said I was a *riot instigator.*'

'That's so bogan.'

We were both cackling.

'I *am* a fuckin' bogan, if you haven't noticed.' She set the beer down by her feet and set her hands flat on her thighs. 'Okay, deep one.'

'Here we go,' I winced.

'*V card.* I was seventeen.' Off my raised eyebrows, she said, 'I know, shocking I lasted so late. But out of all the things I'd done, it was the one I wanted to save.' Her expression darkened. 'I wanted it to be special. I was seeing this guy Cam for a month or two because he had a truck and could take me off-roading. We'd tear through the bush — nearly rolled the car a few times going through the national parks, checking out isolated cliffs and beaches along the coast. It was epic. Absolutely fuckin' beautiful. Not everyone gets to see those parts of Australia. He'd just turned eighteen and kept talking about moving to the city.

'One night, he drove us out to a private spot along the shore. He was packing all his shit and jetting off the next day, and he said he wanted me to come. We'd get our own place in Perth, fuck off school and everyone else… He said he was gonna take care of me.'

She reached down, fetched her beer, and took a long gulp.

'We had sex in the front seat,' she said. 'Windows down. Sea breeze. It was *almost* romantic. But he didn't even have a condom and he went in so quickly, just sort of…' She paled.

'Put it right in. Fuck, it hurt. I still remember that. To stop from totally freaking out I just reminded myself we'd be together the next day, and we could get the pill at some point. And it was just our first time, it would get better. All those little lies.

'Afterwards, he dropped me off at home and said he'd see me in the morning. When I woke up… I waited. Crisscrossed on the grass like a fuckin' kindergartner until noon. After he still didn't show, I decided he'd probably chickened out.'

She wasn't looking at me, instead tracing the shape of the dingo on the side of the beer.

'But nah. He went to the city. He just… didn't take me with him. And now I know how depressing buying plan B can be. Especially when you're alone.'

'That's awful,' I said. 'I'm really sorry, Daisy.'

'Don't be sorry. I'm not.' Her eyes flickered back up to mine, offering some sort of proof it was nothing to her, but I could see the pain that still lingered. 'It gave me the determination to make it out on my own. I started working, saved up to buy a car, drove myself to Perth, and when I ran into Cam on a night out, I lied and told him he'd actually gotten me pregnant, but I aborted the baby. I think that gave him a good scare. His family were a bunch of religious nuts and he felt *so* guilty.'

I blinked. 'Right. Well. Fuck him.'

'Fuck him,' she agreed and cocked her head to the side. 'And you? When did you lose it?'

'Ah…' I shifted uncomfortably. 'Mine's a bit boring, really. Nothing fancy.'

'That's alright.'

I set my beer down on the concrete. 'I was a bit of a lonely kid. I think I'm a bit of a lonely person, actually. And I hit puberty pretty early — by year eight, men were already noticing me. Even at restaurants or walking home in my school uniform. And I noticed them back.'

I felt Daisy watching me, but I avoided her eyes.

'I was horny. I was lonely. The other gay guys at school were all in the closet, nothing much happening there. I wanted to be with someone, properly, but I was too young to go to clubs or bars so I just... got on Grindr. They don't check ID or anything, you just set your age and that's it. Free reign of the entire platform. Instant messaging of whoever you want. So yeah. I lost my virginity at fourteen to some thirty-year-old guy in a hotel room whose name I can't remember. End of story.' I touched the back of my neck. 'Or the start of it. I don't know. I was a bit promiscuous from that point on.'

'That's heinous,' Daisy said.

I couldn't bear to make eye contact. I just barreled through. 'I'm not a victim or anything. I was in control of the situation every time. No one forced me, right? I sought it out on my own. And I liked to think they weren't paedophiles. That they believed me when I said I was eighteen. Though sometimes I look back on photos of myself at that age, and I feel a bit sick. That *child* was having sex with fully-grown men who'd probably sought me out, preyed on me. It's really hard to spin it any other way. I basically just... enabled my own assault. About a hundred times over.'

'Austin, that's not... I mean, you can't *enable your own*... No.' Daisy shook her head in my peripheral vision.

'Yeah,' I said. 'I guess not. It's just sort of insane though, thinking back on it. And now, being a bit older, but still not even the age of the guys I used to sleep with, I see teenagers around and I can't... I can't even fathom anyone being attracted to them. They're just kids. *I* was just a kid.'

Daisy was quiet for a long time, until she asked softly, 'Do you think that messed you up a bit?'

I sighed, though it sounded like a self-deprecating laugh. 'I've definitely developed a couple of bad habits, but at least I'm aware of them, I suppose? I know I only use sex to self-soothe, or to feel less numb, or less lonely, but I'm pretty sure that's why most people have it too.'

'I think we're supposed to do it because it feels good,' she said. 'Because it's nice to be with someone in that way.'

I chewed my lip and frowned at her. 'Do you believe that?'

'Nah. Not really,' she admitted.

'Yeah,' I said. 'Neither do I.'

19

*

Sierra somehow flourished under Karrinyup shopping centre's fluorescent lighting; with her hair dyed from red to blonde, layered thick and silky, she was a dead-ringer for my sister from certain angles. She had suggested we escape the GT for the afternoon, opting to drive twenty-five minutes across Perth for the same shops we had in the next suburb over. Claremont Quarter was too stuck up, she explained; too many PLC girls haunting the food court or judging each other through the display windows.

'I know we talk a lot of shit, but it was a great school,' she tacked on. 'So many lovely girls. It's just a few bad eggs that might've left a bad taste in Jules' mouth, but I think she'd find that at any school, not just the private ones. Everyone's a dick at that age.'

I'd gotten used to her histrionic way of speaking.

She led us through the complex, clearly well-versed in the layout. 'At least we were never as bad as the all-boys schools.'

'I went to an all-boys school,' I muttered. 'It was a glorified circus.'

I thought of the itchy uniforms, ties tight against the throat, blazers badly thermoregulated, perpetually too hot or too cold. Chapel every Wednesday, those looming ceilings and stained glass windows, Jesus pinned up, crying and bleeding. I always found the depictions so morbid. It all seemed like a waste of time, standing there and reciting prayers I didn't believe in. I wasn't a rebel, I wasn't popular, but I wasn't an outcast either. I mostly just kept my head down, avoiding slurs and bashings, the threat of violence hanging around each corner. Other boys weren't as careful, presenting too feminine, solidifying a target on their backs.

I could remember the smell of urine and bleach in the boy's bathroom where I used to give handjobs in the disabled stall, pre-Grindr days. Perhaps it was out of boredom, or a kind of self-preservation, like being someone's prison bitch. Prove useful, and they'll protect you. And they did – too often it was the closeted ones who were the most aggressive, the most violent. I traded favours and discretion for safety. From school, the biggest lesson seemed to be that it was the people around us who decided who we were. Their perceptions and their projections made up our fabric of being, while whatever we thought and felt privately took a backseat. If no one was around to perceive us, was there any point in existing?

We came to a stop outside a menswear shop and Sierra said, 'That would suit you,' nodding at a shirt draped over a mannequin.

'I can't remember the last time I bought clothes for myself,' I admitted.

'Maybe worth spending your money on something other than drugs.'

I didn't have a defence for that, and she was already walking into the boutique, so I had no choice but to follow.

She combed through the racks, pulling out shirts and jeans without my approval, and all but pushed me into the changing room.

'It's really good to see you,' I said through the curtain as I undressed.

There was a long pause before she replied.

'I thought you were going to cancel on me.'

I pulled the first steel-blue shirt over my head. The cotton was soft and crisp, and made my shoulders look broad in the mirror.

'Why would I cancel?'

'Because I'm refusing to be your dealer.'

I pulled a pair of jeans off the hanger and stepped into them.

'I'd feel awful if you thought I'm only using you for that.'

'Well, to be honest, I *have* felt that for the last few months.'

I buttoned the jeans and parted the curtain to stare at her, emphasising my hurt. She met my expression with ambivalence, before surveying the outfit she'd chosen, hands on the hips of her silk skirt.

'That looks great,' she said. 'You need to get both.'

'I'm not a user.'

'You've been a bad friend.'

'I've been a bad person,' I said. 'And I'm really sorry. How can I make it up to you?'

She tried to fight it, but a smile crept back onto her face. 'You already are by being here. And by not talking about *him*.'

I glanced down at the linoleum floor, chewing on the inside of my bottom lip.

'It's been hard being around you lately,' Sierra continued, not unkindly. 'You were either looking to get high or needing someone to rant to. And I get it, breakups can feel like the world is ending. But I've done this routine already, with Marion and everyone else who exiled me, just to relive it all over again through you.'

'That's more than fair enough. I've been selfish.'

'You're twenty. You should be selfish,' she said coyly. 'Just don't be pathetic.'

It was the assurance I needed, and I found myself returning her smile before retreating into the changing room. We ended up leaving the store with four outfits and a pair of $600 sunglasses.

'Why are we constantly shamed for having money?' Sierra said in an attempt to remedy our consumer guilt. We rode the escalator down to the food court, shopping bags draped over our arms.

The section with the renovated shops was all shiny and spotless, containing a little outdoor courtyard littered with overpriced pubs and a brand-new HOYTS. They had fitted in a massive skylight to brighten up the complex, though the weather outside was black and heavy with rain. At least in Melbourne there was a vibrancy even in the wintertime. We went out to clubs and checked our heavy coats at the door, we ate at restaurants where red meats and wines were a source of heat and comfort. Without the sunshine, Perth was only more empty and depressing. I missed my ocean swims terribly.

'Aren't you sick of downplaying yourself for other people's comfort?'

I gazed at her through my new polarised lenses and nodded. 'Yeah, I am actually. I feel like I've been treading on eggshells since I moved here.' Was I the kind of person that wore sunglasses inside now? It was certainly something to try.

'And it's outrageous because everyone knows how money-hungry Ezra became after dating Callum.'

I found it somewhat amusing she was the one bringing him up this time.

'The obsession with nice cars, going out to dinners…' She

rolled her eyes. 'Ezra pretends he's too good for it, but it's his biggest motivator. I'm sure it was the main reason he got back with Callum. He wanted to be taken care of.'

I kept expecting to run into him somewhere. Perth was so small, it was certainly possible, but I started to believe that there were higher powers keeping us apart. I never saw him the nights I went dancing at Connections or The Court. He wasn't at the restaurants or bars we used to frequent: Queens, Besk, Sí Paradiso. His socials had gone private. A Callum-sized black hole had opened up and swallowed him completely. It was for the better. It had to be for the better. The mantra repeated at night to fall asleep was one of my few sources of comfort. I wondered if he hated me, or missed me, or thought of me at all.

'Are you seeing anyone?' I asked Sierra.

'Perth boys aren't worth my time,' she said, side-eyeing the *eshays* with oversized t-shirts and audacious sneakers that were riding parallel to us.

'You should try men.'

'I should,' she agreed, and we stepped off the escalator and onto solid ground.

We found a table at the sushi train in the corner of the complex. Our plethora of shopping bags were piled up by our feet like we were housewives after a divorce. Sierra immediately plucked a plate of sashimi off the conveyor belt. The fillet was pink and fat.

I'd barely snapped my chopsticks in half when I heard a tentative, 'No kidding. Hey guys.'

Marion's distinct huskiness pacified my movements and I blinked up at her in a daze. She was unchanged, as if the last time I'd seen her had been days, not months ago. A blonde girl I'd never seen before lingered just behind her.

'Marion?'

'Been ages!' she said with a forced enthusiasm, perhaps overcompensating for her abandonment of me. I was speechless, my ventriloquist dummy mouth opening and shutting stupidly. Seeing Marion was like seeing an echo from another life.

Sierra combed a hand through her hair and said, 'Haven't seen you since–'

'Down south,' Marion nodded.

'Yeah. You look well.'

Blush painted both of their cheeks.

'Um… This is Izzy,' Marion continued, offering up the blonde girl as a consolation prize. 'My girlfriend.'

Izzy might've been the smaller, rounder version of Sierra if she had circle-rimmed glasses and dressed like a librarian. Her hair was thin and shoulder length, pale pink lips set into a smile I hoped was sincere.

'Heard so much about you both,' Izzy said, and Sierra stiffened.

'Nice to meet you,' she replied icily. I found it briefly amusing that she might be jealous, before I felt a sudden surge of panic.

'Is… Is he here?' I blurted out. 'With… him?'

'Ezra?'

'Yes. With Callum.'

'No, of course not.' Marion's arms knitted across her chest. 'They're not together. That crashed and burned pretty quickly.'

My face must have broken like dawn because she reached out to touch my arm with genuine remorse. I could feel the apology through her fingers, even if she didn't speak it aloud. 'He misses you. We all do.'

I hadn't even thought to consider the possibility of their second attempt failing. I'd accepted his silence as a declaration of success.

'He wants to reach out, but he thinks you hate him.'

'I do hate him,' I said.

Sierra snorted from across the table.

'But nothing happened,' Marion continued, choosing to ignore the smarmy attitude.

'They hooked up. He chose Callum.'

'It wasn't that simple. Maybe just… give it some time?'

'I've had time,' I muttered. 'And I've moved on.'

'He talks about you constantly,' Izzy added, a lame endeavour at reassurance.

Marion nodded to cement this. 'He hasn't been this sullen since… Well, since Callum first left him.'

A pang of despair reverberated deep within me, buried in a box I never wanted to open again. I looked to Sierra for her reaction, but her phone was out and raised like a shield to defend herself from participation. She tapped away at the screen, pretending to be engaged with something important.

'I miss him too,' I admitted finally. 'But I don't know if there's anything worth salvaging.'

'I think you both need to swallow your pride and have a conversation.'

'It's not about pride,' I said, but as the words left my mouth, I realised I wasn't certain of that anymore. Every time I searched for his face in crowds, my pride suffered. Every time I fell asleep thinking of what I should've done, my pride suffered. What else did I have, except my last shred of dignity? Staying away was the only course of action I could muster. I refused to relinquish simply because Marion said I should.

'If Ezra wants me back in his life, he can grow some balls and reach out,' I said coolly, and relaxed my clenched fists.

Sierra beamed at me from behind her phone in obvious

approval of the response.

Marion shrugged us both off. 'Well, it was good to see you anyway.'

'You too,' I said politely, and then she was gone just as quickly as she'd appeared, Izzy chasing her shadow.

20

Just as the weather was getting to me, momentary warmth broke free from clouded shackles. Bathed in a patch of sunlight and with various dips from Coles and a large slab of focaccia between us, we had an unbroken view of Matilda Bay and the city skyline, all the way across the south foreshore. Perth might've been the most beautiful from this vantage point; the Swan River a thick tendril curling around the city, Mounts Bay Road snaking into Elizabeth Quay, thousands of tuart trees knitted into a lush blanket of green, and all zoomed out to hide the imperfections of empty streets and stark storefronts. I'd been told the sunset was breathtaking, but we still had another hour until then. Alé retrieved a lukewarm bottle of Prosecco from Juliana's bag, popped the cork, and poured it into our plastic cups.

'I feel like royalty all the way up here,' he said. The bottle was set down and he lounged on his back, propped up by his left elbow.

'Maybe that's why they call it Kings Park,' Juliana said and took a sip. Her red lipstick matched the cup.

I stretched my legs out on the picnic blanket, flexing my feet, relaxing them again. My sneakers were an untarnished white, a small present to myself – though if I was being honest, I was milking a newfound confidence to spend money. Daisy couldn't care less, and Sierra appreciated that someone could keep up. Clothes were fitting just right, my HITT classes were rebuilding the muscle I'd lost while depressed, my skin and hair had never looked better due to top-shelf products. Was it so tactless to admit how greatly money could improve a situation, a life? And what was so wrong with that?

I traded shame for confidence, shouted dinners, drinks out, always took someone home, and sex became less degrading when I was the one topping. They submitted to me as though they owed me something, and there was power in that. For too long I'd been held hostage to self-imposed subservience, or was frugal for the sake of others' insecurities, constantly forced to downplay my own status. I found myself retroactively bitter by letting it happen in the first place. Pretending to be like everyone else – what was I thinking? I was surely better than most.

Yes, everything was preferable this way. Only my eyes betrayed clarity. I couldn't seem to clear them up. They were perpetually blood-shot and dark-ringed, but that might've been the drug use or the occasional sleep paralysis I'd been experiencing. It would start with the feeling of floating, rising from the bed, and then I'd be screaming internally, trying to wake up, but my joints would be locked in place, frozen in terror. How quickly flying can become falling. Just before some kind of impact, I'd be released, gasping awake, trying to catch my breath in the dark. Sometimes I'd feel a threatening presence in the corner of the room, but I never turned my head, fearful of what would meet me in the moonlight. People often talked about visions of demons or spectres during episodes like this, and I knew whatever my brain could conjure up was sure to traumatise me. I made no effort to change my party habits, however. I still needed my vices, I tended to them fondly, and if this was the side effect of an otherwise entertaining few months, so be it.

'Did you hear from Sierra?'

I nodded. 'She's in Sydney for the weekend.'

'Oh,' Juliana said, clearly miffed she hadn't been privy to the information, but she smothered the reaction with a quick smile. 'I suppose you guys are closer than we are these days. I'm glad you have her.'

'Glad to hand her off, you mean?' Alé said, and Juliana shot him a look I couldn't pinpoint.

'She's been a great friend to me,' I said curtly.

'Didn't mean much by it,' he shrugged. 'Just slightly relieved to be done with those GT girls. Back with the Brazilians. Back with our people.'

'Shouldn't Juliana get to decide who her people are?'

My comment clearly struck a nerve for both of them, because Juliana looked out across the bay as if she hadn't heard and Alé just snatched up the prosecco bottle and refilled his cup in silence.

'I'm sure she would've been here if she knew it was my birthday,' I added quickly, salvaging the moment.

'You didn't tell her?'

'I didn't want to make a big deal of it.'

'But you're twenty-one!' Juliana said. 'You should enjoy yourself.'

'Oh, I will,' I assured her. 'Daisy has a handful of caps waiting for me later.'

'I thought you were scared of MDMA.'

'When did I say that?'

'Ages ago,' Juliana said, but her voice was tinged with uncertainty. 'Something about a psychological break?'

'I was probably joking.'

'Hmm. Right.'

I took another long sip from the plastic cup and watched the white sailboats in the bay, riding the wind like a scene in a picture book. I didn't even notice the shadow that eclipsed our sunlight until Juliana waved and said loudly, 'You made it!'

I shifted around slowly.

'Sorry I'm late.' She was backlit against the sun, cradling a small box in her nimble arms, a beautiful blonde hallucination. I attempted to blink her away but she remained.

'What are you doing here?' was all I managed, shell-shocked.

'Wasn't going to miss my little brother's twenty-first,' Sabrina said, plopping herself down on the grass beside me as if everything was perfectly normal. 'It's such an important one.'

'We're Australian,' I said flatly. 'Twenty-one is a nothing age.'

'Pretend we're American for the next hour and it'll justify the flight over.'

She opened the box and there were six cupcakes, red velvet with cream cheese frosting, my favourite since we were children. She embraced Juliana, and then Alé, exchanging niceties and introductions before handing out the cakes with a PTA motherly finesse. She looked like the old Sabrina, the one from years back, pre-divorced parents, but a woman instead of a girl, bright-coloured clothes, tortoise-shell sun-glasses covering her eyes. Her cheeks were full and her lips were rich in colour, smiling, an act so foreign to the Sabrina I was better acquainted with.

'Finally meeting the other cousin,' Juliana said.

'It was a great suggestion,' Sabrina agreed, peeling the paper from the side of a cupcake. Another disorienting image. I hadn't seen Sabrina consume carbs or sugars in a decade. 'Thank you. You know, for the messages, the updates. And for being there for my brother.' She took a large bite.

The wind was knocked out of me. Her presence in itself

was shocking, and this *version* was more so. Was it an act, a deception? Was it part of some revenge scheme for abandoning her? Had she come to take me away, put me in a rehab, or a conservatorship? Anything was possible.

'Respectfully, this family has some incredible genes,' Alé said surveying the three of us, and the girls laughed. I continued to stare at them in a daze, waiting for the mirage to falter, but Sabrina was hardly paying attention to me, chatting animatedly with Juliana and Alé about Perth and their lives. They briefly turned to me for reactions or responses, but mostly I just nodded dumbly throughout their exchanges until the sun touched down, spilling amber light over the clouds. The sunset was lacklustre from the now-overcast weather, and the wind had picked up. I shivered and watched Juliana and Alé begin to pack up the picnic around us.

'Have you got dinner plans?' Sabrina asked me. Her sunglasses rested on her head, exposing her olive-green eyes, razor-focused upon me.

'No,' I said, squeezing my arms for warmth. 'Just meeting a friend later.'

'Great. I'll take us out.' She smiled with such earnestness, it almost felt threatening.

*

'How long are you staying?' I asked over the rocket salad and stracciatella-covered pears.

We'd ended up at Il Lido in Cottesloe, a favourite of mine. Amidst the frenetic energy of the dinner rush, it felt more private than a quiet restaurant where intimate conversations had to occur in whispers. We could be discussing murder plots at full volume and no one would notice, all tucked into the back corner by the wine wall. Sabrina had selected the first shiraz that had met her at eye-level.

'Only for the weekend,' she replied, gripping the stem of the glass tightly in her hand. I thought I noticed a tremor, a potential detail that would prove she wasn't as amiable as she'd tried to appear at the picnic. Any moment she would shed this skin and revert back to her cold, hard self.

'You know how Graham gets when I'm away too long.'

'He loses all purpose.'

'Exactly,' she chuckled and drank measuredly. I hadn't expected her to take the joke in stride. Usually she would sneer or roll her eyes at a comment like that, but she simply placed her glass softly down on the table.

'Juliana's great.'

'Yeah, she is.' I was cautious of every word, every movement, determined to unravel her agenda before the ambush. I reached for the salad, but she pulled it out of my grasp before I was able to touch the plate. She served herself first, and then me.

'She's worried about you. And so am I.'

'Right. So that's why you're here,' I said with belligerence. 'An intervention.'

She didn't bother to pick up her fork. Her hands folded together on the table. 'I've been meaning to come for ages. She just gave me a bit of a push.'

'I'm fine.'

'You're a bit dead in the eyes.'

'I know, since the funeral.'

'This is different. You've got *drug-addict*-pupils.'

'That's not a real thing.'

'But you're doing drugs, aren't you?'

I shook my head incredulously. 'Did Juliana tell you that?'

'Are you?'

'How is it any of your business?'

'Because you're my brother and I love you.'

I remembered the last time I'd heard her say that. Sometime after our parents announced their separation, when the sun was streaming through the Palladian windows in the front room with the piano.

I was at the baby grand, tapping the same note over and over as if it would change anything. I didn't hear Sabrina approach, she just materialised at my side to share the stool. Like an angel. Our parents were locked in a screaming match in the kitchen after Dad had showed up unannounced with papers to sign. Sabrina's head leaned into me. 'I love you. It's gonna be okay,' she said.

The screaming in the other room got louder, and I couldn't play piano very well, but Sabrina could, excellently. She got me to scoot over so she could stretch her slender arms across the keys, and then she began to play a sonata I didn't know the name of. It began slow and gentle, but as our parents carried on she picked up speed, her fingers striking the acrylic bars with ferocity, louder, until music flooded the room and washed them away. She played for an hour leaving her fingers raw and trembling. They'd stopped screaming by then.

'I love you,' she said again from across the table, 'and I want to make sure you're okay.'

'You're about ten months too late.'

Her eyes brimmed with tears before they were downcast at the table. 'I suppose I deserve that.'

'Where was this concern at the funeral?' I muttered, unmoved, taking a stab at one of the pears. 'You were a fucking robot in that church.'

'I tried to tell you on the phone, but I… It all came out wrong.' She wiped any moisture away before her mascara could run. 'We both struggle with honesty. Therapy was very eye-opening.'

'So this… This person… A bit of therapy and problem solved?' I shovelled the fork into my mouth and chewed.

'You should try it sometime. But no, Austin,' she sighed. 'I'm not fixed all of a sudden. I've changed my antidepressants and I've finally cut Dad out of my life, but progress is fucking slow.'

'You cut out Dad?' I said with my mouth full of food, blinking in shock.

She grimaced. 'It was long overdue. God, he's a fuckhead. So many years spent messed up, so much to untangle, even before the divorce, but *especially* after Mum… did what she did.' She reached for the wine again. 'Yeah. I was a bit traumatised. There wasn't space in my brain to be there for you, and I'm sorry. But look at our parents, for God's sake. Dad was abusive and Mum was probably borderline.'

I physically recoiled at her choice of words. They sounded so harrowing out loud, but she continued on with little acknowledgment of my visible reaction. 'Inheriting psychological issues was inevitable.'

'*I'm fine*,' I said again.

'We will never be fine. We will carry this grief in some shape or form until we die, but at least we can carry it together. Halve the weight. And sometimes that's good enough.' She set the glass down again and reached across the table to squeeze my clenched fist. I hadn't even noticed how hard I'd been digging my nails into my palm.

'I should've never let you leave Melbourne. We needed each other.'

'I needed to go,' I said. My bottom lip was quivering.

'I don't see you happy here. It's not your city.'

'I know that.'

She looked surprised by the admission.

'I've *always* known that, even if I wanted it to be true for someone else.'

'That Ezra guy?' she prodded gently.

I should've felt betrayed by Juliana going to her behind my back, but instead I was relieved. There was no need to replay the supercut. She'd done it for me. Juliana had done all this, gotten Sabrina here, made this conversation happen, for me. She was as much of a sister as the one sitting opposite.

'Imagine getting your heart broken by a Perth boy,' Sabrina said, and her tears and my trembles were replaced with laughter. We laughed harder than was appropriate for the comment. It just felt cathartic to do so.

'Embarrassing, I know,' I said, regaining control. 'But it's temporary. Everything's fucking temporary.'

'Then why are you still here? Mum's house is just sitting there gathering dust and mould, waiting for us to do something with it.'

'That place is haunted.'

'Yeah, no shit.' She picked up her fork at last, but only to play with the rocket leaves. 'Come back and help me sell it.'

I shook my head. 'I promised myself I'd do a full year.'

'Why? You have nothing to prove to anyone.'

'I have something to prove to myself. Figuring out who I am and what I want before I can come home and be a real person again. Before I can be a good brother to you.' My eyes swung through the restaurant, imagining the Perth that lay beyond, from the ocean to Nollamara. 'It's all purgatory.'

'As long as you know that.'

'I do. I think everyone can sense it too. It's why I can't seem to put any roots down.'

'Perth is weird,' Sabrina said flatly. 'Not quite a city, not quite a town. I can't imagine Mum growing up here.'

'Our uncle said she never fit in. But she didn't fit in Melbourne either. I think she was very lost, probably her whole life.'

She gazed at me with pain in her eyes. 'I'm scared that you'll be like that too.'

It was my turn to reach across the table and squeeze her hand. 'I won't. I promise, I won't.'

'And the partying?' She was back on her mothering, but I wasn't so resistant to it this time. It felt, for the first time, comforting. 'Will you calm down a bit?'

'I'm twenty-one, Sabrina. Can't you let a guy live a little?'

'I guess I was a bit wild when I was your age,' she admitted.

We turned our attention down to our plates, ate in silence, and it was almost as if years of suffering had been put to bed before the mains arrived. I knew it would never be that easy, but even for an hour, there was an air of hope it *could* be.

After dinner, we stood out the front of Il Lido, sea breeze clawing at our clothes, waiting for an Uber to take her back to her suite at the COMO. Sabrina looked at me and said, 'It wasn't your fault, you know? It wasn't anyone's.'

Regardless of whether I believed that to be true, I exhaled and said, 'Thank you.'

We hugged tighter than we ever had, merging like a cast to mend broken bones.

'I'll see you tomorrow before I'm off.'

'Okay.'

'And you'll come home when you're ready,' she said against my ear, more as a reassurance for herself, rather than me. 'When you remember you're too good for Perth.'

'No one's too good for Perth,' I decided as we broke apart. 'It's just a place.'

*

We took two caps each in the queue for Connections, and

Daisy introduced me to her housemate, Steve, who was all pale skin stretched over long limbs, skeletal. His face reminded me of a rodent, still good-looking but with the potential to revert back to non-human form at midnight. They lived together in Scarborough, and a few times a month they would end up having sex after a big night. Daisy said she wasn't even sure what his penis looked like, having hardly remembered the encounters the following day, which I found concerning.

Steve tried to fist-bump me, but my hand was open, expecting a handshake, and his knuckles collided with the centre of my palm.

'Oh,' I said, closing my hand around his fist. He found it hilarious.

We made it up the stairs, immediately met with the familiar Connections musk of locker rooms and soiled undergarments, aggressively masculine. Techno music throbbed and strong shoulders and backs swayed in silhouettes. Most of them were clothed, though a few were clad in leather harnesses or naked from the waist up. Familiarity haunted their faces, some from the other times I'd attended, some from Grindr, others from Steam Works. Did they recognise me too? Or was it paranoia? Was I already feeling the MDMA?

We pressed further into their den, and I could feel my shoes peeling themselves from the sticky floor with each step. The chandeliers made of LED bars rippled with colour above our heads and ricocheted off the various disco balls in technicolour beams. A kaleidoscope of energy. I hated to admit that I enjoyed this sweaty pit, the various characters that threaded between each other, a freak show and a gladiator ring all at once. Good-looking men, strange-looking men, some neither men nor women but something else entirely, labels or conformity held no power here, a lawless land. There was anonymity in the darkness, but also danger – hands could grope you and disappear before the culprit was caught, you were at the mercy of the amoeba. It was both thrilling and violating.

The drugs took less than an hour to hit Daisy. I wasn't surprised considering how little she was. She kept touching her ribs like something was digging its way out and gawking up at the ceiling as the lights flickered and spun. Steve was next, eyes bulging from his skull, pupils wide as dinner plates. He was gurning too, jaw popping and distending before he finally put a piece of gum between his teeth for his mouth to fixate on. I knew mine was coming with the ache in my stomach. That was always how it started. The lights – all at once – were so bright, the colours oversaturated. My body lit up like a fuse box. I could feel every nerve, every muscle, isolated and functioning at full capacity. Each singular blood cell bouncing in my arteries. The caps were stronger than the ones I'd had before.

The three of us turned in to face each other, making a small circle in the mosh. We found a childish playfulness in the lurching of our bodies, in the screwed-up expressions on our faces. Sweat-stained torsos brushed against us, but we hardly noticed them. It was our little ring of euphoria. I felt moisture on my cheeks. I touched my hand to my eyes and examined the tears drying on my fingertips. I couldn't understand why I was crying, but the sob began to shudder through my chest before I had time to stop it. I kept dancing and the music kept building, heading towards a crescendo. The anticipation was almost painful.

'I'm so happy,' Daisy said when the beat dropped.

'Me too,' I wept.

'I love you, dude.' Her hands made fists in my shirt.

We jumped up and down with such force that my tears were thrown from my face and discarded into the crowd. My cotton shirt threatened to rip in Daisy's fervent hands. Steve put his arms around us both. He kissed Daisy, and then me. I was taken completely unawares. His tongue was warm and sloppy, and when he pulled away, he squinted.

'Why are you crying?'

I felt heavy in the chest again. The tears were spilling with conviction. I stepped back and pressed my fingers against the tear ducts in an attempt to plug the leak. The men in the shadows watched me. There was a hunger in their dancing. Someone pressed up behind me with an erection and held my hips. Fingers inched their way into the waistband of my jeans.

I pushed the stranger off, drawing even more attention to myself as the pack began to sniff out an outlier. They could all see me crying now. I needed to get away. I receded from the crowd, from the dance floor, from Daisy and Steve and the music, to the stairs leading further up. They coiled into the darkness, an iron serpent. I took them. Another turn, the shape of a door, and freedom.

I emerged out onto the rooftop deck, thick with the smell of cigarettes and the sound of gossip. The night was cool on my face. I sucked in oxygen. Men clustered together, flirting, smoking, chatting, vaping. A drag queen adjusted her wig. A barback in a tank-top stacked half-drunk cocktails onto a precarious tower. Two people made out in the corner. Using the wall like a handrail, I slowly felt my way across the roof. The texture was sharp and brick dust coated my fingertips. I closed my eyes and studied the roughness of the ridges. I let it soothe me. I let my breathing slow. I didn't notice someone behind me.

'Hey,' he said, 'happy birthday,' and I turned to face Ezra.

21

'Oh. Hi,' I said coolly, straightening up and pushing the hair from my forehead.

'Your pupils are huge.' Ezra crossed his arms and leaned against the brick, gazing at me with a glassy kind of uncertainty. His hair had grown out long past his ears since November and I hated to admit how well it suited him, less clean-cut and more relaxed and masculine. Had it really been seven months? Our time apart felt simultaneously endless and startingly brief. A blur of drugs, sex, and tedious café shifts had that effect. If he was still suffering, there was no trace of it in his face. Part of me had hoped he'd been crying himself to sleep each night spent without me, while the other part was relieved to see him looking healthy.

'Did you know I'd be here?' I demanded.

'No. Of course not,' he frowned. 'I'm out with Matteo for a dance but he ditched me for a boy he's been chatting up.'

He nodded at the couple in the corner. I looked closer, realising it had been Matteo locking lips. He and the stranger devoured each other drunkenly, like flames against dry wood. Ezra was clearly discontented with the situation.

'And it's not like we have many other options to go out. Or maybe this is fate.' He smiled like it was all one big joke. Like everything was fine. Like nothing had happened.

I thought I might punch him, but instead I said, 'I've missed you,' almost against my will. It just slipped out, sounding somewhat strangled in its delivery.

'I've missed you too. Can I hug you now?'

'Yeah.'

Folding back into his arms was like finding solid ground after months adrift. He was skinnier than before, the muscles in his arms slightly deflated, but he smelled the same.

'You're shaking,' he said.

'I can't believe you're here.'

He pulled away from me, only slightly, and then held my chin between his thumb and forefinger, investigating the size of my pupils again.

'Are you on drugs?'

'No.'

'Okay.'

'How did you know it was my birthday?' I drew back from his accusatory stare and gentle fingers.

'Because you told me. Months ago.'

'And you remembered?'

He looked wounded that I questioned this. 'Yeah. I remembered.'

I was tongue-tied behind clenched teeth, half-convinced the caps were laced with PCP and Ezra was simply a drug-induced apparition that would soon dematerialise. First Sabrina, then him... psychosis seemed a digestible answer.

'Are you having a nice night?'

'Yeah,' I said. 'I didn't expect to see you.'

'Me either. I'm really glad I did though.' He dispersed weight from one foot to the other, a rocking motion, like one that would soothe a baby. 'How are you?'

'I'm great.'

'I wanted to reach out, I really did. I just—'

There was raucous laughter from the table beside us as someone started shaking their ass to a Doja Cat song on the overhead speakers. The group of gays that surrounded egged them on with snaps of affection and cheers of approval. I was suddenly conscious of how loud the music was, how cold I was in the night air, and how ill-fitting this backdrop was for a reunion.

'Can we talk somewhere else?' I asked, shivering again, hands tucked under my armpits.

'Yeah, sure. Do you need something to eat?'

*

The kebab shop next to Connections was a certain kind of liminal space. Drenched in harsh fluorescents and the smells of several different cuisines, it served as a transitional point to carb-load after a tack-yack or before Ubers were called and trains were caught. We ended up at a rickety stainless-steel table with scuff-marked plastic chairs. My HSP box sat open in front of me, chips glistening with grease, drenched in cheese and dotted with flecks of oregano and pepper. The shredded lamb looked grey and pink in all the wrong places, but with enough milk-coloured garlic sauce as a topping, I stuffed the contents into my mouth regardless. The salt and sodium stripped the moisture from my tongue. Ezra watched me. I didn't offer him any. His jacket was draped over my shoulders, and I could smell his cologne on the collar: woody-sage and lavender, overpoweringly strong and intoxicating.

'Why didn't you reach out?' I wiped my lips with the back of my hand. I was sure I looked feral, but my initial shock of seeing him had waned, leaving behind a kind of apathy. What could he do to me that he hadn't done already? Leave? I felt suddenly invincible.

'You told me you didn't want to hear from me again,' Ezra answered slowly.

'So?'

'I thought that meant you didn't want to hear from me again.'

'No, it meant I was pissed off, and you should've kept trying to make it right until I wasn't anymore.'

'Pissed off seems like an understatement.'

'Don't flatter yourself.'

He sighed and shook his head. The fluorescents were making my head spin, so I reached into my pants pocket and withdrew my new sunglasses to set them over my eyes.

'Those are nice.'

'They're DITA,' I said. 'Japanese titanium or something.'

'Um… Okay?' He sounded put-off by the explanation. I decided it was probably the jealousy of not being able to afford a pair. 'You're definitely on drugs,' he added.

'So what if I am?'

'I've been worried about you.'

'I'm perfectly fine,' I shot at him. 'My life didn't end because we stopped talking.'

'Right.'

'I moved on really quickly, actually.'

'Okay.'

'You're not that special, you know?'

He just sat there and took it. Berating him was satisfying.

'Actually, I do know that,' he said, chastened. 'I fucked up. And I'm sorry.'

I played with my food and thought about how I'd been collecting apologies over the last few hours like church donations. The plastic fork brushed against the meat but I didn't skewer any pieces. Around us, the ambience hummed with slurred words and the sounds of things sizzling on grime-covered stoves. We inhabited the only pocket of calm.

'I still kind of hate you a bit,' I muttered.

'I'd understand that completely.'

'Callum's a bastard.'

'Yeah, he is.' Ezra watched the traffic stall in the road. Cars honked and lights flashed, red and orange. 'We only slept together that one time and then he fucked off again.'

'Only once?'

'Yeah. And that was it.'

Though Marion had prefaced this, I hadn't expected it to be so cut and dry. I almost felt bad for him, but instead I shrugged half-heartedly. 'I told you that would happen.'

'The classic *I told you so?*' His eyes were back on my face. 'Marion, Nadia, and Matteo already beat you to the punch.'

'So they have some use. Colour me shocked.'

He ignored the remark. 'I made a mistake, Austin. A fucking *monumental* mistake. The last few months have been awful, not because I miss Callum, but because I miss you.'

'You're a pussy.' He reddened at the obscenity, but I barrelled through. 'I ran into Marion and I made it crystal clear the ball was in your court–'

'Yeah, she told me. I just wasn't sure how–'

'You could've called. It was that bloody easy–'

'I know. And I'm *so* sorry.'

Despite my lingering anger, it was impossible to ignore how simple he'd made this, how perfectly he'd said all the things I'd needed to hear. It was as if he'd taken a peek at my non-existent diary, or seen right through me into my wants and hopes.

'I was terrified you'd ignore me,' he continued. 'I kept hoping to run into you somewhere so we could just talk face to face but–'

'It never happened.'

'Until now.'

'Right.'

He rubbed the back of his neck. 'I just want us to be okay

again. Please. You won't see me begging for many people, but I'll beg for you.'

That made me abandon the fork altogether and cross my arms.

'We can't go back to what we were doing,' I said.

'Oh, believe me, I know,' he nodded vigorously. 'We're never sleeping together again.'

'Wow! Thanks for that.' I leant into the sting.

'I just mean—'

'I have no desire to sleep with you either, for the record.'

'I'm actually relieved to hear that. It's for the best.'

Daisy appeared at the window, waving me down, with Steve following close behind. They ducked past the line forming at the counter and approached our table, their eyes delirious yet simultaneously hyper-focused. Daisy's shirt was falling from her shoulder, and her dark lipstick was smeared all over Steve's face. There was an obvious roughness to them exposed in the light. I suppose it had always been there, but I hadn't properly noticed until they were juxtaposed against tame, sanitised Ezra, with his crisp collared shirt and quaffed hair.

'Dude, what the fuck?' Daisy ran a hand through her hair. It was matted and shiny with oil. 'I looked all over Connies for you.'

'Can I have a chip?' Steve pleaded. He was gazing down at my half-finished HSP like it was a newborn baby, the miracle of life brought into the world.

'Yeah, finish it,' I said, pushing it towards him. He snatched it up eagerly, using his fingers as kitchen tongs.

'Sorry,' I directed at Daisy, 'I got a bit overwhelmed in there. And then I ran into… This is Ezra.' My hand flourished lazily in his direction.

She went very still for a moment, eyes quickly darting

back and forth between the two of us, unsmiling, before shooting a placid, 'Hi,' at him, and then to me, ''Kay. We're gonna go home.'

'What? Are you sure?'

'Yeah. Was just making sure you weren't dead,' she affirmed curtly. 'I'll see you at work.' She tugged on Steve's shirt and began her swift exit from the kebab shop.

'See ya mate,' Steve waved with a grease-coated hand, the box of chips tucked under his arm. They both disappeared from sight, lost somewhere in the crowd. Ezra followed their departure over his shoulder and then turned back to me with eyebrows raised.

'What?' I said.

'Well, she fucking hates me,' he laughed.

'No, she's just cooked.'

'Is she the one giving you drugs?'

'She's not *giving me drugs*. Her name is Daisy, and she's a great person.'

'Okay,' he surrendered, hands raised. 'Sorry. I'm sure she's… Yeah.'

We fell silent.

Did I truly want this? There was too much inventory taken up in my brain to know for certain, even without the effects of the high. I was devastated, horny, angry, and desperate all at the same time, scrambled, blended, a potluck of chemicals reacting together and bubbling over.

'I need you back in my life,' he said before I could procure a sentence. 'Not as a boyfriend, or as a hookup. As my best friend. Whatever way to make it sustainable.'

I took my sunglasses off my eyes and placed them on top of my head. I was tired of fighting, of waiting, of torturing myself. He was a fever I thought I'd burned through, yet it had returned twice as strong.

Reluctantly, I said, 'I want you back in mine too,' and I despised how good it felt to admit it to his face.

He exhaled in relief. 'So… Can we do this? As normal as possible?'

'When have things ever been normal between us?' I chuckled darkly.

'We can try. We can establish some ground rules.'

'*Ground rules*,' I repeated. I leaned closer, all the weight on my elbows, smiling in spite of myself. 'Like what?'

'No sex, obviously. Or kissing.'

'*Obviously*,' I repeated. 'Sleepovers?'

'Might lead to sex.'

'Fair.'

'Cuddling is okay.'

'Absolutely not. Leads to sex.'

'Really?'

'Yes.'

'Fine. We probably shouldn't drink together then.'

'Won't be able to help yourself?'

'I can. You might not.'

'Fuck off. We can drink together. I just won't pass out in your bed.'

'Fine.'

'Great.'

We were grinning at each other, like a dare, like a taunt, both determined to be the one who held steadfast in this scaffolding of a friendship. We had that much to prove to ourselves, to each other. It was a new game, more delicate than the first time around – and this time, Ezra was not only aware of it, he was playing too.

22

Sabrina was already in the living room with Juliana when I emerged. They were both clad in cool-toned leggings and windbreakers, their takeaway coffees with lipstick stains on the lids abandoned on the kitchen counter. I rubbed the sleep from my eyes and waved lazily. My jaw was sore, and the inside of my cheeks were raw from chewing into them so vigorously. It would probably take a few days for the scar tissue to heal over.

'How was last night?' Sabrina asked.

I contemplated whether to confess my reunion with Ezra, but I knew how strongly they'd both disapprove, so instead I said, 'It was good. You guys are up early.'

'It's after nine. There's a cinnamon scroll from North Street for you.' Sabrina nodded at the paper bag beside her. I plopped down on the couch and yawned.

'We went for a good walk along the coast,' Juliana said. 'Catching up on lost time. Shit-talking our boyfriends.'

I tried to imagine what the three of us growing up together would've looked like. Probably the girls bickering away like sisters over their choice of Barbie dolls while I ran around in their hand-me-down princess dresses (much to the dissatisfaction of my father), begging to be included. We might've taken our bikes with tassels on the handles down to Albert Park lake, throwing breadcrumbs at ducks and swans, climbing trees and subsequently falling from them. Maybe we could've kept our parents civil.

'I'm breaking up with Graham, by the way,' Sabrina added.

'Oh?'

'Juliana convinced me.'

'Don't blame me,' she said. 'I was just calling a spade a spade.'

'And if by spade, you mean scumbag–'

'Overdue, if you ask me,' I said with a polite smile. 'I'm happy for you.'

'Fresh start for everyone,' Sabrina affirmed, regarding me specifically. 'No more moping or drug benders, or I'll be back to smack you over the head again.'

'I hope you come back,' Juliana said.

'Or you could come to Melbourne. You can stay with me any time you'd like.'

Family used to be a perpetually fragile word that nicked me like a blunt razor whenever it was thought or uttered, but as I gazed at Sabrina and Juliana with our newfound warmth, I decided the word was beautiful. We were not our parents. We could choose a new ending.

When I dropped Sabrina off at the airport that afternoon, neither of us cried, and we didn't hug either. We'd surrendered more than enough vulnerability the previous night and, akin to the moments after a hurricane, an eerie calm had settled. We stood there on the pavement in silence, watching the planes hurtling into the overcast sky above our heads.

'I wish you were staying longer,' I said.

'I've got a life outside of you, you know?' she said. 'You'll be okay. Just don't be an idiot.'

'What does being an idiot entail?'

'Whatever you've been doing for the last few months.'

I wondered if she could see it in my face, that snide accomplishment, because she was examining me with suspicion, trying to see through the tinted lenses of the sunglasses. I refused to give her the satisfaction of another lecture, so I smiled with what I hoped was assurance and put my hands in my pockets. She visibly relaxed and said, 'Take care, okay?' and dragged her miniature suitcase off to the terminal.

*

Daisy was hiding under the veranda behind the café, taking shelter from the downpour of rain. The plastic chairs were drenched, so she sat on an upturned milk crate. I joined her side, but I couldn't find anything to repurpose into a seat, so I remained standing. The veranda was thin, only a metre or two of space from the wall. The tips of our shoes teased the puddle's edge.

'How'd the rest of the night end up?'

'Good, thanks,' she said in a stale tone.

'Had fun?'

'Sure. Was alright.'

I swallowed a clump of saliva, concrete-thick. 'Are you upset with me?'

'I just hope you know what you're doing,' she shrugged.

'With Ezra?'

She smoked, staring straight out at the rain. It was coming down harder now, each drop exploding into a little spray on the concrete. 'Yeah.'

'It was just a chat, Daisy. You don't need to be so possessive.'

She laughed, a harsh, callous sound, and threw the rest of her dart into the drain and went back into the café.

*

We danced right back into things – how could we not when

the steps were so familiar, ingrained into our bodies. Things as simple as driving back to Nollamara, no need for navigation, my parking spot on the patch of dirt still reserved for me. He said with a laugh that he could always hear me coming – my music was so loud it wafted down the driveway and through his open window. Things as simple as knowing which cupboard had the crackers to go with the cheese and meats I'd brought, before settling into my familiar spot on the couch with a bottle of wine and two glasses. Like I'd never left. I set the glasses on the coffee table and poured.

'Is that from The Boatshed?' Ezra nodded at the spread I'd put together. It looked quite elaborate for the two of us, cured meats coiled neatly, apples sliced with precision, assorted nuts and chocolates scattered for pops of colour and texture. I wasn't sure what I was trying to prove, but I felt big-headed over the finished product.

'It is.'

'I love that place, but it's far too expensive.'

I shrugged and picked up the knife to hack away at the aged cheddar. A large chunk crumbled away and I popped it right into my open mouth and chewed.

'That's right,' he sighed to himself, 'Forgot, you have money all of a sudden.'

'I always had money,' I said and then swallowed.

'But now you're just… embracing the fact.'

'We already talked about this with the whole Tesla conversation.'

'I know, it's just–'

'Do you want the expensive cheese or not?'

'Yes please. Sorry.'

That satiated him momentarily. I clutched my wine glass to my chest like it was a stuffed animal and kicked my feet up onto the ottoman. He built a cracker sandwich with the prosciutto and blue, held the remote in his other hand, and scrolled through Netflix.

We were on complete opposite sides of the couch, that was an unfamiliar step. I could feel the distance like a searing pain, and immediately regretted saying yes to a movie night – an occasion far too intimate and far too soon for my liking.

'It's only as awkward as we make it,' he'd said, but the lack of coaxing into our new stasis was apparent for me. No kissing, no touching, no staying the night. This was what we agreed, and I was supposed to be happy with that, but I couldn't help but loathe every boundary established. It was fundamentally awkward, knowing how good our sex was, only to force me into the timeout corner where I had to hide my erection under a pillow. If he gave me the slightest green light, I'd be tearing off my clothes, because now that it was forbidden, it was all the more erotic. But I couldn't lose the game. I couldn't give him the satisfaction of sighing and tutting, 'I should've known you were too immature for a platonic friendship.'

I refused to let him win. And I missed him. I missed his company. Sex would ruin everything.

'You don't have to make such an effort for me,' he said. 'I like you whether you bring expensive cheese and wine, or not.'

'Did you consider that this isn't for you? And simply because *I* wanted a nice cheese or wine?'

He stared straight ahead. 'I've just noticed a change is all.'

'Yeah, I stopped feeling guilty and decided to enjoy my financial benefits. I didn't realise that was a crime.' I took a pointed sip of the pinot noir that was about half his weekly rent. I didn't make a show of it when I'd set the bottle on the counter, but I silently hoped he was going to google the label and be horrified by the price. Was this who I was now?

Someone who got off on other people's shame or envy? Maybe it was the only way to establish status with him. He might be morally superior with his squeaky-clean sexual history and well-intentioned friendship, but I was now everything he hated and everything he wanted, flexing the muscle he could only dream of building.

Instead of delivering a sharp retort, he smiled. 'I only ever wanted to know the real you. So as long as you're being yourself, I'm more than happy.'

'I thought you wouldn't like the real me,' I said quietly.

'I'm sorry that I ever gave you that impression.'

I set the wine down. He set the remote down. We both looked at each other across the pillows in silence. I couldn't read the expression on his face. It wasn't apologetic, but it wasn't probing either, an expressionist painting that swirled and contorted the harder I looked.

'When we met, I decided I wanted to be someone you liked.' I said slowly. 'And I thought that would be impossible if I was wealthy, or had baggage, or was overly-sexual–'

'So you lied?' He blinked, not accusingly.

'I wasn't authentic.' I stared at the cheese board with a sudden distaste. 'I'm still not. This isn't me either, being so showy.'

'Yeah I can tell,' he laughed. 'But it is good cheese.'

'I'm a bit fucked up, okay?' I said.

My bottom lip was trembling again. It was time, it was long overdue. Now that Sabrina had unearthed it all and we'd confronted it together, I was feeling brave enough. 'I've wanted to tell you about–'

'About how many guys you slept with while we were apart, yeah. I know.'

I froze. He was clearly trying his best to not look disappointed or patronising.

'No, I mean…' I mumbled. 'Who… Who told you?'

'It's Perth. Word gets around.'

'Look–'

'I don't care, Austin. Especially because we're just friends.'

'That wasn't–'

'It doesn't matter. Honestly, it never really mattered, but especially not now. Matteo's a slut too, and I give him shit for it, but it's out of love. Hopefully we hit a point where you feel comfortable with me teasing you about it.' He leaned across the couch and squeezed my shoulder, presenting his winning smile like there were no more secrets between us.

I was speechless, trying to figure out how to manipulate the conversation back to a dead mother, but the moment had slipped out of my grasp again.

'Honestly, I think I always knew. You were shockingly good at sex. That doesn't happen without a bit of experience.'

'Yeah,' was all I managed.

'Just be you. Don't overthink so much. And if we hate each other in a few months, at least we'll be ourselves while we do it.'

I picked up my wine and took another quick and nervous sip. 'Why do you want to be my friend so badly if you don't know who I am?' I licked the dregs from my top lip which had the consistency of dirt.

He chuckled, shook his head, and went back to browsing on the TV. 'I know who you are, Austin. I can see all the parts that are already there, just hiding, or taking a while to settle. Call it an investment in the brilliant fully-formed person you'll be soon enough.'

*

I cried on the drive home. I didn't mean to, but a song we

used to sing in the car was at full blast, a country rock deep cut from 2013 that Ezra once said reminded him of Callum, and my chest started to heave and moisture began spilling from my eyes. I knew it wouldn't always be this hard. Soon the distance between us on the couch would be second nature, and I would forget the taste of him and the feeling of his sheets and his arms around me, and the limerence would drain from my system. I wondered if he'd thrown out my toothbrush, or if it was right where I'd left it, in the holder under the mirror. I didn't think to check, and now I was scared about what it would mean if he *had* left it. Was he waiting for me to claim it after we fell into old patterns and haunts? Or was the toothbrush meaningless, belonging to no one? Was he unaffected, determined to embrace this new status quo as if it wasn't excruciating?

And then I was turning the car into a familiar street, and messaging someone to see if they were still up, and being invited in, and going inside the house, and taking my clothes off, and letting myself be fucked senseless until the questions stopped.

23

This time I was on my stomach, face buried in the pillow, the feeling of someone's knees pressed into my shoulder blades, holding me down, smothering me. *Get off.* I was screaming. *Someone help me.* It was the dark presence that usually lingered in the corner but now it was on top of me. It had never done that before. The weight was so heavy, crushing me. *Please stop. Please.* And then I was released. My muscles were responding again, I could move. I turned over and breathed haggard gasps of humid air. I hadn't done any drugs since my birthday, so the pattern was inconsistent. There was no sure root of the cause, which made it all the more sinister. I was being tortured in my sleep. And I knew I deserved it.

*

Ezra took one look at me and said, 'You look rough.'

'Thanks,' I said flatly. 'Have you ever had sleep paralysis?'

'No,' he frowned and leaned against the counter by the coffee machine. 'Should I be worried?'

'I'll live.'

A plume of steam rose from the stainless-steel jug. I held it on an angle and poured the contents delicately into the paper cup of espresso, trying to make the action look effortless. Ezra was watching closely, silently grading my skills, but when I finished, the foam was sitting perfectly bouncy on the top. Gold star. I slid it across the counter to him.

'You're a full barista now,' he said, obviously impressed.

'I have been for a while. You've just never visited me at work.'

He looked sheepish while he sipped the oat flat white. 'You know how much I love the GT.'

'Well, in a normal, balanced friendship, you come to my area as much as I come to yours.'

'Hence why I'm here.' He winked, far more flirtatiously than I'd expected. I blushed and retreated behind the coffee machine.

Daisy passed in the background, shot a cold look at Ezra, and kept walking. Her contempt was making work almost unbearable. I wondered if she'd been in love with me, and I'd completely missed it, too busy cooking my brain and feeling sorry for myself. She had to have known the kisses between us were just friendly, attention-seeking. I'd never even spoken of sexual attraction to women, but she might've thought she was the exception. Whatever the reasoning, our friendship rusted away like old sheet metal.

'Give me five minutes and I'll be clocked off,' I told Ezra. 'Wait for me in the bookshop.'

He took his coffee with him and sauntered out, long blonde hair rippling in the soft breeze. He made a left and disappeared from view. I rubbed my sore eyes and sighed. This setup was stranger than the first; movie nights, *get-home-safe* texts, visits at work – it felt closer to dating than whatever we had before, yet the sex was glaringly absent. Perhaps this was how best friends were supposed to behave, but I was unfamiliar with the concept.

'He's a good-looking fella,' Leslie said, her head poking up from behind the bar fridge. She rose to her feet laboriously as the fridge swung shut.

'Yeah,' I murmured. 'He is.'

She picked at the band-aid on her left index finger, peeling it back to inspect the quality of the fresh burn beneath it. Her hands were covered in these sorts of lesions. 'Good for you, kiddo.'

I blinked at her. 'Oh. We're not, I mean…' I swallowed the explanation, choosing instead to reply with an innocent and genuine, 'Thanks, Leslie.'

'Feel free to finish up early. There's nothing left to do.' She took a crate of empty milk cartons into her arms and left me by the machine. I took advantage of the moment, convinced she'd change her mind if I was still there by the time she returned.

Inside the shop, I found Ezra by the non-fiction table, examining the back cover of a book about cryptocurrency.

'If you need a recommendation–'

His eyes darted up to me. 'You know I don't read. We're here for you.'

'I already have a massive pile to get through.'

'I don't care. It's your extremely late birthday present. Pick anything.'

He set the book down where it belonged and followed me to the fiction shelves. I could feel his eyes on me as I ran my finger along the coloured spines, relishing the slick feeling of the laminate, coming to a stop at a title I had seen on the nightstand of a guy I'd once slept with. I pulled it out and examined the cover; a black and white close-up of a man, eyes closed in clear agony.

'He looks like he's having fun,' Ezra said with a laugh.

'It's supposed to be very depressing.'

'Right up your alley.'

Ezra bought it with cash and signed the inside cover as a birthday card, making me promise not to read it until I was alone.

'Why? Is it dirty?' I grinned, tucking the novel under my

arm when he gave it to me. We exited the bookshop and began the all-too-familiar stroll back to the apartment.

'Worse. Heartfelt.'

I made a face. 'Didn't think you were capable.'

'I've been heartfelt lately.'

'A rarity. And you used to say you didn't have any feelings.'

'I think that's all you,' he shrugged.

'Me?'

'You helped. Opening myself back up to emotions and…' He started going red and shook his head. 'It's all coming across very cheesy.'

My eyebrows hovered in surprise. 'I was under the impression I was just an absolute nuisance most of the time.'

'Not at all. We've had a lot of fun together.'

'We have.'

'Speaking of.' He smiled tactfully at the reminder. 'We're having a little house party at ours on Friday. Just the group and Izzy. You're welcome to come.'

'Are you sure they want me there?'

'Of course they do. They've always loved you.'

I stifled a laugh. 'Huh. Okay.'

'Trust me. They wouldn't let me invite you if they didn't.'

I said I would come, and we hugged goodbye outside the apartment. One arm held the book tight, and the other ended up around his waist. My chin fell on his shoulder. I inhaled the trace of YSL behind his ear and then broke away before he could give me an erection. Pressing up against him had that effect, like I was a teenager again, buzzing with hormones. Ezra looked surprised I'd shrugged him off so fast, but he didn't say anything about it except, 'See you then.'

'See you. Thanks for the book.'

He looked overjoyed with my contentment. We parted ways, him back towards wherever he'd parked his car, and me up the red-bricked steps to the apartment and through the flyscreen door. Juliana was in the kitchen, standing by the window that looked out onto the street, a mug of what was probably hot tea cradled in two hands. Her eyes were narrowed.

'So,' she said, and took a sip.

'Save the lecture, we're just friends,' I said, tossing the book down on the counter, and the sound was much louder than I'd intended. She looked startled, but I carried on. 'Everyone's been giving me shit, and I just don't think it's fair.'

'Sabrina will be disappointed, and Sierra will be pissed.'

'Why can't any of you be happy for me?' I snapped. 'Or do you prefer it when I'm fucking miserable, so you all get to take turns mothering me, just to feel better about yourselves?'

Juliana's eyes went even wider. She blinked slowly. 'Okay.'

'I just mean–'

'Do what you gotta do, Austin. But don't use me as a shoulder to cry on when it all goes to shit again.' She put her mug in the sink and strode past me and off to her bedroom.

I nearly yelled after her to put her dishes away for once in her life, but the door had already shut. I groaned and pressed my hands into the linoleum countertop, head bent and staring down at the book. I thumbed the edge of it and then opened the front page to display Ezra's note.

Happy big 21. You're a full adult now! It's not often that incredible people roll into your life, and even less often when they take you back after a falling out. I can't say I regret our ups and downs because I think it made us stronger than ever. You've helped me find myself again after a long time being lost, and I'll always be thankful for that. I'm expecting you'll be in my life forever, so here's to many more years of friendship. Ezra x

I ran my finger over the impression made from the ink, fascinated by the way his messy scrawl looked as though each letter was tripping over the one proceeding. I forced a smile. It wasn't painful. I was happy and this was okay. It was better than nothing at all.

*

Sabrina called me on the drive. I'd only just hurtled past the Dog Swamp BP when her contact flashed on the Tesla's interface. Juliana had probably told her about Ezra, and I could see the headache approaching like a pothole in the road. I tapped the screen and answered. 'Hey.'

'I meant to call earlier. Are you okay?'

I sighed. 'Yeah, I'm fine. There's no reason to–'

'It's the 18th.'

And all at once I couldn't breathe. I pulled on the wheel and brought the car to the side of the road. Horns honked at the aggressive intersection change, but I hardly noticed them with the ringing in my ears, the throb of my heartbeat in my throat. I opened the door for a clear shot of the street if I needed to vomit, but nothing happened. I closed the door again and steadied myself by clinging to the wheel. It was better now that I wasn't in motion. More cars whipped past, their headlights strobing.

'You didn't realise.'

'No,' I said quietly. 'I'm a horrible person.'

'No, you're not,' Sabrina said. 'I shouldn't have reminded you, but I was worried you'd be–'

'I'm on my way to a house party.'

'Turn around.'

'Yeah. I will.'

I leaned back against the leather headrest, swallowing deep breaths. How quickly it had come on, like a hangover, or food poisoning – a gut punch of nausea.

'Do you want to–?'

'No,' I muttered. 'I'll be fine.'

'Are you sure?'

'Yeah. I'm sure.'

Sabrina's silence was tinged with uncertainty, but she must've decided pushing further would hinder rather than help. 'Call me if you need anything.'

I hung up and contemplated what to do. Beads of sweat were crystallising on my forehead and I had a sudden desperation to smother myself beneath a stranger's naked body or with a substance, but I couldn't ask Sierra – she'd barred me from her supply. I might've outsourced on Grindr, though most of them only offered meth. I'd never done it before, unless it had been laced with other drugs I'd taken, but I was willing to try it now if it meant obliterating myself for the rest of the evening. How quickly good behaviour can falter. Despite barely admitting it to myself, I'd only stopped my drug use for Ezra's sake. His friendship was intertwined with my sobriety, which I knew was far too much pressure to put on one person.

Now it felt as if the tightrope of temperance I'd been balancing on had snapped beneath me and I was in freefall, desperate to cling onto something, anything. Something to do, or someone to fuck, or something to take, or somewhere to go. Then Ezra texted me.

Are you close?

And I couldn't say no to him. I wiped my moist brow with the back of my hand, shifted the car into drive, and continued down Wanneroo Road, pushing a door closed on a hallway flooded with water. I could brave it. At least there would be liquor, that was the only thing keeping my foot on the pedal – liquor and Ezra.

The front door was unlocked. There was an opened bottle of cheap tequila on the kitchen counter which I poured into a plastic cup filled with ice cubes. Everyone was already outside on the sandstone patio, the fairy lights strung from the canvas awning barely illuminating their faces in the night. I settled into the empty seat beside Ezra, bestowing placid *his* and *nice-to-see-yous* and took a long, sobering drink from the cup.

'You okay?' Ezra asked aside.

I nodded with all the enthusiasm I could muster, and let the conversations wash over me as if they might drown the thoughts still circling the perimeter of my brain. Such vapid and contrite background noise, a reminder of the reasons I disliked this group setting – pointed comments about each other, inside jokes I'd missed during the time I'd been away, complaints about Perth and their banal lives. It was the same regurgitation as last year.

None of them asked me how I'd been doing, or what I'd been up to since that day at Sí Paradiso. I was just part of the decor. Marion's new girlfriend seemed nice at least, though she wasn't able to get much of a word in either. We were kindred spirits that night, the plus-ones on the outskirts.

By the time the ice had melted in my cup, Matteo suggested we play a drinking game, and we all agreed since we didn't have any other ideas or grounds for refusal. Ezra peeled the plastic off a box of cards he'd received for Secret Santa a few years ago and had forgotten about in the bottom of a drawer. The cards were black and shiny and he shuffled them clumsily.

'Who needs another drink before we get stuck in?' I said. Everyone raised their hands.

'I'll help darl,' Matteo sighed, which surprised me, and he followed me into the kitchen. We divided and conquered. I made drinks for Ezra and Izzy while he made them for Nadia and Marion. The counter was sticky with dried pineapple juice and cordial. I poured another tequila on the rocks for myself and set it aside. Matteo wrinkled his nose, and asked, 'Are you drinking that straight?'

'Maybe.'

'You're on a warpath, aren't you?'

'One of those Fridays,' I muttered.

'One of those years, it seems like.'

I blinked at him. 'What would you know about it?'

'I'm not judging,' he smiled, thinly lipped, almost taunting. 'I've seen you at Steam Works. I go too, every now and then.'

My eyes darted back to the patio. Ezra was turned away from us, and the music playing from the Bluetooth speaker suppressed any conversations. It wasn't a shock that Matteo frequented the sauna, but the thought of him lurking in the shadows observing my naked body sent a sudden chill down my spine. How often had he seen me being pleasured by various men? How often had he reported what he saw to Ezra?

'You never said hi.'

'And what would you do if I had?' He set the booze down and stared at me with a piercing hunger. 'If Ezra knew how bad I wanted you to fuck me, he wouldn't be pleased.'

I felt faint again, this time from the repugnant scent of his vanilla perfume and the way he stressed the 'k' in 'fuck'. There was something dehumanising in his gaze too, like I was a thing instead of a person. His hand crawled spider-like across the counter, stopping at mine. His index finger traced my knuckles. I withdrew immediately.

'Well then, maybe you should keep it to yourself,' I said

coolly, picking up three drinks in two hands.

Matteo flushed with the heat of rejection. 'Noted.'

We rejoined the table as if the exchange hadn't happened, and Ezra explained the rules of the game. A player drew a card and read a question aloud. The other players either guessed the reader's answer, or passed by taking a sip of their drink. The reader would then reveal their answer to the question. If correct, the players were safe, but incorrect players would have to take two sips. Izzy and I were immediately at a disadvantage due to our lack of history, but I'd anticipated getting drunk, I was determined for it. I could already feel the tequila sloshing in my stomach, rendering my speech to a sloppy drawl.

The first few cards were fairly tame – liquors that got you the most messy, a song that made you hit the dance floor – and I ended up drinking for all of my incorrect guesses. Izzy pulled, 'What's my biggest red flag?'

'I'm gonna pass on this one,' I said and had a sip. We went counterclockwise for our guesses.

'I'll throw out… being a lesbian?' Ezra said, and everyone laughed.

'Bad eyesight?' Nadia shrugged.

Marion was next. 'She's a tradie. That's definitely a red flag.'

'Yeah, that's good,' Matteo agreed. 'But I'd say being from Brisbane.'

'What's wrong with Brisbane?'

'Bad vibes.'

'You've never been, how would you know?'

'Okay,' Izzy giggled. 'I have to agree with being a tradie.'

'Shocker.'

'So the rest of you drink twice, except for Marion and Austin.'

They drank and it was Nadia's turn to draw a card. 'What gives me the ick?'

'Oh,' Marion said, 'When men won't let you peg them.'

More scattered chuckles.

'Gosh, I don't know,' Izzy said. 'Come back to me.'

'Answer or pass.'

'Pass, then.' She drank.

'Boring,' Matteo sighed. 'But the answer is weak men. Like… physically weak. She nearly broke up with Ben when he broke his leg and couldn't do anything for himself. Hobbling around on crutches, asking for help. Completely emasculating.'

Nadia smirked into her drink. 'That's correct.'

'You're supposed to wait until we all answer,' Ezra said with irritation, but sipped anyway. I followed suit, relieved by how the tequila seemed to burn a hole through me, borderline masochistic. I was dizzy and swimming in the numbness. No one seemed to notice.

Ezra pulled a card. 'Who's the best sex I've ever had?'

I could feel everyone's eyes on me, even though it wasn't my turn. Ezra flushed in his discomfort. Izzy passed again and drank. Nadia did the same. Marion said, 'Austin,' and Matteo said, 'Callum.'

'Yeah, I'll go with Callum too,' I said, my words slurring. Why did I feel so low? It was only a question, and yet the implications of it felt heavy. Even if I believed myself good in bed, how could I fully compete with Callum? I might've been a slut, but Callum was the love of his life. The ghost of him had haunted Ezra's yearnings from the moment we'd met, and ever since.

'Well, you're both wrong,' Ezra sighed. 'Marion's right.'

Colour returned to my face as Marion gave herself a loud clap of self-congratulations. 'I'm good at this game!'

I drank twice.

Ezra was probably more embarrassed than I was, but when he caught my eye, he flashed a grin like we were sharing a private joke, which only made my face feel warmer. Of course it was true, there was no reason for me to be surprised. He'd almost said it himself. Our sex was addictive. It was one of the reasons it was so difficult to walk away from each other in the first place. It had taken him months to detox from me, yet still he felt that forbidden want, as strongly as I did. I could see it in his smile, his gleaming eyes, that same hunger Matteo had. We would do it again. We would fuck. And from then, it was only a matter of time until someone got hurt again. Or maybe I was just drunk, and bitter, and horny, and sad. Maybe he didn't want me, and this was completely one-sided. I should've gone home, but I didn't know where home was anymore.

'Austin, your turn,' Nadia said.

I lurched forward, going for the pile of cards but I missed them completely.

Ezra laughed. 'Someone's a bit tipsy.'

He fetched one for me, placed it in my hands, and steadied me upright in the chair, reinforcing the dynamic of grown-up and child.

I squinted at the text. 'What was… a nickname that caught on in high school?' I put the card down and groaned. 'That's a boring one.'

'No, that's good,' Marion said. 'Nadia, you first.'

'*Autism?*'

'Wow. Thanks,' I said sardonically. I was dizzy and swirling in my chair.

'We had a kid called Austin in junior school and that was his nickname,' she shrugged.

'Maybe something to do with… I don't know. Pass.'

'Izzy! Every time.'

'Sorry.'

'How about *Ozzy*? Kind of basic, but–'

'We're all thinking it. Fag?'

'Matteo–'

'It's a classic.'

'That's a slur, not a nickname.'

I was hardly paying attention to who was talking. I held the table for support. The floor was swimming right there, daring me to kiss the surface and fall into it. *Go on.* Sweet numbness teetered precariously on nausea.

'I honestly have no idea,' Ezra sighed. 'I might pass.'

'Boring! All of you!' Matteo was shaking his head in disappointment.

'It was Bates,' I said at last. I slumped in my chair.

'Bates?'

'Like… Norman Bates.'

'The serial killer with the motel?'

'Yeah.'

Ezra blinked in surprise. 'Okay.'

'How did you get that? Were you a total psycho in school?'

'Or a mummy's boy?'

'Yeah,' I mumbled. 'That was it. Mummy's boy.'

'I bet he still is.' Matteo sounded smarmy. It set something off within me.

'Actually,' I said, 'My mum's dead. She killed herself exactly a year ago today.'

My head lolled against my chest. I was aware of everyone staring at me, but the tequila was like quicksand, or a pool of honey.

I sank further, lost in the painfully sticky drowning. I wasn't sure how much time passed from the point of admission, but soon after I'd spoken, the game was over. Ezra was trying to get me to my feet, but my legs weren't responding. The feeling of his hands on me was nice. Strong and gentle hands. If I got myself drunk more often, he would touch me, that was the key. And then we were on his bed and in my drunken blindness I thought, *yes, I want this, take off my clothes and do whatever you want to me*, but I couldn't move my mouth to say the words. Or I did say it, because someone unbuckled my belt and pulled my jeans off, and that was momentarily thrilling until I wondered if the person might be Matteo, and then I felt panicked, but I couldn't move my limbs or open my eyes, they were too heavy, and it was the sleep paralysis all over again but different, darker, drifting further away from consciousness. If someone penetrated me, I didn't feel it. I didn't feel anything tangible except the texture of Ezra's bed sheets. The warm cotton enveloped me, strong with his scent, and it was the last thing I thought of before I faded away.

24

I opened heavy eyes to a glass of water and a packet of painkillers on the bedside table. I reached for them with shaking hands. I was all dry lips and tongue, frail. My hand closed around the glass and I brought it to my mouth, almost moaning at the relief of rehydrating my desiccated corpse. The pill tasted like nothing. I washed it down with another greedy gulp and some water dribbled out of the corners of my mouth.

'He's alive,' Ezra said flatly.

I sat up in bed, wiped my mouth dry, and set the glass back down. The overhead lights were off, but the room was drenched in morning.

'Was I embarrassing?'

'You chugged so much tequila, you were a goner by ten.'

I glanced at him in his oversized t-shirt and plaid pyjama pants. He was avoiding my eyes, fingers fidgeting with each other on top of the duvet.

'Did we...?'

'What? Have sex?' His head snapped to meet my eyes with sudden fury. 'No Austin, I didn't rape you.'

'That's not what I meant–'

'What the fuck is wrong with you?'

I blinked dumbly. My brain was rotating on an axis, still dizzy from the night before. 'Why are you so angry?'

'Were you ever going to tell me about your mum?'

Of course I'd done it in the worst way. My deflection and

avoidance was a ticking time bomb. It was cowardly at best, almost sociopathic at worst. I should've known it was an inevitability, this ugly truth emerging. Like a dam with fissures expanding up the sides, the longer I waited, the more devastating the collapse.

'It just never came up.'

Ezra shook his head at the wall in disbelief. 'You're such a fucking liar. All the time, about everything—'

'I tried to tell you. A week ago when we were on the couch and then the whole sex conversation happened—'

'You're obsessed with sex,' he snarled. 'The fact that you thought that was more important—'

'*I'm* obsessed with sex?'

'—than telling me something fundamentally traumatic—'

'*You're* the one who's obsessed with sex.'

'—is insane, and it's like—'

'So judgmental about it—'

'—I don't even know you.'

'—as if it's morally corrosive.'

'*Morally corrosive*? You're such a wanker.'

'Read a fucking book, Ezra!'

He rose from the bed and I thought he was going to storm out of the room, but he began to pace back and forth alongside the mirror. It unnerved me, like there were now two of him ganging up on me.

'Maybe you should think about why I didn't feel comfortable telling you,' I threw at him. 'It says more about you than it does me.'

'Wow,' he laughed bitterly and stopped his pacing. 'I told you about my bipolar.'

'Okay? And?'

'I deserve to know… things.'

'*Things*,' I repeated, tasting the word in my mouth.

'Things about you.'

'I didn't realise our relationship was so transactional.'

'We're supposed to be friends.' He sat back down on the edge of the bed, surveying me closely. 'Friends who share everything with each other, friends who are honest–'

'You weren't honest when you promised nothing was going to happen with Callum,' I hissed.

'Don't even go there, that's so fucked up.' Then his eyes went wide. He saw it coming before I did. 'Are you gonna–?'

'Yeah,' I said quickly, feeling the blood drain from my face. My stomach churned like an ocean tide about to expel debris onto the shoreline. I clamped a hand over my mouth and slipped out of bed, bolting for the toilet. I managed to drop to my knees and fling the seat up before I hurled. It was gushing out of me in hot chunks, and my eyes were wet with tears. Another wave, more vomit, even more painful than the one before. I spat out the bits that lingered on my tongue. That was it, surely that was it. I took a few sharp inhales. Another one came. I was retching, and then coughing, and then crying. Ezra was on the floor beside me, rubbing my back, slow circles between my shoulder blades. His palm was flat and I could feel the heat radiating. He was the only thing keeping me sitting upright.

'You should've told me,' he said quietly.

'I didn't want you to pity me,' I choked out.

'You'd rather I don't trust you?'

'Out of the two? Yeah.'

I lifted my head from the toilet bowl pathetically, and used some toilet paper to wipe the bile from my mouth and the tears from my eyes. His hand was still pressed into my back. I turned to look at him, at how confused and hurt he was, which was a far worse display than anger. It made me feel guilty, and I couldn't weaponise any of it for my own defence.

'I don't pity you,' he said. 'I'm… sad for you.'

'It's the same thing.'

'It's not.' His hand slid all the way up my spine, coming to a stop at the base of my neck. He leaned forward, and I thought in alarm he was going to kiss me – which would've been okay in any other circumstance – but then his forehead pressed against mine and we held there. 'But I think I understand.'

'You do?'

'Why you came to Perth, why you've been so lost. It makes sense, I suppose.'

I let my head fall deeper into him, nuzzling the crook of his neck, losing myself in his comforting smell. His arms wound themselves around me. I didn't fully realise I was only in my underwear until then. The tiles were cold against my bare thighs, gooseflesh splashed down them like paint. I held him tighter, burying myself into his t-shirt, and quite immediately I was erect. He would be able to see if he looked down, considering my cotton briefs hid so little. Maybe I wanted him to look. How deranged was I to be aroused in this situation? Rehashing trauma was becoming a kind of foreplay.

He continued making circles on my back. We were on the bathroom floor for ten minutes like that. I thought again about kissing him, but the aftertaste in my mouth gave me pause. It was just nice to hold him. I shouldn't be so greedy.

He got me back into bed and we didn't speak of my mother or the various lies I'd told. He just made me a herbal tea, let me sleep off more of the hangover, and when it was lunch time, he popped out to get us takeaway. Alone in his bed with food on the way, I felt like royalty or a sick patient, adored and nurtured. How quickly I'd been raised from rock-bottom to a pedestal, and I couldn't understand why. Did he want me this way? Weak and needing him? Perhaps he was simply feeling sorry for me. Did the reasoning even matter? We were coexisting in a bubble that had yet to pop. I wanted to stretch it out as long as possible, dreading the thought of going back to the apartment to face Juliana's austere judgement. When he returned, we ate burgers – careful not to drip sauce on his fresh sheets – and started watching the first *Twilight* movie, which Ezra had somehow never seen before. Two hours of longing glances and pine trees desaturated with blue filters before the credits rolled. Ezra glanced at me, seemingly amused by the melodrama of it all and asked, 'Should we watch the next one?'

I smiled weakly and nodded, and we moved onto *New Moon*. Hours flew by, and I was slipping in and out of consciousness, catching clips here and there; a passionate kiss, a run through the forest, a wedding. How were we already on the fourth movie? What time was it?

'You've been out so long,' he said gently, stroking my head. I rubbed the sleep from my eyes and gazed up at him.

'Do you want me to go?'

He smiled. 'Not at all. You can stay tonight again if you want. Do you need dinner?'

I shook my head. He shrugged and turned his attention back to the film, fingers still combing through my oily hair. I wasn't miserable anymore, far from it. His constant touch was enough to make me want to stay indefinitely.

Most of the weekend existed in the confines of his room. I didn't eat much, I was asleep for most of it, but I received back scratches and head rubs as a reward for my docile disposition, like I was his pet. My brain was scrambled from emotional exhaustion so I had little power to interrogate why Ezra was allowing this. It was as if he'd simply decided to be the person I needed, and perhaps it could be as easy as that;

making a choice to do the right thing for somebody else. Because you loved them. He went out for a few hours to run some errands and hit the gym, and I remained half-naked and buried in his sheets for nearly all of Sunday too, only venturing out a few times to refill my glass of water. Marion caught me in the kitchen and said with surprise, 'You're still here.'

'Sorry. Ezra said it was okay. He's out for a while.'

'Totally fine with me. You're always welcome.' She looked like she wanted to say something sensitive, but the idea expired behind her eyes. Instead she said, 'It's date night tonight, so Izzy and I are out. You're welcome to take up the couch instead of hiding away in the bedroom.'

After Marion departed, I took a shower, rinsing the sickness and the rot that had developed into an invisible layer over my body. This was one of the instances a warm shower could, in fact, fix everything. Steam rose from my flushed-red skin, and I smelled of Ezra's eucalyptus body wash. I was brand new.

And then I saw my black toothbrush in the holder under the mirror, exactly where I'd left it all those months ago. I felt unmoved by its presence, realising how little it meant in the grand scheme of things. It was just an object. The constant touch, letting me stay, the feeling of home – those were real, tangible moments that told me where we both stood.

Ezra found me on the couch wearing his hoodie. He had a paper bag full of groceries that he set down on the counter before he said, 'Thought I'd cook us all dinner if your appetite is back.'

There was a patch of sweat around his chest, staining the nylon top a darker shade of grey. His forearms looked veiny and inflated, and upon noticing this, I felt my mouth sapped of moisture.

'Marion's not home tonight,' I said.

'Oh.' He began unpacking the groceries. 'That's alright then.'

'Do you need any help?'

'Um…' he scratched his head. 'Yeah, actually. If you want to dice some onions while I take a quick shower. I probably stink from the gym.'

'I can't tell,' I laughed, which only seemed to make him flustered.

'Right. Yeah.'

I joined him at the counter and extracted a knife and a cutting board from their respective drawers. He slipped past me, hand grazing my lower back on the way out, and I was left alone in the kitchen. I didn't cook very often so my dicing was poor, a glaring admission of privilege, always ordering in or going out for dinner. The chunks were uneven and going everywhere, and the scent of onion was so strong tears sprung again. I'd cried more over the last few weeks than I had in months. Ezra said I was opening him back up to emotions, but I felt he was doing the same to me.

My phone buzzed on the counter, and I wiped the onion tears from my eyes and gazed down at the screen, only it wasn't my phone but Ezra's, and the notification was from Grindr. The illusion shattered immediately. I put down the knife, washed my hands in the kitchen sink and sat on the couch with an all-encompassing emptiness. I had no right to be angry if I had the app too, yet my brain was whirling with possibilities and paranoia. Was he really at the gym the whole time, or had he slipped out for sex? Maybe he smelled of it, and that was why he took a shower. He always showered after sex. Who was he to call Matteo and I sluts when he was chasing the same thrills? I was suddenly furious at his hypocrisy, furious at how tenderly he'd been treating me all weekend only to fuck other people behind my back.

I had the TV on when he returned. His hair was still wet and he got straight to work in the kitchen, very house-husband while I quietly contemplated my tactic. Confrontation would get me nowhere. He was defensive by nature, and I would look jealous and desperate. I'd calmed down a bit and hypothesised he wasn't fucking anyone yet, but if he was on Grindr, it meant he was horny or lonely or both, and I could use that to my advantage. Nothing he'd find there was better than me. *The best sex you've ever had.* I had to remind him of the fact.

We ate in front of the couch in silence. I cleaned the dishes and sat back down beside him, closer this time. He was wearing his black gym shorts, the ones that showed off his fleshy pale thighs dashed with blonde hair. I stretched my legs out into his lap. Skin connected to skin. His hand dropped to my foot, squeezing it and leaving it there. I wriggled my toes against him. His eyes stayed trained on the TV, but he stroked the metatarsals. My heel pressed into his groin.

'We've got one more *Twilight* left,' he murmured.

'Throw it on,' I said. 'We've come this far.'

The opening credits rolled. He abandoned the remote and used his other hand to massage the ball of my foot. Both hands worked in tandem, moulding and sculpting, extracting any tension from the joints. My nails went to my mouth, nibbling as I watched him. They were already blunt, so I was mostly chewing into skin. Ezra met my gaze.

'Don't give me that look,' he sighed.

I dropped my hand. 'What look?'

'The one you get when you want to kiss me.' He curled his fingers so they were claw-like, and dragged them in circles around my ankles.

'That's a bit presumptuous of you,' I said stiffly.

'You think I don't know you well enough by this point?' He let his hands slide further up my leg. 'I know when you're pissed at me. I know when you're upset. I know when you're lying. And I know when you're horny.' Under my foot I could feel his erection.

'I'm not upset,' I said slowly. 'But I did see a Grindr notification on your phone.'

'Right.' His voice contracted, like he was anticipating a blow.

'It's fine. I just wish you told me you were on it.'

He continued rubbing my feet and frowned. 'Aren't you on it too?'

'I am. So I can't say anything, can I?'

'No. You can't.' He shrugged casually. 'I just use it when I'm bored.'

'Am I boring you?'

'Walked right into that one,' he laughed, more to himself. 'No Austin, you're not boring me. I'm just having a look. It doesn't mean anything.'

'And what if I did want to kiss you?'

Submission darkened his face, like he knew he was at the mercy of my desire. 'Are you taking the piss?'

'No,' I said deliberately.

'Then I would say it's a bad idea, and you know it.'

'Maybe I don't care,' I said.

'You only want it because I'm talking to other people. You're marking your territory.'

I withdrew my feet from his lap and sat up straighter, almost offended. 'You think I'm that manipulative?'

'I *know* you're that manipulative.' He let his head loll against the pillow and his face broke out into a grin. 'But part of me loves that about you. You're not afraid of going after what you want.'

I leaned across the couch and slipped my arms around his neck and planted an open-mouthed kiss against his closed lips. He tasted nostalgic, and he wasn't surprised. He let it happen. I kissed him hungrily, licked his lips, his cheek, sucked on his neck.

'We're supposed to be friends,' he said but I kissed him again, more determined this time. 'We shouldn't be doing this.'

I pulled myself onto his lap, knees straddling either side of his hips. Our erections rubbed together easily, the loose cotton of our shorts wasn't much of a barrier. Then his hands were sliding up around my ass, under the hoodie, and he pulled me closer, kissing me back. Crushed lips and feverish tongues. Devouring each other. 'God damn it, Austin.'

'Why are you fighting it?'

'Because you know what kissing leads to.'

'I do.'

'We can't. We've been so good.' But when I rolled my hips into him, he moaned. 'Fuck. Alright. Alright, fuck it.'

Our clothes left a trail to the bedroom – our shirts and shorts forgotten in the hallway, our underwear discarded on the floor by the bed. He all but threw me on the mattress, nipping his way up my familiar body, stopping at my hips, mouth warm around my cock. I gasped and my spine curled. I turned my head, watching us in the mirror, his silhouette of firm legs and strong shoulders, the slightest round of his stomach. We looked so good together, we looked right. The foreplay was urgent, rushing towards that pressure and tightness of penetration. He didn't even bother to grab the lubricant, he just spat on himself and pushed inside. The noise I made was subhuman. He almost ripped me open and the pain was specific and dizzying, the kind of pain I'd spent months chasing in darkened rooms, the kind of pain no one else but him could replicate. My legs were up around his shoulders and he rubbed his face against the bottom of my foot, kissing the arch, before taking my toes into his mouth. Watching him do that was so filthy and erotic, and there was something obsessive in his need to taste every unorthodox part of me. I was drunk with the idea, with the feeling of his tongue attending to these sensitive spots. While I cursed and moaned, he was thrusting with aggression, but there was an obvious restraint, clearly trying not to finish too quickly.

'I missed this so much,' he said, panting.

'I missed you.'

My legs dropped to the bed as he reached down and cupped my face. Our mouths were brought together and he bit down hard on my lip, and I tasted blood, sharply metallic. The thrusts became harder, deeper, he was desperate to bury himself in me. I played with my cock, jerking furiously as he made that face, the pained one, and we both let out a weighted gasp as we came in synchronicity. I sprayed all over my navel. He fell against me and stayed there, breathing in the scent of our sex; it might as well have been opium fumes. We were wet and warm and blissful. The moment could have lasted forever if we'd wanted it to. I almost cried at the relief of it, the catharsis of being dragged back into the riptide, back into him.

Just don't leave, was my silent prayer in the darkness. It was a futile request. Maybe I had to let him know it was okay to abandon the sweetness. Someone had to eventually.

'Do you need to shower?' I said after a few minutes, my way of providing an exit route.

'I'm okay for now.' He trapped me between his legs and nuzzled his face into my collarbone, surrendering to the haze. This took me by surprise, but I refused to overthink it. Then he whispered, 'That can't happen again. I'm serious.'

I stroked his feathered hair jovially. 'Okay.'

'That was the last time. Just to get it out of our system.'

'Yeah. The last time.' I smiled up at the ceiling and began pasting daydreams on the plaster.

25

The glass was wet in my hand. The bartender had done a rush pour, and the soda water bubbled over the rim and dribbled down the sides. I carried it back to the corner I'd been haunting for the evening, leaned against the brick, and watched from across the rooftop deck as Ezra morphed into a version of himself I'd never seen before: the desperate-to-charm host, the extrovert eagerly greeting high school throwbacks, university acquaintances, and ex-co-workers – all with an over-exaggerated throwing back of his head and a rupture of laughter that I knew was performative.

There might've been fifty people in total, enough to fill the rented space, but I could only count five that I knew. Juliana, Sierra, and Alé were supposedly en route, but it was after ten and I hadn't spotted them yet. One girl wearing a fur stole said something to Ezra, and he began clapping and hollering like a seal performing tricks. I wondered if he'd done a line of coke, causing him to act so showy, but it was unlikely given his hatred for the stuff. No, he was overcompensating. He was deeply unsettled and feeling insecure and making up for it by darting around like a madman and attending to everyone except for me.

I could have thrown myself into the ring of conversations, but a definitive pettiness allocated me to the corner. I needed Ezra to notice me on the outskirts, retrieve me of his own volition, present me and announce, 'Everyone, this is Austin, the guy I've been fucking regularly for the past month, and it's been going so well that we both deleted Grindr and stopped seeing other people,' but the little world he'd built for himself tonight didn't seem to include me. It wasn't fair to hope, or to expect anything. It wasn't my birthday, after all.

I thought we'd fall apart when the truth about my mother came out, but perhaps he thought that I was in fact so fucked up, we were no longer equals, and the power had returned to him. It was all a game really, chess pieces scattered across the board, especially in our sexual dynamic. I was on some kind of physical offence while he remained guarded and reactionary. I never wanted to force his hand, and yet he refused to make a first move on me. I was the one to lace our fingers together. I was the one to press my lips against his. I was the one to slip my hand into his pants. And he obliged, meeting me with an open mouth or an erect cock, but never by his design. At best, I felt unwanted, but mostly I felt like the kind of person that coerced their partner into affection, unable to take no for an answer.

'I need you to initiate sometimes,' I'd said to Ezra one night, my face still warm from sex. 'Otherwise it makes me think you don't want it.'

'Of course I want it,' he replied, breathless, and pushed his damp fringe off his forehead before laying back against the pillow, one hand trapped behind his head. 'I'm just trying to be smart.'

Whatever that was supposed to mean, I wasn't sure, but I noticed subtle improvements in the days following; leaning his head on my shoulder, squeezing my thigh, giving me a kiss on the forehead before he left for work in the morning. It was nice actually, a reminder that our relationship didn't have to be so perverse.

'Your present was a bit much.' Nadia snuck up beside me,

holding a large goblet she'd taken from the gin-tree. *A tree of gin*, I'd thought, *how outrageous*, but the venue certainly scored points for presentation with the fake ivy wrapped around the metal bars that held each cocktail in place.

We'd been drinking since brunch – or at least the core four, plus Izzy and I (the tentative six, I privately dubbed us) – though the drinks were weak and full of sugar. Ezra had sat at the end of the table with large silver balloons attached to his chair as we went around bestowing our gifts. Despite harbouring a dislike for the group as an entity, I appreciated the collective effort they put into birthdays, especially for a milestone such as thirty. Ezra looked mortified that the day had arrived, and spent most of brunch making self-deprecating comments about wrinkles or grey hairs, but he seemed to relax once he'd received his presents; a watch from Nadia, a spa treatment from Matteo, a new Bluetooth speaker from Marion and Izzy, and then it was my turn. I handed out the printed itinerary of the Airbnb and everyone went quiet.

'Eagle Bay,' Ezra said down to the paper.

'It's just for a weekend,' I shrugged. 'We can change the dates if you need to.'

'Probably my favourite–'

'Your favourite place in the world. Yeah, I know.' I still remembered our first full conversation, innocently wandering through vineyards in Margaret River, back when the only complications we faced was an age gap.

It was an extravagant gift, but more than that, it was a declaration of our evolving relationship, and I knew that by presenting it in front of his friends, he wouldn't be able to ignore what was being set into motion: us, as a concept, as a unit. Yet there he was, doing exactly that for the entire evening, pretending as if the gift didn't exist, pretending as if I didn't exist, like I wasn't the person in his life that knew him best, that loved him most.

'It's not a big deal,' I said to Nadia.

She took a sip of her gin and tonic and surveyed the scene with me. 'Callum's family has a house in Eagle Bay. That's why Ezra used to spend so much time there.'

Between her and Matteo, they always knew how to poison a moment, yet I couldn't deny it gave reason as to why everyone had responded with such hollowness. They knew the implications.

'Great,' I laughed bitterly. 'I'm an idiot.'

'How would you know?'

'I should've guessed. Everything he loves is stained with Callum.'

The jokes wrote themselves, they had from the beginning – manufactured and whispered behind my back. *Poor Austin.* I could see it in the eyes of everyone observing us from the outside.

'Should I cancel?'

'I don't know.' She inspected the split ends of her hair unhappily. 'But for what it's worth, he's an idiot for dicking you around. You're a good person, Austin.'

I blinked in surprise. 'That's very nice to say.'

Was it true? Or was my altruism only in service of the things I wanted from other people?

Matteo found us and made his way over. 'He's trying too hard, it's embarrassing,' he said in Ezra's direction once he'd reached our wall.

'Who are these people anyway?' Nadia grunted.

'A lot of Callum mutuals we used to hang out with. They petered off after the breakup, but I guess all is forgiven now.' He nodded to the group Ezra had been hovering over for the last half-hour, the ones painted bronze with fake tan and adorned with expensive necklaces and watches.

Ezra was widely gesturing with a cocktail he kept spilling on his shirtsleeve to a man in loafers. He was growing increasingly drunk, that was clear.

'He wants everyone to think he has more friends than he actually does.' Matteo brought out his vape and sucked on it. The exhaled cloud smelled like bubblegum. 'At least brunch was nice. But there's something you should know about Eagle Bay–'

'I already beat you to the punch,' Nadia said.

Clearly they found their mental overlap hilarious because they both laughed. I didn't join in.

'Can I have some?' I nodded at the vape.

'Sure.' Matteo passed it over and I took a long pull. It wasn't the same relief as the darts Daisy used to roll for me, but the burn in my chest gave me enough of a buzz to pretend I wasn't hating myself.

'Oh wow,' Nadia said. 'His parents came.'

Ezra's mother had translucent skin and a bend in her spine, and his father's once handsome features withered away beneath tired eyes and greying hair. They were dressed too casually for a nice event, almost as if they'd stumbled in by accident. Nadia waved them down and they approached with jaded smiles.

'Looking well Nadia,' the mother said. 'And you Matteo.'

'How are you both?'

'Good, we're good,' the father mumbled. I couldn't determine if they were South African or New Zealanders. 'Just popping in for a quick hello for the big thirty. Who's this?' He extended his hand out.

'Austin,' I said, shaking it. His grip was firm.

'Did you go to school with Ezra?' his mother asked me.

'No,' I said quickly. 'I'm a new friend.'

'How nice.'

Should it have hurt that they had no idea who I was? I was becoming indifferent to the entire night; numb, borderline sober, and still somewhat embarrassed from the last time I'd gotten wasted, which was certainly holding me back. I would've loved a bump of something, but I'd managed to avoid the stuff for a while, and I could only imagine the shitstorm that would erupt if Ezra caught me. Instead, I stayed muzzled with my weak vodka soda, and hoped someone would rescue me from this depressing display.

Ezra's parents said their goodbyes and Nadia and Matteo abandoned me to meet Ben by the bar. I drained my drink in silence until I spotted Juliana, Alé, and Sierra all arrive at once. I was surprised by how relieved I was to see them. I beelined over, discarding my empty glass on the way, and embraced Juliana first, then Alé, who gave me a few claps on the back in the way straight men did to somehow reaffirm their masculinity. Sierra's black dress was strapless and floor-length, with a slit that exposed her left knee. She certainly turned heads, especially Marion's, whose sight was pulled like a magnet from the table she was sitting at with Izzy.

'You look great,' I told her as we hugged. 'You all do.'

Juliana smiled at me with one hand clasped around her wrist. 'You look really well yourself.'

'Less drinking, no drugs,' I said.

'I guess we have Ezra to thank for that.'

'Is he your boyfriend yet?' Alé asked, so impertinent.

'No,' came my shrewd reply. 'Not yet.'

'Listen,' Juliana said, pulling lightly on my elbow and dragging me away from the others. 'We need to have a chat about something. I've hardly seen you.'

'If it's about Ezra—'

'It's not. I promise. Something else.' She surveyed me again, a certain sadness in her eyes despite the smile plastered on her face. 'Nothing to freak out about. I do hope you're happy, though.'

'I am,' I said. 'And we will chat. After the party.'

She squeezed my arm. 'Okay.'

'Shall we get a drink?' Sierra asked over Juliana's shoulder, who nodded and led the way to the bar, linking her arm with Alé's as she went. Sierra and I trailed behind.

'You know,' she said, 'I had a solid chat with Jules before we came here. And I finally expressed how I've never felt like I've been taken seriously. Sometimes people treat me like I'm too dumb or too vapid to deserve respect.'

'I don't think you're either of those things,' I said earnestly.

'I wish I could say the same for others. Even tonight…' She gazed around the rooftop with a furrowed brow. 'What am I doing here? Ezra doesn't care for me. Marion and I aren't friends anymore. I've only been kept around because it's easier to be fake, rather than cause issues with a falling out. You know how it is in Perth. Inescapable.'

We reached the bar. Juliana ordered a round while Alé's attention was directed down at his phone. He looked – or perhaps just felt – very out of place, and the bubbling tension between him and Juliana seemed obvious to me.

'Well, I'm really glad you're here,' I said to Sierra. 'I've hardly spoken to Ezra all night.'

'I think we need to stick up for ourselves a bit more.' She put her hands on my shoulders and stared into my eyes. Sometimes I felt as though she truly saw me. 'I genuinely love you and I just hope you're doing what's best for you.'

'Tequila,' Juliana announced before I could respond, passing us shot glasses.

I grimaced instinctively, my own vomit still fresh in my memory, but I tried to push the image down. Sierra let her hands slide off me and took one, careful not to let the lime wedge balancing on the rim fall to the ground. The tequila was yellow and smelled like gasoline. We waited until everyone had one in their hand before we made a small circle, clinked the glasses together, and knocked it back. I sunk my teeth into the lime and sucked. The citrus was a salve.

The night slipped away with the help of a few more rounds. Juliana and Sierra were waved down by some of the girls Ezra had been talking to, and they reluctantly sauntered over to say hello with Alé trailing behind, a miffed shadow. Ezra was elsewhere, continuing to rotate around me. I was growing more brazen in my drunkenness, ready to confront him for his avoidance, but my bladder was heavy with liquid, and so I went to the bathroom instead. The fluorescence was harsh and the urinal smelled repugnant. I opened my jeans as the disabled stall opened behind me and Matteo emerged, wiping his nose.

'Hi,' he said. I nodded at him curtly and turned my attention back to the wall. 'Do you want some coke?'

'I'm good, thanks,' I replied over my shoulder.

In my peripheral vision, I saw him lean forward to check out my flaccid cock, and then he left without a word. I shook my head at the audacity of it all, finished urinating, and went to the sink. I looked tired in the mirror. Someone had written *hoes mad* on the glass with a black marker. I traced over the phrase, wondering if it was a fresh addition, but the ink was dry.

As I left the bathroom, I nearly hooked the corner back out to the deck when Ezra's voice made me pause. 'I didn't realise you knew those girls.'

'We went to PLC together,' Juliana replied coolly.

'Ah. Of course. Well, it's nice to see you after all this time.'

'Thanks for the invite.'

I stayed hidden behind the wall. Awkwardness lingered in their silence.

'Alé looks a bit unhappy,' Ezra said. 'He doesn't seem to like me much these days.'

'I'm not sure *I* like you much these days.'

'Oh.' Even from that one word, he sounded mortified.

'I'm here for my cousin. To be honest, I'm pretty concerned with what's going on, considering how badly you hurt him last time.'

'I know, and–'

'How could you know? You weren't there. He was miserable, completely off the rails.'

'I hope you understand how much I regret my actions last year, but whatever's happening now, between me and him… Austin's commanding the ship. I'm just going along with it.'

And there it was. He'd curated the innocent bystander role, blameless for whatever outcome we found ourselves in. He didn't stop the relationship because he hadn't chosen it. I had, and I continued to do so.

Juliana didn't seem to agree with my logic. 'You're old enough to know better. You are *thirty*, after all.' She punctuated his age like it was an obscenity. Ezra would've felt that cut deep. 'He's fragile, okay? I'm not sure if you've heard about his mum, but–'

'Yes. I heard.'

'You can't string him along. You just can't.'

'I feel so much for him,' he said softly. He sounded so vulnerable. 'It's confusing, but I think I'm in lo–'

'Don't. Don't you dare say the word unless you're sure.'

I held my breath.

'I can't promise that it's going to work between us, but I can promise that I'm trying,' he murmured. 'Is that enough?'

Juliana took a long time to decide on an answer. 'I

suppose if it's enough for Austin, it has to be enough for me.'

Ezra took this in. 'He's really lucky he has you.'

'Yeah. Well. Happy birthday,' she muttered, indicating they had nothing left to discuss. I waited until I was confident they'd parted ways.

When I rounded the corner, Juliana was alone by the wall, arms folded over her chest.

'All good?' I asked her.

She pushed a long curl of hair out of her face and forced a smile. 'Do you wanna get out of here? Alé's being a dick and we're over it.'

'What's happening with Alé?'

'There you are.' He emerged from the bar like his name was a summon, putting his hand on Juliana's arm. 'Let me take a piss and then we can talk.'

'I'm not in the mood,' she said to him.

'I was only saying you don't have to pretend in front of those girls.'

'I wasn't pretending. I know them.'

'Yeah, but you were doing that private-school performance bullshit again.'

'Excuse me?'

They ignored the fact I was standing directly in front of them. The row was clearly too pressing. I dropped my gaze to the floor and slipped my hands in my pockets.

'Batting your eyes, bragging about what you've been up to. It's not us.'

'*Not us*? God forbid I'm not Brazilian enough for you.'

'That's not what I said.'

'That's what you've been implying for weeks.'

'Sierra got in your head, didn't she? Now that you're best friends again.'

'Go and take your piss then, like you piss on everything.'

Alé rolled his eyes and stormed past us. I raised an eyebrow quizzically at Juliana, but instead of saying anything, she gently took my hand and began to lead us towards the stairs. I didn't think to protest. I snuck a glance over my shoulder at the dwindling crowd that lingered; Marion and Izzy seemed to be arguing about something, Nadia was at the bar, Ben and Matteo passed a vape back and forth. Ezra was still talking to that man in the loafers and the girl with the fur stole, but she was typing away furiously on her phone with two tiny thumbs. I could see Ezra's increasing desperation to steal the attention, to get her to choose him over the screen, but his flailing only seemed to make her more disinterested. I felt sorry for him. No one noticed Juliana push on the fire-exit door and take us into the stairwell. Sierra was waiting on the top step.

'Yeah. He's being a cunt,' Juliana said, her voice reverberating off the concrete walls, big and echoey.

'So what are you going to do about it?' Sierra challenged with a daring smile, like she must have done back when they were in school. Juliana mirrored her expression and squeezed my hand tighter. I could picture them all those years ago in their plaid skirts and collared shirts, sunhats and scrunchies. I imagined they'd cut their uniforms short and skipped classes to meet up with the Scotch College boys, smoking cigarettes at lunch and copying each other's homework. Their raw rebellious spirit must've been something to behold, the kind only found in youth. There was so much shared history between them. I didn't have anyone in my life who knew me so intimately, not even Sabrina. Certainly not Ezra. Did he know me at all? It appeared so, but then I'd slip through his fingers like sand. It wasn't my intention. I wanted to be solid, to be caught and held, instead of perpetually falling.

'Let's disappear for a dance and not tell anyone.'

'Yes!' Sierra rose from the steps.

'No boys. Just Austin.' Juliana stood straighter, taller, more self-assured. 'Fuck 'em.'

'Let's go before Alé comes back.'

My phone buzzed in my pocket and I pulled it out.

Where are you

Everyone wants to go to the court

The girls were looking at me expectantly as I read Ezra's message. My teeth dug into my bottom lip.

'Well?' Juliana murmured. 'Are you coming?'

I'm sorry I've been so distracted tn

But I really want to dance with you

'Um.' My chest deflated. 'I…' They exchanged a glance that punched me in the gut, but there was nothing else I could think to add except, 'It's his birthday,' as if I would've chosen anything else.

Juliana shook her head and dropped my hand.

Sierra spoke for both of them. 'Enjoy your night, Austin.'

They descended the stairs without looking back. The clomps of their high heels echoed all the way down until they were gone, and I was left in silence.

'There he is!' Ezra beamed when I returned, throwing his arms around me and kissing me on the cheek. It was sloppy, leaving a wet stain. He smelled sourly of different liquors. The man with loafers and the girl with the fur were gone, leaving the core four, Izzy, Ben, and a few other stragglers.

'You're wasted,' I said into his ear.

'Yep,' he nodded, hands still locked around my neck. 'A lot of people are leaving.'

'So are we.'

'Yeah, but they're going home.'

'The people who love you will stay with you.'

Marion made Ezra chug some water before we left, and then we huddled together, all seven of us, the others flanking Ezra and I like security personnel, and we made our way through Northbridge on foot. It was lightly sprinkling, another warm rain, and Ezra clung to my hand for stability. The streets were stuffed with people lining up for nightclubs; Paramount, Geisha Bar, Rapture. We passed Connections, and the neon Northbridge sign in capital letters, the state library, and the renovated museum with its modern developments consuming the remnants of the historical red-brick. At the end of the block was The Court, all too familiar. *Back where it all began*, I thought quietly to myself.

I was worried the bouncers would think Ezra was too intoxicated to be let in, but he managed to pull himself together as we got to the front of the queue. I paid for his entry, and for a round of vodka sodas for everyone still standing. There was an expectation these days now that the group knew I had money, a silent *I'm sure Austin will get it*. It was a feeling I used to dread, but now all I felt was apathy. Who gave a fuck anyway? We carried our drinks to the mainstage as the DJ played *Dancing On My Own* which made Ezra light up with joy. He knew every word. We dove headfirst into the huddle of people, forcing space for the seven of us, and he did his drunken dance, so charming and ridiculous at the same time, shoulders and hips rotating in synchronicity. He reached for my hand and twirled me in. We were chest to chest, nose to nose, and I was singing every lyric back to him. His cold shoulder was scrubbed from my mind, and it was just us in the crowd, no one else. His eyes were distant, yet somehow clear at the same time. His drink spilled down my back and I shrugged a shiver away.

'In a couple of years, when we've got our shit together,' he began to say through slurred words, 'we're gonna have kids, and they're gonna be the cutest things ever.'

It made my heart swell. We stayed pressed up against each other, swaying side to side.

'That's kind of impossible for us, you know?'

'I know.' He looked immediately forlorn. 'I hate being gay.'

'Really?'

'Don't you?'

I kept a steady hand on his shoulder while the other clutched my drink. Back and forth, step-touch. 'Parts of it, I suppose. Not all the time.'

'Well, when you hit this age… Fuck,' he sighed. 'You realise how much you miss out on. How much harder it all is. You'll wish you were born normal. I could've had a family by now if I was normal.'

I flinched at that. It was such a miserable thing to say. *Normal.* What was normal? A feeling? An expectation? We were long past that, sexualities aside. I didn't care for normal. I just wanted to be happy.

'You still can,' I said. 'Have a family, I mean. Whenever you want.'

'Callum never wanted one.' He was searching my eyes for some kind of answer that would ease his panic, his restlessness. He'd sought it out many times, but I always managed to disappoint him when I answered truthfully. 'Would you? One day?'

'Maybe,' I said, my mouth going dry. 'One day.'

And then I saw Callum just over Ezra's shoulder, hovering in the background by the edge of the crowd. He was always somewhere, watching over us like a bad omen, a phantom. I stared him down, hatred burning in my eyes, and then I cupped Ezra's face in my hand and kissed him, claiming what was mine. I knew Callum saw. It felt victorious.

26

Our first stop was the Bunbury farmers' market, which Ezra swore was essential to the trip. It was laid out like an IKEA showroom, one long fluorescent-lit hallway of black and white striped awnings and shelves snaking through different sections. The fresh produce had plump red tomatoes and pumpkins the size of infants. Every kind of meat lay marinating in various oils and seasonings, and the baked goods were piled high in neat pyramids.

Ezra approached me and popped a brownie straight in my mouth. His fingers brushed my lips. 'Taste tester,' he said.

I chewed into the fudge, sweetness round kicking my pallet. I licked my lips and nodded in satisfaction.

We bought steaks for dinner and a pie for dessert, and then we piled back into the Tesla, Ezra in the driver's seat (as if that was ever up for debate). The conditions worsened when we approached Eagle Bay. Rain pummelled the windscreen and the trees shook violently. I knew I was safe in Ezra's careful hands, but there were some things even a skilled driver wouldn't be able to avoid. The road was treacherous and winding, and I felt the car sliding around each bend. Ezra put his hand on my leg and squeezed my knee reassuringly. I forced myself to relax.

The pristine views of the ocean boasted about on the Airbnb listing were hidden somewhere behind the storm clouds that charged across the sky like stallions, thundering and spitting rain as they went. I turned to Ezra with apologies on my tongue, like the weather was something I had control over, but he was gazing around the property with stars in his eyes. He admired the dark oak panelling and the enormous plush sofa, before running his hand over the dining table, which was large enough for eight people and made of a rich heavy wood. There was a crystal pendant light hanging above it, glowing amber.

'They have a reading nook for you!' he exclaimed.

I'd already seen it when I booked the listing, but it was even more quaint in person, covered with turquoise velvet pillows. The views be damned, if Ezra was happy, I was happy, and his child-like wonder and ear-to-ear grin told me I'd done well.

'There's a hot tub under the balcony,' I said. 'Hopefully it's sheltered from the rain.'

'Austin.' He turned very grave. 'This must've cost a fortune. It's too much, it's—'

'You think I can't take care of you?' I said.

He blinked in bewilderment.

I leaned forward and kissed him softly, and then I took the shopping bag from his hand and went to the kitchen, leaving him to gawk. The fridge was hidden in the panelling, nondescript, a small iron handle jutting out of the wood like the entrance to a secret passageway. I unpacked our groceries while Ezra wandered deeper into the house. Was he comparing it to the one Callum's family owned?

It didn't matter, as long as my version was better.

*

Ezra's head lolled back against the edge of the hot tub, exposing his neck. Rivulets of sweat descended the curve of his Adam's apple until it was caught by the concave above his collarbone. I had a primal urge to lean over and taste his perspiring body, licking the chlorine off from head to toe. He would probably let me. His gut was full of steak and pie, and there was a pleasant smile painting his lips that told me he was happy. How stupid of me to let Nadia and Matteo's cynicism get in my head. Everything in their reach turned to dirt, but I was determined to run my fingers through Ezra's life with a Midas touch. It wasn't a matter of wealth, it was about comfort and company, spending time with each other in beautiful places. The rain persisted, but there was something cosy about it now, a woollen jumper kind of weather, fireplaces and red wine. Much more intimate than a summer sky.

'I really needed this,' he murmured.

'Me too,' I said. I propped my elbows up on the lip of the tub and let one leg float out in front of me. My foot brushed his upper thigh and he grabbed hold of it, rubbing it with two hands. The bubbles hid my erection. I was perpetually hard around him, it was maddening. Some people had that effect, a quiet sexiness which felt personal, even private – so private he seemed unaware of it himself.

'Do you think you'll stay in Perth?' he asked.

I frowned. 'I don't see why not.'

'But do you like it? Living here?' He wasn't looking at me, just staring down at my foot through the water. 'I realised I haven't asked you that in a long time.'

'Why do you ask?'

'You're so evasive.' His chuckle was listless.

'Sorry.'

'I'm asking because I'm just not sure if I should be protecting myself.' His eyes flicked up and I held his gaze cautiously.

'Protecting yourself from what?'

'From you. Leaving me.'

I pulled my foot out of his grasp and let it sink to the bottom of the tub.

'Do you think I'm going to leave you?'

'I think you have the capacity to.' His mouth was tight at the corners, unease slanting his brows. Everything was very hot, my face, my body. The steam drifting between us gave him a ghost-like quality, as if he were made of vapour.

'I would stay if I was…' I began to say. 'If someone…'

'What?'

'I don't know.' I pressed my wrist to my damp forehead. 'I think the hot tub is making me light-headed.'

'Do you wanna get out?'

'Maybe.'

He swam over to me with concern and took me by two hands. We rose, water cascading down our torsos. He stepped out first, and then me next. Stability flooded back with the feeling of cold air and the sound of rain. Our towels were folded on the sunbed. He turned away from me and I watched the muscles in his back swell and tense as he dried himself, wet boardshorts clinging to his firm ass. There it was again, that primal urge, even stronger. Why fight it? We had the property to ourselves, nothing could be seen beyond the black of night. I approached quietly, dug my fingers under the waistband of his shorts, and pulled them down his thighs.

'Austin—' he said over his shoulder, somewhat startled, and then I sank to my knees and buried my face in him. He made a noise – a strangled sort of gasp – and bent over, holding the sunbed for support. I could feel his legs trembling as I kissed and licked. We had never acknowledged the existence of his asshole before, of it being played with or penetrated. When I tried to eat him out, he always steered my head back to his cock, or if I ended up between his legs, he would stare at me aghast, petrified that I might just stab him with it unprompted. It was either the Catholic guilt, or he was clinging to his last shred of purity, his obsession with being 'normal' – as if not taking it up the ass made him any less gay – but now he was moaning and reaching around to hold my head in place, arching like a figurehead, and I knew whatever wall he'd been defending had come tumbling down in a matter of seconds. I felt somewhat vexed that it had always been this easy, or perhaps a major switch had occurred – a singular moment where Ezra had decided he was willing to submit to me.

When we went upstairs to the master bedroom, there was no conversation needed, he just threw me the bottle of lube and crawled onto his back, legs up in the air, the yearning in his eyes speckled with nerves, anticipating pain.

'Are you sure?' I asked.

He closed his eyes and nodded. Surely that was affirmative enough? I was too horny to deconstruct it and already crawling to him. I hadn't realised how desperately I'd needed this, how long I'd sought the feeling of being inside him. It might've given cause as to why I'd kept seeking out other sexual outlets, subconsciously frustrated by his lack of versatility. The final threshold I was desperate for us to cross.

I kissed from his ankles up his calves, dragging my tongue across his warm and still-damp thighs. I sucked on the flesh there, nipping playfully and leaving a mark, before lubing up and positioning myself. He was breathing hard, clutching the linen sheets. I caressed his happy trail with the back of my hand, a reassuring gesture before pressing myself against him and slowly inching inside. My jaw fell open, elated by the feeling of him throbbing around my cock. Anguish ravaged his face and I waited for him to breathe through it, to set the pace. It took a long time, a lot of coaxing and waiting, not very sexy at all, but eventually he was more assertive, giving me that green light, and deeper inside him I found that warmth of friction and pressure, all the way in, my hips against his glutes, his legs up on my shoulders. I began to thrust, slowly at first, and he was whimpering, which almost made me ejaculate right away. How disappointing would that be? Close to a year of build up only for it to be over within a few minutes. No. I needed to savour it. I felt my body stiffen, retreating from the climax, while still trying to keep some semblance of pace.

Bottoming was easier in a sense, I just had to lie there and take it, no floodgates to hold shut, no sweaty exertion required, though the tightness around me was euphoric and unbelievably warm, worth every drawback.

'Does it hurt?' I murmured.

'Yes.'

'Do you want me to stop?'

'No.'

Writhing beneath me, legs shaking, his willingness to please me made it all the more arousing than it had any right to be. I'd felt the same with him, that unflinching desire to be used and loved in this painful and vulnerable way. It told me this was real: how much we were willing to suffer for each other.

'Fuck,' I groaned, elongating the vowel, stressing its weight. I leaned forward to bring our faces closer. His legs slipped off my shoulders but one of my hands caught his thigh and held it while my other hand made a fist, punching into the mattress beside his head. I rolled my hips into him, picking up speed until it was more of a pounding, as relentless and as punishing as he'd allow, all that yearning being exerted, all those whimpers mutating into moans, his body begging for it, as mine had done for him time and time again. His face was red and covered in moisture, eyes open, pleading, *more, more, more*. Sex wasn't a game, as I'd always thought. It was a battle for dominance, and Ezra had surrendered.

*

We ate at Meelup Farmhouse for breakfast, under the cover of a bamboo roof and wicker chandeliers while the rain persisted. A chubby chocolate labrador threaded her way through the tables, stopping by us for pets or scraps from our plates. The staff seemed accustomed to her existence, simply stepping over her or giving her a gentle push to continue on. We finished our meals and Ezra rose from his seat with a wince. I laughed and told him not to be such a baby.

'Some of us can't take it as well as you can,' he said.

'Some of us aren't as big as I am.'

I thought it was funny, but he looked somewhat offended. Truthfully, we were more or less the same size, but I wasn't aware it was such a contentious point of conversation. Our classic male ego, always boiled down to measuring dick size. I thought he might say something in response, but he kept walking towards the host desk. I could see him rifling for his wallet in his back pocket and I took a few quick strides to cut in front, ApplePay already out on my phone. He hardly had time to react before I'd completed the EFTPOS purchase with a little *ding*.

'I can afford breakfast, you know,' he threw at me as we exited.

I smiled innocently, batting my eyes as if it was an apology, but he was having none of it. He huffed and led the way back to the car, breaking into a half-jog to escape the downpour.

'You could say thank you,' I said.

'Thanks,' he said. 'I'm an ungrateful twat, I know.'

'*Twat?* Who says twat?'

'I don't know. The Brits.'

'We're not British.'

'Can you please get off my dick?'

'I am off your dick,' I retorted playfully. 'But you're welcome to get back on mine.'

'Fuck off,' he said sourly and got into the driver's seat, yanking the car door closed. He'd been short with me throughout breakfast, and I was convinced that picking up the bill or cracking jokes would smooth things over, but instead it was eroding everything. Had I gone too far the night before? Too pushy, too aggressive? Guilt enveloped me, nauseating, all those whimpers now sounding harrowing in the playback. Did he want it, or did I give him little choice? Was I evil, all my fears of coercion made true?

I climbed into the passenger seat timidly. Ezra shifted the car into drive, and we swerved back into the bush. There was no music, just stale silence. I'd certainly fucked up. I'd chosen selfishness over respect and ruined everything. Again.

'I'm really sorry,' I said quietly.

'About?' he said to the windscreen. The wipers made a churning noise, working overtime to keep the glass free of rain splatter.

'Last night. I never should have–'

'Austin, we really don't need to–'

'We do,' I said. 'You didn't want it, and I shouldn't have–'

He glanced at me with mirth. 'Do you think you took advantage of me or something?'

'Maybe? I don't know.'

He began to laugh loudly, and I didn't have time to decipher if it was genuine or begrudging because a tree had fallen halfway over the road and we both saw it at the same time. Ezra wrenched the wheel to swerve us out of the way and with such speed, there wasn't a moment to yelp in alarm. The car skidded and I held my breath, the branches drawing near, threatening to pierce the windscreen and impale our fragile bodies, but in those last vital seconds, Ezra avoided it by a hair. The only collision happened at the front left tire, which made a loud popping noise before the screech of metal on asphalt. The console screen lit up with warning signs. Ezra swore loudly and veered the car off the road. He killed the engine and we sat there, breathing, shell-shocked. I was about to ask if he was okay, but he was already flinging open the door to inspect the damage.

He walked around the front bumper and squatted down in the mud, drenched immediately from the rain, his grey jumper clinging to his body like papier-mâché. I got out too, arms squeezed tight around myself to trap warmth. I hardly cared about the tire or the scrapes along the side of the door, I just stared up at the sky and scowled. A higher power was smiting me, ensuring nothing would ever be as good as what Callum once provided. When was it time to admit defeat?

'I'm so sorry,' he breathed.

'It wasn't your fault,' I said, already shivering. 'Just get back in the car and let me call Roadside.'

He was inspecting the tire, running his finger over the sizable hole and the debris that had gathered around it. 'I've changed a million tires.'

'It's bucketing down. You'll catch a cold.'

He squinted through the rain. 'That's a myth, actually. You can't catch a cold from being rained on.'

'Whatever. What are you trying to prove?'

'That I can do things. That I'm capable.'

'Was that ever up for debate?'

'Can't you just let me be the man?'

I blinked in disbelief. '*The man?*'

'I'm older than you. I should be taking care of you, not you of me.'

'I'm not *taking care of you*. This weekend is your birthday present. I'd do it for any good friend.'

He rose to his feet. 'Is that what we are, are we *good friends*?'

I took a step forward. 'What are we then?'

'You know we're not just friends.'

'Then tell me what we are.'

Panic flared in his eyes. 'Well, what do you want to be?'

'Don't answer a question with a question,' I said.

'Hypocrite.'

'Yeah. We both are.'

I got back in the car and slammed the door. He couldn't say it, and neither could I. We were as cowardly as each other, and whether that broke my heart or filled me with rage wasn't clear, but my inability to cry made me think it was the latter. It wasn't long until he too receded back inside.

'I just remembered Teslas don't carry spare tires,' he said quietly.

Instead of answering, my face turned away from him and I watched the rain streaming down the passenger window like a network of rivers.

We waited in the silence, at least a few minutes long, almost holding our breath until Ezra sighed. 'I've been in love with you for a while now, but I'm really fucking scared because I don't know what to do about it. And I don't know if it'll change anything, because you're still young, and I'm still emotionally stunted, and maybe it would be a huge mistake. Or maybe it would be the best thing to happen for us.'

I stared at him. He looked exhausted, as if the simple act of expressing himself had drained the life from his face.

'Huh,' I said, and he flinched.

'If a noise is your only response, I'm going to be physically ill.'

There was a speech I'd privately rehearsed a million times, all the perfect things to say to him in this moment, but the lines had been blacked out like a classified document.

'Do you think I'm not scared and confused too?' I blurted out, running on instinct. 'It feels wrong to be happy when I should still be grieving. Maybe I *am* still grieving – but I don't know how I'm supposed to process it, or what it's supposed to look like. And maybe there is no right way, but for some reason I keep seeking out things that make me miserable, like drugs and sex, and I lie to myself that I don't think about it, or that it doesn't mean anything, but it does. It feels disrespectful and wrong to her memory, carrying on like this – but I keep doing it anyway, because that's how I've always dealt with things. Since I was fourteen, it was just a part of my coping mechanism. I didn't see a good enough reason to stop. Until you. Because I *do* care about sex, especially sex with you. Because it makes me happy. Because I love you too.'

His face lit up. 'Really?'

'Don't pretend like you weren't completely aware of that the entire time,' I breathed, almost with contempt. 'You've always had the power.'

'That's not true. You don't realise how weak I am with you.' His gaze lowered to a point above my knee, too embarrassed by the concept of inferiority to maintain eye contact.

'Is that a bad thing?'

'I don't know,' he said. 'I don't know anything anymore. I don't know if I have enough to make you happy.'

'Forget about money–'

'I'm not talking about money. I just mean me. The life I offer in Perth. Will it be enough to make you happy?'

We held another tense stare, achingly long and confronting.

'I'm happy now.'

'Is it enough?' he asked, even more gently. My mouth opened and shut. I blinked dumbly. The lack of an immediate response made him shrink in his seat and he swallowed hard. 'I don't have it in me to fail again. I have to get it right.'

'You can't control that, Ezra. We don't know what's going to happen.'

'I'm trying to be smart–'

'Be stupid!' I cried. 'The label is arbitrary at this point. We're together, aren't we?'

He groaned in frustration and then leaned over the console, took my face in his hands, and smashed his lips against me so forcefully, I thought our mouths might merge into one entity. It was a cementing act.

'Yeah,' he whispered as he pulled away. 'We're together. Whatever that means for us.'

And it was like the world stopped for a perfect moment.

27

'Daisy! Wait!' Those words might have been carried away by the wind, but the slightest stiffening in her shoulders let slip that she was ignoring me. She had her hood up, and her body was lost under the shapeless form of her oversized canvas jacket. Considering my legs were nearly twice as long as hers, I caught up halfway down the block.

'Oh. Hi,' she said dismissively. 'I can't miss my train.'

'Can I walk you to the station?'

'Alright.'

I didn't give her much of a choice, already glued to her side. We pressed on as the wind whipped around us, penetrating our clothes and drilling deep into our bones in a very Melbournian way.

'Did I do something to you?' I asked. 'I thought we were friends but you've hardly looked at me in months.' It sounded so confrontational aloud, but I suppose that was the intention. I should've been braver as soon as she'd turned cold, but I'd let it fester to our detriment.

Daisy kept her pace, bouncing in her Docs, eyes ahead. 'I just don't think we have anything in common,' she said.

'Seriously?'

'We only hung out all the time because you didn't have anyone else.'

'That's not true.' I turned to look at her, earnest. 'I really enjoy your company.'

'You enjoyed someone listening to you.' She delivered this

with a sharp flourish. 'I know people like you. You latch onto someone when you're at your lowest, dump all your shit on them. And then you get back with the person that caused all the shit to begin with. You won't stay in Perth. You'll probably head back to Melbourne, or maybe try Sydney, or anywhere else in the fuckin' world. And I'll be here. At the café. Always.'

'You don't have to,' I said quietly. 'You have a choice, Daisy. You're smart, resourceful. You can choose better for yourself.'

'The fact you see it as such a failure is part of the problem,' she said, coming to a stop and trying to tame the loose strands of hair slipping out from under her hood. 'Some of us are happy to make coffees, and put down food, and wait for people to say good morning, and smoke darts, and drink at the pub. Some of us are happy to live in Perth, where it's quiet, and nothing really changes. I know it's not good enough for you, but that's what makes me happy.'

'I never meant to—'

'You don't need me. You'll be fine.'

She continued her walk to the station, and I didn't follow. It seemed final. I made a left en route to the apartment and texted Leslie to let her know I wasn't coming back to work. There was relief in the act, and an unexpected appreciation for Daisy pushing me to that finality. I should've done it months ago. In fact, I never should've worked there in the first place. All those meaningless hours and for what? Itchy hands from cleaning chemicals and t-shirts ruined from coffee stains.

I'd been afraid of too much time, and now I was seething over how I'd squandered it. There were other things I could do to fill the vacant gap in my life. I could read more, exercise more, get a different job in something I was actually passionate about, volunteer somewhere… Wasn't that what rich people with too much time on their hands did? At some point I would have to grow up and do something with the privilege I'd been given, but when I thought too hard about it, I was rendered dizzy.

I tried to conjure up Ezra and I living in a nice apartment in Cottesloe (depending on whether I could convince him to move to the GT) but there were too many missing puzzle pieces to render the picture. I could feel new cities whispering: Copenhagen, Tokyo, New York, even a return to Melbourne – but Perth was a white out, a floating question mark, and it made me feel sick.

How would Ezra and I find commonality in the long run when our futures were at war? Ezra was stubborn, holding steadfast to the life he'd worked to build while I meandered in the potential of one. We ignored those caution-taped truths and questions, opting to bask in the warmth of routine; dinners on his couch in front of the TV, a glass of wine, good sex, morning coffees in bed before he kissed me on the forehead and slipped out to his windowless office.

How long we'd fretted over the concept of commitment, and yet nothing had really changed except for our outwardness of affection. I was happy, I hadn't lied to him, but I was also aware there might come a time I would outgrow Perth and look for an escape route. I only needed him to join me and he would see what else was out there. He wasn't like Daisy. He had tasted the other world. Surely I could change his mind if Callum nearly had.

I told Juliana I'd quit my job as soon as I found her in the living room, and she looked happy for me until she asked what I was going to do next, and I had no answer for her. I could see concern simmering in her eyes, but she held back from commenting on it, instead shifting gears to reveal what she'd tried to tell me at Ezra's birthday.

'The landlord is raising the rent in November,' she said. 'Prices are going up everywhere, even food and bills, and I need to scale down.'

'Okay,' I nodded slowly. 'So—'

'Alé's put a deposit down on an apartment in Maylands. And he's offered for me to live there with him.'

It wasn't clicking in my brain. 'We're leaving the GT?'

'Well… I am,' she said with a wince. 'It's a one bedroom. My savings aren't anywhere near what I want them to be, so I just thought—'

'Oh.' *She* was leaving, and I hadn't been asked to come.

She folded her hands in her lap. 'I'm more than happy to help you find a new housemate. Or you could always live here by yourself! Turn my bedroom into a library or something.'

The idea seemed ridiculous considering how little time I spent at the apartment. In the almost-year since I'd met Ezra, he had never slept in my bed, or even stepped through the door, a fact I was well aware of and sought to change that very evening. I'd invited him over without telling Juliana, hoping some quality time all together might be a proverbial olive branch.

'I thought you and Alé—'

'We're fine,' she said firmly. 'He can be childish and possessive, but he loves me. Our fight the other weekend made him understand that I need my own life, a life that includes people like Sierra. And he can take care of me, something no other guy in my life was capable of doing.' The subtle bitterness alluded to something deeper than a past relationship. I wondered if she was referring to Ray.

'What if I paid your rent for you?' I asked. 'Would you stay?'

She immediately shook her head. 'I've got too much pride

for that. And I think if there's one thing we've learned from our parents, it's to keep money and family separate.'

I felt a pang of mourning for the life we'd established – not that there'd been much of one, considering how deeply Ezra had permeated my very existence. That was the sacrifice I'd made without realising it – Ezra over Juliana. Ezra over everyone. Potentially justifiable for true love, if there was such a thing, but I was all-in with a weak hand of cards, praying the bluff would pay off. I needed it to be worth something, the investment and anguish, every shitty thing we'd said and done, every precious moment we'd shared. All those hours spent beside each other, the months missing him. Being together in a more conventional way was all I'd wanted, and now I had it, so why did I still feel so unsettled? I couldn't trust happiness. As soon as I found a warm stasis to land, something else seemed to shift and the mirage would falter. I just wanted to freeze time and trap the moment.

'How about Ezra? Would he move in?'

I laughed callously. 'We've only been officially together for a week.'

'You've been on and off for a year,' Juliana retorted. 'I think that counts for something.'

I bit my nail and avoided her eyes. 'I invited him over for pizza tonight. I hoped you might stick around and make an effort with him.'

Her eyes narrowed at the prospect of an ambush or perhaps the suggestion she hadn't been trying. 'I've already got plans, sorry,' she said quickly. 'But you guys enjoy.'

'Yeah. Thanks.' I sounded hollow, and I felt it.

She leaned over and squeezed my arm, an attempt at reassurance. 'It's been really nice living with you. I hope I didn't blindside you.'

'Not at all. You have to do what's best for you.'

She surveyed me. 'I'd say the same to you.'

'When have I ever known what's best for me?' I smiled, hoping she'd laugh, but perhaps the joke was too close to an uncomfortable truth to be humorous. She just nodded with a kind of melancholia, and later, managed to time her departure a mere fifteen minutes before Ezra arrived, as if she had a sixth sense.

When Ezra stepped into the entryway, he examined the apartment with muted surprise. He carried a backpack that contained a change of clothes and his meds, both straps tight over each shoulder like a student on their first day. I kissed him on the cheek and he set his bag down on one end of the couch.

'I expected something else,' he admitted as we both sat down.

'What do you mean?'

He glanced around again. 'I mean it's… two twenty-year-olds in a sharehouse.'

'Well,' I blinked, 'Juliana and I are two twenty-year-olds in a sharehouse.'

'I assumed it would be all… *bourgeoisie*.'

'Now who's the one using big words?' I chuckled.

'I got that one from TikTok,' he said sheepishly, and I shook my head in amusement.

'I didn't want to take over the place,' I explained. 'It's all Juliana's stuff. At least until she's gone in November.'

He had started unlacing his shoes and frowned down at them. 'Gone? Where?'

'She's moving to Maylands with Alé.'

'Are you staying?'

'I don't know.'

He kicked his shoes off and folded his legs up against my thigh. 'Would you rent here on your own?'

'I don't know,' I said again, stressing it harder this time. 'I don't really want to think about it right now.'

'Okay,' Ezra murmured, staring at an unfixed point on the wall, perhaps noticing the black marks on the plaster, unless he didn't pay attention to those sorts of details. 'Should we order pizza?'

We ordered a meat lover's (typical homosexuals, I'd said) from a place around the corner, which was a perfect balance of salty and greasy. We managed to avoid the topic of my future in Perth and the uncertainty that lay ahead. We laughed about how I quit my job and could finally achieve trophy wife status, and then he joked about me being both a trophy wife and a sugar daddy simultaneously, and I asked if he was okay with that, and he said yes. We started making out, tasting the remnants of cheese and garlic on each other's lips. We cracked a bottle of shiraz and I put on a HAIM album, and after half an hour of disconnected tangents, I asked him where he'd travel if money wasn't an obstacle.

'Paris!' He exclaimed, nearly spilling his wine over himself. 'I don't care how basic of an answer that is. I want to see it!'

'It's beautiful,' I agreed. 'I went once as a kid. I still remember the hot chocolates. It's all thick and far too rich and they give you the whipped cream separately to stir in.'

Like teenagers with the world at our fingertips, we began constructing a dream European travel itinerary that started in Paris, then all the big cities Ezra was desperate to check off his bucket list, some I'd never been to before – a route threading through Amsterdam, Dubrovnik, Rome, the Amalfi Coast, Barcelona, Lisbon, London. All the iconic restaurants and clubs, the most picturesque beaches, the museums, the landmarks. We didn't have a date or a budget, just a yearning for bright colours and culture and life.

We could have it all, I realised. We could swim in the Perth fishbowl, in our simplicity and comfort, counting down the days until we escaped to the chaos of the outside world, then retreating back to safety when we were homesick. We could do it together. Wasn't that the ideal life?

He knew so much about each prospective city, that I was painfully late to realise our itinerary was a carbon copy of the trip he had once planned with Callum. My mouth went dry, and my excitement receded.

Ezra noticed immediately. 'What?'

'Nothing.'

'Tell me.'

I couldn't look him in the eyes and confront him. I couldn't snarl and say I wasn't a fucking idiot, I couldn't tell him how furious Callum's constant presence in our relationship made me, how deeply sickening it was to be in a threesome with someone's ghost, so instead I just leaned in and kissed Ezra's neck to hide my face from him.

'Oh?' he said, taken aback.

I slipped a hand inside his pants, groping the outline of his cock through his underwear, and he quickly abandoned any acknowledgment of my mood shift. Sex was safe, an embankment to retreat to, a well-timed weapon. Once he was fully hard, we went to my room, stripped each other naked, and while he fucked me, he wrapped his arms tightly around my torso and whispered he loved me. I held back tears.

I couldn't finish. He tried lazily stroking my deflated erection until I lied and said I'd masturbated too recently to go again. He accepted this and excused himself to the bathroom, probably to wash his cock in the sink. I was sitting upright in my bed sheets that were so rarely used, they felt unfamiliar, and my head was swimming in jealousy and sadness. The lights were off. Ezra returned and leaned against the doorway, backlit by the hallway light. His arms were crossed over his chest, his head bowed. I couldn't tell whether it was out of modesty or shame.

'Um. This is a bit of a mortifying question but…' He was drenched in shadows so I couldn't see his face. 'Have you been feeling a burning sensation when you take a piss?'

28

I could feel the horns strapped to my forehead digging into my skin. I knew at some point throughout the night, whenever I took them off, there would be an impression of two small red circles, like an octopus had suctioned itself to my face. I made a mental note to never attend a Halloween event again where the most recognisable part of my costume was an uncomfortable accessory.

'You guys look great,' Marion had said to Ezra and I, me with my devil horns and black jacket open to a bare chest, and Ezra with his white singlet, wings, and a halo. The irony wasn't lost on me – of course I was the demon trailing behind angelic Ezra – but he looked pleased with the compliment, and it was one of the few times he'd smiled in my presence over the last few weeks. Matteo was a few people ahead of us, leading the way inside, dressed as a vampire (fitting, I'd thought), though it was a lazy effort considering his costume consisted of a flimsy mesh black shirt and 5-inch Lululemon shorts with fake blood running from the corner of his mouth. Marion and Izzy went as Velma and Daphne from *Scooby-Doo*, their costumes made of shiny polyester, and Nadia was the *Corpse Bride*, with the wedding gown cut well above her knees. Seeing them all dressed up around me, I wondered what age people were supposed to grow out of these sorts of events, all of them now in their thirties or fast approaching, but the Connections Halloween party was a yearly ritual, one of the few times they bothered to step foot in the venue.

It was a newfound agony to enter a room and be unsure of who I'd hooked up with. The last time I was here with Daisy and her friend Steve, I was off my leash, Ezra a mere afterthought. Everyone was a possibility, another tally in the black book. Now, they were reminders of my shame, each flicker of recognition a wound split back open, and I was paranoid Ezra might notice these silent exchanges as we passed through the crowd. The room was hazy and disorienting, bodies brushing past in outfits that ranged from disturbing to arousing: a zombie in a jockstrap; a guy in a *Spider-Man* suit that wasn't a suit at all, but head-to-toe body paint; more vampires; someone in a gimp suit; the list went on. I wondered if any of them had given me an STI, which led to me giving Ezra an STI, which led to the worst fight we'd had thus far, one which came throbbing back to me even weeks later.

He hadn't moved from the doorway of my bedroom, frozen and silhouetted, his shadow splashed across the carpet. I was in bed, hugging my knees, physically holding myself together.

'I blame myself for trusting a twenty-year-old,' he'd spat to the floor.

'Don't talk to me like I'm some kid that's disappointed you. This is a relatively normal occurrence for people sexually active in the gay community–'

'This isn't normal. This should never be normal. And I'm not *sexually active* in the gay community, by the way. Some of us don't need to degrade ourselves for attention.'

'Nice one.'

'I've got a lot more where that came from.'

'If you were so paranoid, why didn't you use a condom?'

'Because I had faith that you were careful enough, or

smart enough to test regularly, or even have the decency to let me know—'

'I usually take care of it, but in the months before—'

'You know what? You and Callum… You're the same. Thinking you're invincible, no regard for other people—'

'And I bet you love that! You love how similar we are. It gets you off.'

'Fuck you.'

'It's true! You're still obsessed with him.'

'And you're constantly trying to *be* him! Do you seriously think that's what I want?'

'You changed your tune about me as soon as I starting paying for things, so—'

'Are you actually listening to yourself?'

'Are *you*? You've always had dollar signs in your eyes, Ezra. You're just too fucking self-righteous to admit it.'

'So typical, putting blame on other people, gaslighting…'

'You wouldn't know the meaning of the word.'

'Oh yeah?'

'Yeah, and I bet you pulled it from fucking Tik Tok too.' I couldn't stop. I couldn't submit. The train was running off the tracks but I steamrolled ahead. 'I'm aware that I'm in the wrong, but your reaction is genuinely insane. You haven't even gotten a positive test yet, and you're already self-diagnosing and jumping to conclusions.'

'It's pretty obvious what this is. You've put us at risk, Austin. Have you properly grasped that in your under-developed brain? Neither of us are on PrEP. Imagine if it's more than just the clap, but HIV, or—'

'No one gets HIV anymore.'

The silence was deafening. He stared at me in disbelief, and then said, 'Christ, you're young.'

'I fucking know! My god, I know. And you hold me to an

impossible standard where I can't act my age and make mistakes. I always have to be functioning about eight years ahead, and if I slip up, I'm a disgrace. It's exhausting.'

'Did you ever experience homophobia? Like at all?'

'What does that have to do with STIs?'

'I'm honestly curious.'

I took a breath through my nose. 'Maybe not as bad as other people, but I still remember being called a fag a handful of times through school, and–'

'That's it? You just live in this little bubble where everything's okay and normal.'

'We *are* normal! That's your bloody trigger word, isn't it? I'm sorry for being born a few years later and missing out on your generation's self-hatred. And for the record, my dad wasn't all rainbow parades. He told me it was a choice. It wasn't easy to hear that.'

'Did he kick you out of the house? Threaten to bash you up if you ever brought a boy home? I don't think so. You have no idea.'

'So I'm a bad person because I wasn't threatened with hate crimes?'

'No, you're just an arrogant one! Completely naive to how difficult the world can be. And that's not even a gay thing, that's just you. In everything. Entitled, spoiled, like Callum–'

'Stop saying his fucking name.'

'I'm just hammering the point.'

'Point hammered! I'm young and I'm stupid, and you hate me for things I have zero control over.'

'No, Austin, I love you, which is why I'm so unbelievably furious that you weren't careful with me, that you didn't tell me you hadn't been tested since we started sleeping together again, and every time I think we're done with the lies–'

'It's impossible to be honest with you when you have this

whole judgmental approach to anything that has to do with sex!'

'You're blaming *me*? Really?'

'It always comes back to this! I'm not the perfect innocent guy you wanted me to be.'

'You were the one that put on that act in the first place! You set us up for failure.'

'So that's it? We're a failure?'

'It's a pretty bad sign this early in the relationship. So, I don't know.'

And the rest I don't remember as clearly because a tidal wave of panic surged, and I wasn't able to breathe, and I was crying and begging him not to end it, to give me another chance like a sinner in confession seeking absolution, and I'd never been so snivelling and pathetic before, but it certainly made him pause. He didn't forgive me, and instead of staying the night, he dressed and went home, but he hadn't broken up with me – not yet anyway.

I was half-certain I'd just delayed the inevitable, that he was worried I'd kill myself if he did it too soon. My other half-certainty was that his bipolar was acting up, and his down had coincided with our fight, or our fight had triggered the down, or the pills we took to cure what ended up being the clap had some side effect which sent him to that cold distant place I could never reach. I conjured up just about anything in my brain in an effort to self-soothe. We still watched movies on his couch. I was still invited to pre-drinks. We still attended the Halloween event in our prearranged costumes, but the wall was up each time. I continued to cradle the idea of us in my hands, though we were little more than broken glass by that point, and the harder I squeezed, the more I bled.

I watched the men dancing, sweat dripping from their

pecs and arms, smiles on their faces, hands caressing themselves and each other. They were lost in the music, the
pulsing, throbbing techno. They looked so free in their
sexuality, they revelled in it. They loved themselves with
shamelessness, the kind of pride Ezra and I might never
have.

The group had floated to the bar without telling me and I
was now alone in the crowd, wishing I could be anywhere
else. *I could just go home*, I thought. *No one would notice.*

Instead I went to the bathroom and stood in front of the
sink, splashing water on my face, trying to sober up, and as I
leaned over, my horns hit the mirror and made my head ring.
The glass was scratched up and graffitied, but I found my
reflection and paused to examine my misery. I looked stupid.
I felt it too, stupid and powerless. It was a similar suffocating
feeling to that day at Sí Paradiso, a mad scramble to stay in
control when there seemed nothing I could do to fix things.

I was about to leave when Matteo entered, drink in hand,
a clear liquid which I assumed was a vodka soda. We made
eye contact, very direct and haughty, until I said, 'Do you
have anything on you?'

Matteo looked surprised, but then his eyes shined.
Opportunistic. 'I sure do.'

He led the way into the cubicle, and I followed with the
same foreboding of someone sentenced to the electric chair.
He set his drink down on the toilet roll dispenser. We were
nearly pressed up against each other, boxed in by the black
walls, his body heat making the enclosed space even more
sticky and suffocating. I despised everything about him, from
his smirk to his unduly vanilla odour. The scent was
overpowering – intermingling with the traces of piss and
faeces, it almost made me gag. He looked victorious while my
face was warm with shame.

'I've got MD.' He slipped a hand into the pocket of his shorts and pulled out two capsules. 'But you have to earn it.'

I expected as much. I swallowed the lump in my throat.

'Just don't tell Ezra,' he added slyly. I couldn't think of anything to say.

The stall was spinning, closing in. Matteo reached out and took a hold of one of the horns on my head and used it to push me to the floor, on my knees in front of him. The floor was wet, I could feel it seeping through my pants. He towered over me, asserting his power, his other hand offering up the pill. I plucked it from his palm and placed it on my tongue.

Three months clean, gone in an instant. I immediately knew it was a mistake. He took the other pill, and began to pull his shorts down, his erection tenting in his briefs. I wanted to disappear. Ezra was right. Every good part of myself was an act. I would always be this person, sad and disgusting and unlovable. Ezra wasn't a paragon by any means, but I was a black hole, a detour down a dead end. I wasn't like Callum either, I was worse in every way. I couldn't hide behind childish mistakes anymore, this was deeply embedded behaviour, intentionally malicious, seeking to inflict maximum damage. I was old enough to know better. Why Ezra ever bothered trying, I'd never understand.

Making a choice to do the right thing for somebody else. Because you loved them.

Was it really that easy? Perhaps it was.

I spat the pill to the floor and wrenched myself away from Matteo. His pants were around his ankles and when I pushed on his thigh, he tripped over himself and fell back against the toilet seat, cursing as he bumped his head on the wall. His drink slipped off the dispenser and shattered on the tiles. I rose to a standing position, pants sopping wet, the fabric clinging to my knees. My hands hurried with the lock on the door, and I flung it open as Matteo yelled, 'What the fuck is wrong with you?' but I slammed it behind me and left him there.

I needed to find Ezra. I needed to make it right. It wasn't over yet. I could be better, we could *both* be better. Every tribulation had the potential to make us stronger, and if I'd forgiven him for Callum, he could forgive my indiscretions. No more lies. No more masks. I had to believe that I was capable of it, that I could start on the path of change, of growing up at last, even if it had taken so much time. But I would promise him I was committed to being a good person, a mature person, cemented with the weight of an oath. We could be happy. I conjured up the vision of our Perth apartment, of our European trip, all the other silly dreams and fantasies we ever shared with each other. Where was Ezra?

I emerged onto the dance floor, but the throng was so dense, it was almost impenetrable. Bodies pressed down from all sides, tangles of arms and legs and loose hair tossed about. A revolving maze, doorways opening and shutting every few steps. The crowd thinned; the bar just ahead.

And there he was.

At the edge of the bar Ezra wasn't alone. A man was with him, enclosed in his feathered wings. Their heads were moving in a strange, rhythmic way I couldn't comprehend, until it hit me. Ezra was kissing him.

I felt the world haemorrhage. Everything was stripped bare and left a raw and bloodied rage, thick and nauseating.

The man was unknown to me, but I immediately thought of the story Ezra told me, the one where Callum kissed a stranger on Valentine's Day in plain sight, pointedly, just as he was doing to me now. And so I did what Ezra himself had deemed deserving of the act.

I picked up the nearest empty glass, and I threw it at Ezra's head. Beneath the techno, I heard a sickening crack and whether that was his skull or the sound of the glass breaking, I didn't stick around to find out. I pivoted and fled, pushing my way through the costumed crowd and down the stairs to the exit, tears welling up in my eyes, my abdomen tight. *Don't lose it yet*, I thought. *Don't let anyone see you hurting.* No one stopped me, no security guards called out. Ezra wasn't chasing me down. I pulled off the headpiece and threw it to the floor, but whether I was sporting devil horns or not didn't change the fact I felt hellish.

Out on the street, there was only more chaos. A fight had broken out across the road and there were sirens and flashing lights, flurries of bodies passing, unidentifiable smells and noises. Men were yelling, police were barking orders at each other, and a woman was wailing. It was all so disorienting and I was standing too close to the curb when a car honked, making me jump back and collide with a firm body.

'Fuck, sorry,' I said, turning and staring into the person's eyes. A knot tied itself in my stomach.

'You're alright,' he said quietly, one hand in his pocket.

I didn't move.

'You're standing in front of my Uber.' He nodded at the car that had just honked. His broad frame swayed, and his pupils were unfocused. He must've been drunk too.

'Do you want me to come home with you?' I blurted out. I didn't care how desperate I sounded. I needed to get away, I needed him to take me away. 'If that's where you're heading.'

There was genuine surprise on his face, perhaps because the last time we'd spoken, I made him swear we would never address each other again, or maybe he was taken aback by the sheer audacity of the delivery.

'Yeah, that's where I'm heading,' he said, regaining his

composure. He stepped around me, leaned over, and opened the car door. 'Jump in.'

I climbed in first and Callum followed, his hand on the small of my back.

29

On an automatic timer, the canvas blinds rose slowly with a monotone hum, the bay in full view. Rowers passed by on their morning training session. Sailboats were stagnant in the distance, docked at the wharf. Clouds loomed with a grey judgement, tinged with pink and yellow. Callum's room was all high ceilings and white walls that drank the muted colours of the sunrise. With rooms this big, all cement and glass, it was always cold. The times I'd stayed the night, I woke up shivering.

Sleep had escaped me. My stomach was atrophying with regret and the space between my legs was throbbing. I turned my head and examined the other side of the bed. Callum looked docile when he was asleep, beautiful even, someone worthy of love. I decided hatred and desire were two sides of the same coin, and it was still spinning in the air after all this time, unsure of where to land. When he finally blinked awake, maybe an hour after light had penetrated the room, he stretched his long limbs out across the bed and yawned. He was so tall that even on opposite sides of the enormous mattress, his fingers easily brushed along my bare hip.

'Keen for a coffee?' he asked.

I pulled the sheets tighter, hoping that bundling myself in the cotton might help me disappear. 'No thanks,' I said.

He propped himself up on his elbows and gazed at me curiously as if trying to place an actor he'd seen in an obscure movie.

'You did this last time,' he said. 'Begging for it in the moment and then turning ice-cold in the morning. Why don't you just sneak out before I wake up like a normal person?'

'I think I like to rub my nose in it,' I murmured.

'It's just sex. It's not a big deal.'

'Of course it is. This is fucked.'

'Says who? You guys aren't boyfriends.'

'We are, actually. We have been for the past few weeks.'

I could see that took him by surprise, but he seemed to maintain his defence with a deliberate scowl.

'I only sleep with you to get back at him,' I continued, more to myself than to him, the kiss I'd witnessed in Connections still raw in my memory. 'Or to hurt myself. It's both sadistic and masochistic.'

'I know,' he laughed. 'But I don't mind being used. Especially when the sex is so good.'

I despised that he was right, I despised that it was so good, better than what Ezra and I ever had. I would've argued it was only because of how abhorrent it was, how much was at stake if we were exposed, but the hard truth was that I'd finally met my match with Callum. We were twin flames or toxic fumes, reacting and burning everything around us.

I wanted to believe that I wasn't a monster, considering I had met Callum prior to Ezra, just another warm body whose soft sheets I'd folded into those first weeks I moved to Perth.

We'd exchanged our first names between kisses and fluids, and then we went our separate ways. I never thought of him again until we were down south for Marion's birthday and Sierra had mentioned his name and divulged their history. I thought to myself, *Perth can't be that small.* And yet after not much digging, I found a photo on Ezra's Instagram posted within the time frame of the relationship. There was nothing particularly romantic about the image, which I assumed was why Ezra had left it up, but it was proof enough. Still, I wanted Ezra, and he wanted me, and I decided it didn't matter if I'd slept with his ex once, all those weeks ago. We could laugh it off, jest at how painfully small the Perth pool of available gay men was.

I was so naive. I didn't foresee the contempt and mourning Ezra held for Callum, the vitriol toward anyone still associated with him, and I realised I'd lose him if he ever found out about our encounter. I was convinced Callum would dob me in when he and Ezra started talking after Sí Paradiso, but he stayed silent. That was one thing I appreciated about him. He could keep his mouth shut.

I promised myself I would never have sex with Callum again once Ezra and I had reconciled, but I lied to myself just as much as I lied to other people. Those platonic movie nights with Ezra had me tearing apart at the seams, such harsh reminders of everything we couldn't have. The distance was harrowing, his kindness was cruel, and I needed to feel alive, or I needed to die, just a little bit. I left Ezra's place in Nollamara and drove straight to Callum's. It wasn't right, and it wasn't fair, but it was the only power I had – power over my own body, to use and be used, to weaponise sex in petulant retaliation. After that last fuck, Callum and I had laid together in this very bed, both of us catching our breath and covered in sweat.

I'd stared up at the ceiling and said, 'This can't keep happening. It was different before, but now… even if I message you first… You have to say no. Don't respond. Fucking block me, even. Alright?'

Callum had looked at me and said, 'You really love him, don't you?' which caused me to break out into a violent sob. He'd elongated his body across the mattress and wrapped me in his large arms until I stopped shaking, his lips on the back of my neck, knuckles caressing my outline. Gentle, soothing motions.

'It's okay,' he whispered. 'I won't tell.'

I knew his comfort was manipulative. It had to be. He wasn't supposed to be capable of empathy. It didn't fit with the person I'd created in my head, the man I knew so much and somehow so little about: frankensteined from Ezra's memories, from my own brief encounters, from the things I wanted to be true and projected upon him. It made me hate Callum even more, this theft of my constructions, and it solidified the determination that he would never see me vulnerable or naked again.

Then last night happened. I lost control, or I never had control to begin with, always at the mercy of the people around me, suffering beneath the weight of their decisions. No, I had a choice, and I chose to be violent, to behave in that barbaric way. Ezra might've been maimed, brain damaged, rotting in a dark hospital while I was bundled up beside his ex. So evil, so *stupid*. There were cameras in nightclubs and I would be identified and charged if something serious had happened. I certainly deserved whatever punishment was coming my way. Meanwhile, Callum was unaffected, blind to those details and basking in the morning glow of a good root. He even looked pleased with himself that his allure was so tenacious, I would risk so much for him.

'Did you know we were at Connections?' I demanded to know. It was too well-timed, too much of a coincidence. It had to be intentional.

'Why? Do you think I followed you?' When I didn't answer immediately, Callum narrowed his eyes. 'That's definitely something Ezra would say.'

'Because you're a stalker? I saw you at The Court too, on his birthday—'

'Because he's a narcissist. I wasn't stalking anyone, *he's* the one that can't seem to leave me alone.'

I studied his face for the remnants of a lie. 'That's bullshit,' I said.

'Of course,' he smiled again. 'You've had him in your ear since you got to Perth.' He shifted in the sheets so they fell further down his hips, exposing more pale flesh and definitive hip bones.

My eyes peeled themselves away. 'So none of it's true? Everything he's said about you?'

'I thought you never wanted to talk about him with me.'

'Well, maybe we should.'

'What has he said?'

My jaw was set with contempt and I stared out across the bay.

'I know you're smart. Ezra told me as much,' he continued, aware that he wouldn't get much from me without some coaxing. 'Smart enough to know it's always more complicated than one person's take on things.'

'So you didn't break up with him out of nowhere? And wormed your way back in as soon as you saw us together?'

'You're as full of yourself as he is,' he breathed.

I glared at him and threw my legs over the side of the bed, scanning the floor for my clothes, but Callum reached over and held my wrist softly. I could've easily wrenched out of his grasp, but I didn't.

'Okay, okay,' he said. 'Fine. I was jealous of seeing you two together, but I never meant to ruin things.'

I let him pull me back until I was settled against the headboard, though I left a leg hanging out, ready to make a break for it if need be.

'Of course it was going to ruin things,' I said icily. 'He's never stopped loving you.'

'It's complicated, having that sort of history with some-one. We're all a bit fucking twisted.' Then he put on a performance of earnestness and said, 'I felt really bad when you guys stopped talking.'

'Right. And then you had to fuck him, just to fuck him over again. An absolute waste of time and energy.' I didn't know where else to direct my anger, and why I felt the need to defend Ezra was beyond me. He had hurt me first, and I had hurt him back – albeit ten times as hard. An emotional hurt versus a physical one. I wanted to believe those cuts were equal, that he deserved it, but there was no justification for that level of violence, even if Ezra had done it to Callum first. Cycles of abuse, the three of us trapped in that spinning wheel. When did it stop?

'It wasn't so calculated,' he said quietly.

'I don't believe you.'

'With Ezra, it's just… zero to one hundred. He expected it would all go back to the way it was. Trying again, picking up where we left off.' Callum shook his head. 'I didn't want that. I was very clear it was just sex.'

'People are fragile. It's cruel to manipulate their feelings for a physical reward.'

'As if you haven't done the same to him,' he said pointedly. 'Or to me.'

'You're not a reward, you're a punishment,' I threw at him, and he made a noise that might've been laughter, but it sounded too malignant.

I took a shallow breath through my nose. 'Ezra thinks we're very similar.'

'He would,' Callum said. 'We're everything he wants to be.'

'You think that highly of yourself?'

'We're intelligent, wealthy, charismatic… He wants to love us, even be us, and yet he has to inevitably push us away because we make him feel inferior. That's why he surrounds himself with the most average people.' Everything out of his mouth sounded over-rehearsed and phoney, an oiled-up politician.

'So what does that make me then? If I've been kept around for so long.'

'You're not average. You're like me, how I was at the beginning. Ezra can still use his age, or so-called "experience" to put you down. But he doesn't know shit about anything. He's as sheltered and immature as they come. It's almost reverse psychology – making *you* chase *him*, when it should be the other way around. You'll be unstoppable one day, and he'll hate you for it.'

'I'm not you, Callum,' I said, choosing at random which thread to pull, which accusation to rebut. 'Even after all the bullshit, I wanted to be there for him–'

'Such a martyr. How's that all working out for you? Feels good?'

'He has his downs, but it's under control. It doesn't define him.'

'Only because of the medication. You should've seen him without it. Insane highs and subterranean lows. It took me months to muster up the courage to end things, terrified of what he'd do to himself. How he'd punish me.' He tilted his head, words now dripping with disdain. 'You can't sit there and say that you know how bad it can get. You don't. You've only known him for a year. You hardly chipped the fucking iceberg.'

'He's not the guy you want him to be. He's not…' My nails dug into my palms, hard. 'He's a good person. And he deserved an explanation at the very least. You just left him, no closure, nothing–'

'Closure is bullshit. Closure is not caring anymore.'

'You bloody ruined him, you know that? I never had a chance. Spending a good part of a year trying to fix him and–'

'*Fix him?*' There was that bitter laugh again, more coarse this time. 'Oh my God. You just want to find someone to blame for your fucked relationship, don't you?'

'Yeah,' I seethed. 'And I blame you. Completely.'

'Blame yourself. And I'd bet good money that you actually made him *worse*, all on your own. Especially when he finds out about us.'

'Are you going to tell him?'

He pondered the answer, temptation lurking in his spiteful glare. At what point would I beg for his silence? Or perhaps I wanted Ezra to find out. It would certainly free me – there would be no reconciliation, nothing left to salvage after burning it all down, and there was something enticing about the idea. If I wasn't strong enough to walk away, I could leave it up to Callum, the arsonist.

My inhale was loud, no longer needing a definitive answer. 'I didn't mean for any of this to happen.'

'Then why are you in my bed right now? Where's Ezra?' His eyes were sharp and convincing. 'That wasn't me, Austin, that was all you. Don't pretend to be a fucking victim.'

I slid out of the bed before he could stop me, stooping down to fetch my underwear. I was determined to dress and leave as quickly as possible.

Callum continued, almost lazily, the rage rescinded. 'Some people are better off alone, you know? And I felt relieved when things ended. Like a weight was lifted.'

I found my pants with the stains on the knees and stepped into them. I buckled my belt and snatched up my socks.

'He begged me to stay. He said he would do anything. That's a lot of power to give someone. Surrendering so much of yourself… It's not romantic. It's pathetic.'

I couldn't find my jacket anywhere.

'But you and me? All that secrecy and tension… Did you ever consider that you chose wrong with Ezra? We would've been a better match.'

There it was, lying in a corner with my shoes.

'I took it a bit personally at first. I'll admit that. I should've stayed away, let you phase out on your own. But as it happened, you both just kept crawling back to me anyway.'

I was fully dressed at last and hovering by the door, which is where I said over my shoulder, 'You're a piece of shit.'

Callum's mouth twitched. 'He told me he'd be at The Court for his birthday. He still texts me all the time. Asks me how I'm going, if I'm seeing anyone, if I want to catch up for coffee. The most recent one was a few days ago. I can show you on my phone.'

I blinked at him in bewilderment. 'Why are you like this?'

He was expressionless. 'Why do you think? You say I ruined him… Well I wasn't so fucking cynical before Ezra. Relationships can wreck either person, regardless of who's the one to end it.' He scratched his crotch, masculine and blithe, as if we were in a locker room talking about the weather. 'I'm trying to save you from a lot of the effort and pain I had to endure. You can do a lot better than him, and you'll never be the person he settles down with. If being a slut wasn't enough of a strike against you, it would be your age, or the jealousy over finances, or the fact that nothing about you screams Perth…' He trailed off, shaking his head. 'Why did you bother trying?'

His blasé callousness should've twisted the knife, but by that point I was so defeated, I felt next to nothing.

'I thought the same thing about him. Why did he bother?'

He shrugged. 'You filled a void. The void I left.' It was

said so matter-of-factly, I doubted he'd intended to get a rise out of me. It was just the truth.

'I think I'm finally aware of that,' I nodded slowly.

'Was Ezra?'

My knees quivered under the weight of myself, struggling to maintain balance. I wanted to grip the door frame for support, but I was convinced the act would make me look weak. Instead, I wavered, woozy like a drunk. My knees locked and I steadied myself at last, picking Callum as the focal point. He played with the dark hairs on his navel, seemingly unbothered once again. I envied that level of emotional control. It was something I was desperate to replicate.

'I don't know,' I said. 'If he did… If he *knew*, and was just using me as a placeholder… then I was wrong about him.'

Callum sighed in a pitying, condescending way. 'When you get older, you'll realise most people are kind of… the fucking worst. They'll disappoint you every single time. You'll just stop trying.'

'I don't want to stop trying.'

'Yeah? What *do* you want, Austin?' He spread his legs wider under the sheets, so snide and effortless. It was an attempt to pull me back in, the curve of his thigh muscles and the outline of his cock fully visible. If I hated myself the slightest bit more, we might've had sex one last time for good measure, a fervent go of it, but I couldn't feel anymore hate. I was numb.

'I want to leave,' I decided.

I walked myself out. The house was a labyrinth, endless hallways of marble and concrete, but I'd performed this exit enough times to know the escape route – parallel to the dining room, left at the billiard room, and if I've hit the second kitchen, I've gone too far. I tried to imagine Ezra in these picture-perfect backdrops, sprawled by the infinity pool, pouring a bottle of Burgundy into a fragile glass, watching his Marvel films in the home theatre with his feet up on the coffee table. It didn't fit. He must've felt like it was a borrowed life.

Once I was out on the street I hooked a right and took the thin path alongside Callum's mansion that snaked down to the bay. He had a private dock with a modest speedboat anchored up. I assumed it was his family's, though I'd never seen anyone else during those few walks of shame except for staff; a maid here, a prep-chef there. The only stranger allowed in our family home was the weekly cleaner. Callum was on an entirely different plane of wealth than I ever was. I clung to the differences between us like a lifeline, however small or seemingly insignificant. I couldn't be him.

I reached the water's edge, kicked off my shoes, and walked straight into the bay fully clothed, which was already a pleasant temperature by this time of year. My first swim in months. I'd meant to undress at some point, but the simple act seemed too exhausting.

The black jacket billowed around me like an oil spill. Seaweed and jellyfish meandered past, taking little notice. I made it up to my chest, the water licking me clean. The water was cool, fresh as the promise of forgiveness, of being made anew. If only it could be so easy, but I knew I was beyond redemption. My choices were mine to live with, marked across my body and invisible to everyone but me. I closed my eyes and sank beneath the surface, reunited with silence. I could have stayed there forever.

30

Ezra and I sat across from each other at the Queen's. It felt poetic doing it here, close to a year since our first date – if we could even call it that. So much of us had existed in the grey areas, the halfway points, the *almosts* and *not quites*. We weren't at the same table, that would've been too pointed. We were in the beer garden under the large tree, other patrons seated far enough away to provide some privacy. Ezra was half an hour late, and I was already on my second pint by the time he sat down. It seemed clear to me he wouldn't be drinking, that this was going to be very brief, straight to the point. I was glad we were in public because I was half afraid of him shouting at me, spitting in my face, or punching me in the gut. It would've been uncharacteristic, but if my last encounter with Callum taught me anything, it was that there were many parts of him I never saw, or ignored for my own preservation.

He looked different somehow, harder, like he'd endured unspeakable things in the days following Halloween, which was also the last time we'd talked. I looked for a welt or a bandage on the back of his head, but I was relieved to find nothing to confirm he'd been wounded. Perhaps all those years avoiding school sports had left me with a weak throwing arm. I was glad. It could've been so much worse. I wondered if he might bring it up, or if he was waiting for me to confess, or if he knew it was me at all, but I decided the topic of Callum and my leaving was much more important.

'So,' I began quietly.

'So.'

'How are you?'

'I've had better weeks.'

It was painful. There was no way to determine how much he knew just by looking at him. *Out with it*, I thought.

'I'm going to go back to Melbourne for a bit.'

He nodded slowly. It seemed he was expecting as much.

'We've received an offer on Mum's house, and I need to be there to help my sister through the process.'

It was the truth, and a highly convenient one. Sabrina had called me two days prior and told me the news. For the first time in a while, the path forward was laid out for me, exit sign and all. She didn't need to convince me. I'd idled too long to renew the lease on the Mosman Park apartment, and the eviction date was drawing near. I had no more reasons to stay.

'I know it's quite abrupt.'

Ezra cleared his throat. 'When do you leave?'

'Next week.'

Cars flew by in rushes of rubber and metal. There was something peaceful about the sound of them gliding over the asphalt. Ezra used to point out the nice ones, back when he cared about things like impressing me.

'Right.'

His cold response should've made my insides curdle, but I was mostly unmoved. 'It's not forever. Or at least… it doesn't have to be. But I think it'll be good to get back to Melbourne, sort some things out–'

'I think that's for the best.' He met my eyes, though somehow indirectly, almost looking right through me. He placed his hands flat on the table. 'Pretty fucking cowardly of you though, having sex with Callum and gearing up to run away. Can't say it didn't sting a bit, but I also saw it coming a long time ago. That's just who you are, I think.'

I picked up my pint and took a long, measured sip before I responded. 'Who told you?'

'Matteo saw you guys leave together.'

Of course, I thought. Disappointing but not surprising.

'Great friend you have there,' I said. 'You know, he tried to get me to suck him off in exchange for–'

'It's actually impossible to believe anything that comes out of your mouth. I think that tends to happen when you've been lied to enough times.'

I blinked slowly and shifted my gaze away. 'I was going to tell you. Why do you think I asked you to meet me?'

But he was hardly listening. 'How long were you planning on doing this to me? Was it… Was it premeditated? Was it all a game from the beginning, figuring out how to hurt me, how to torture me?'

I said nothing.

He continued without missing a beat. 'It's scary how well you lie. I think you might be a high-functioning sociopath, or maybe you're just a very sad person that needs to screw over others to feel good about yourself. Honestly, I knew there was something wrong with you from early on, we all did. The whole *dead mum* thing should've been the clear sign to run – if that's even true – but I guess I justified it in my head because I was desperate to be wrong about you. There's a good chance that you *did* love me, in your sick sort of way, but… I'm not sure you know what love is supposed to be. You're too selfish to fully grasp the concept. And the craziest part is that I'm not even angry, or sad. Just sort of… exhausted.' He cleared his throat again and leaned back against the chair. 'I've already got too much going on in my life, and I can't deal with this too. With you.'

I remained frozen, statuesque in an apathy that had turned me to marble. I sat braving the elements, the pressure, refusing to crack.

'I guess it's a good thing I'm leaving then,' I said.

'I'm pretty relieved, yeah.'

'Fair enough.' I was doing so well, performing so level-headed, until I muttered, 'I suppose you didn't mean it when you said you loved me.'

'I suppose not.'

That immediately hurt to take in. I felt it percolating through my respiratory system, seeping into my bloodstream. I felt it dissolving in my gut. I reached for the beer again as medicine. I nearly downed the rest of the pint.

'And I don't think you loved me nearly as much as you wanted to,' he added.

I set the glass down. 'What do you mean by that?'

'I think you were desperate to love anyone. I don't think you really wanted me, particularly. You just didn't want to be alone.'

'And you? Wasn't I just filling the void?' I almost wanted to confront him further, lay out his own lies, the constant games he played with me, demand an admission that Callum had always been on the backburner, but how could I be sure any of it was true? It was easier to absorb the poison.

Ezra shook his head vehemently. 'I don't need anyone. I'm a full person. I can be alone.'

'Then prove it,' I said. 'Be alone.'

He looked disturbed by the challenge, and I wondered if he might cry or vomit, but then he glared at my almost-finished beer. 'What the fuck was it all for?'

I wasn't entirely certain I knew what he was referring to, but I said, 'I'm sure we have very different answers for that.'

'Yeah? What's yours?'

'I think...' I began slowly. 'I think I have the capacity to change. But maybe I needed someone to see the worst parts of me before I could outgrow them.'

'It's all so tidy for you. A bloody learning experience.'

'I have to look at it that way. Or I'll follow my mum.'

He flinched. Then his rage sobered as he chased down a memory. 'I wanted to kill myself. After Callum.'

Part of me already knew this. It was quietly folded within subtext and inferences, the things unsaid. 'But you didn't.'

'Because there's always more to life than a single feeling, even if that feeling is endless at the time.'

'Did you get that from somewhere?' I frowned.

'No. I made it up just now.'

'You're smarter than you give yourself credit for.'

He cocked his head. 'And you're too smart for your own good.'

'Not smart enough. Too many careless and selfish choices. Twenty-year-old stupidity.'

His tongue slipped out, wetted his lips, and retreated inside his mouth. 'You know, you manipulate your maturity when it suits you.'

'Is that so?'

'You hate being treated like a child but then you hide behind your age when you've done something wrong.'

I opened my mouth, ready with a retort, but instead a breathy sort of scoff emerged, making me sound disgruntled.

'You're a broken person,' he continued, perhaps thinking he'd struck a nerve. 'We both are, I suppose. In different ways.'

I could feel a tightening in my gut, an instinctive refusal of the idea. 'I'm not broken,' I said with some conviction.

'You are.' He was convinced he had me figured out. He'd always been this way, my passive superior, seeming to know everything without knowing anything at all.

'I think we have a choice in that, Ezra. You can choose to be like this forever, wallowing and feeling sorry for yourself, obsessed with the past, resenting the present, but I won't. I refuse to be this person.'

He pondered this. 'Maybe you have time… Being so young.' He was suddenly gentle in his delivery, the thought balancing on a precipice. 'But I think it's too late for me.' It always came back to this, his victimhood, his loss, forever his ball and chain. I realised there was nothing I could've done to free him of it.

'It kind of hurts my heart that you're still the same guy I met last year,' I said.

'I never tried to be anyone else. I can't say the same about you.'

'I only wanted to be someone you might love.'

He shook his head again, much softer this time, fatigue and misery weighing down every part of him, his sparkling eyes, the corners of his mouth, his strong shoulders, they all sagged in submission. 'What a waste,' he breathed.

'It wasn't a waste to me,' I said and knocked back the remainder of the beer. I rose to my feet, arms limp by my sides. 'Would you like anything from inside?' I asked, though I already knew the answer.

'No thank you,' he replied. He was lost in thought.

I nodded stiffly to excuse myself and sauntered to the bar. I could feel his eyes on the back of my neck, burning into me like a lit cigarette, and then nothing. Extinguished. My chest had the heavy feeling of crying but without any tears. I'd cried enough, and in its wake was a clarity, brutal in nature but definitive. There were no tendons still attached, no cells eager to regenerate. A clean cut. I ordered my third beer without sneaking a glance behind me. I knew he would be gone by the time I returned to the table.

31

I wasn't very good at goodbyes, but I endured them anyway. Between packing boxes and moving trucks were the brief sweaty embraces of Juliana, Alé, and Sierra, as we came together on the hottest day in recent memory, and any potential melancholia was set aside for the laborious effort of a smooth eviction. Sierra refrained from any heavy lifting, not wanting to ruin her manicure, but she certainly made up for it with bouts of encouragement and a steady stream of Powerade bottles.

I wouldn't miss the sweltering heat, but I would miss Perth, with its understated beauty and the cleansing nature of its oceans, and I'd miss this family, even if we weren't perfect, even if I'd given up precious time together for a love that was temporary – but Juliana and Sierra's greatest kindness was a refusal to pass anymore judgement. 'We've all been there,' Sierra reminded me. 'One way or another.'

Ray arrived later to provide another set of hands, and though we didn't hug or share any sentimentalities, he was outwardly pleased for me. Whatever guilt still lingered within him, he must've found peace in the knowledge I was reuniting with my sister in a way he never would.

It was all becoming all a bit too easy, this bandaid rip, and I began to feel a false sense of security, but when I expressed these feelings to Juliana, she just said, 'Maybe that means you're finally doing the right thing. It doesn't have to be met with resistance.' I liked that idea and we all knew as much.

Sierra had interrogated the move when we first met, Ezra had said I was more suited for Melbourne, Sabrina had coaxed me to admit it was all purgatory. I stuck it out anyway. I did my time. What those few more months achieved besides a bit of self-flagellation, I wasn't entirely certain of, but there was a stubbornness in me that had to see something to the end. I hated *what ifs*. It was better to know things, even if answers hurt.

My entire life in Perth consisted of three suitcases and two medium cardboard boxes. Inside one of them was the book Ezra had bought me for my birthday, which I had read in two days. The prose was harrowing and soul-crushing, yet I felt indifferent while leafing through it, and upon finishing, I tore out the note he'd written on the title page. It was easier that way, no reminders, no souvenirs.

I removed Ezra and his friends on every social media platform and deleted his number, just in case temptation struck somewhere: drunk in a bar and hearing a song we once danced to in his kitchen; overtaking a white Volkswagen on the highway; seeing Ezra's eyes in passing strangers. I needed to erase him completely.

When I touched down in Melbourne, his absence was jarring. While Perth screamed his name from every street corner, being back home had the opposite effect. The squeal of trams and the bite of cool air in the nighttime, black puffers adorned with AFL scarves, wine bars and bookshops, a sea of red brake lights at rush hour, leaving a nightclub on a Monday morning only to be christened by a brief spell of rain, the way the sun kissed the Yarra – none of these things were his. They were mine, indefinitely. I felt safe in the knowledge that Ezra would never leave Perth, and I would never go back.

The house was sold quite painlessly, and Sabrina and I

celebrated with dinner in a heritage-listed building in the city, fashioned with high ceilings, stained glass windows, and rich leather booths. We sat at a table set for three and popped a bottle of Veuve – Mum's favourite. We poured out a glass for her. It sat untouched throughout the meal, the bubbles slowly dissolving until the liquid could be mistaken for Riesling.

'I'm proud of you,' Sabrina said, which I thought was ridiculous because I hadn't done anything particularly brave or selfless, but I absorbed the praise regardless. How long was I supposed to punish myself?

There was no clear atonement for the choices I made in Perth except to make better ones moving forward. I was still the same person I was, just weighed down with experience and engulfed by that numbness I couldn't seem to chase away. I didn't expect the feeling to linger, or perhaps it was the absence of a feeling, impressed upon me, embedded into my soul. It was all unfinished pages and dead end streets – closure, the fool's errand. I was cold, distant, empty. That was the new Austin that took hold. It was easy to pretend this wasn't the case, hiding behind smiles and humour, doing all the things a now well-adjusted person would do: I made new friends, I went on dates, I behaved myself for the most part, even if I still partook in a few nights out, or woke up in someone else's sheets, but it felt less shameful, a difference in intention. Seeking pleasure instead of torture. Still, I felt adrift, caught between liminal spaces. The cut was clean, but it was a phantom limb – sometimes I could still feel something there, clinging on, leaving claw marks.

I would lie awake in my new apartment in South Yarra, moonlight seeping through the curtains, and picture Ezra in the shadowed corner of the room with that lasting expression etched into his face. Fury or disgust would've been easier to digest, but the exhaustion, the wretched despair, it haunted me. It made it impossible to ever fully move on.

*

I thought the engagement photo would procure a scowl, or sicken my stomach, or force me to flag down Sabrina and Juliana with the desire to spew animosity, but it didn't.

The girls were leaning against the rusted balcony, drinking their limoncello spritzes and flirting with a trio of Italian men, the Altare della Patria a blur in the distance. Ezra would be little more than a footnote to them now – and it was about eighteen months since I physically saw him last. I unpacked the timeline in silence, blinking sun from my eyes. Whoever the fiancé was, Ezra must've met him quite soon after me. There was some satisfaction in knowing he couldn't be alone, that it was all true. I had simply been filling a void. It made it less personal, which both softened the blow and reinforced my apathy.

Sabrina glanced at me around the head of one of the Italians and beckoned me over, but I held up a finger to indicate *one second*. I gazed down at the photo again, spine bent and legs hooked under the chair, examining Ezra's shallow cheeks and hollowed out eyes, his beautiful blonde hair now buzzed short. He looked older, drained somewhat, but happy? It was hard to perceive genuine joy in a single photo.

The fiancé was handsome at least, and after excavating his social media, I determined he was nothing like me; older, salt and peppered hair slicked back, a full beard. He was Perth born and raised, very non-scene. He worked in finance. He had two brothers and a dog. He listened to The Beatles. He went to ECU, graduated with a degree in business. He had a solid swing on the driving range. He was probably stable, easy-going, unchallenging – all the things I wasn't. Maybe Ezra finally let go of his obsession with replacing Callum.

Maybe I was only an abyss to hurl his pain into, and once I was gone, so was his grief, his anger, his bitterness, like a curse passed on. *I needed someone to see the worst parts of me before I could outgrow them.* Maybe it was true for him too.

I thought of Ezra often throughout the trip, considering I'd stolen his dream itinerary. It wasn't intended to be petty, but upon reflection, it was quite pointed, almost taunting him with all the things I could (and would) do without him in my life. The girls never knew, all too happy to relinquish control of planning the route. My socials were public and sometimes I hoped he kept tabs on me, or at least stumbled upon the regularly posted adventures that began in Paris, where Juliana met up with Sabrina and I, before we passed through Amsterdam, and then Dubrovnik, and then it was on a rooftop in Trastevere, west of the River Tiber that the engagement photo appeared on my feed, reposted by Nadia who I'd forgotten to unfriend on Facebook. It was one of those rare glimpses into his new yet same-as-always life. Perhaps this was his revenge; I went to Europe, and he got engaged. Chess moves. I liked the idea of it, that we were still communicating after all this time, just in a new language, each choice we made in our lives another grasp at power, an attempt to shift status on its axis. The game that never ended. It was a deluded thought, but what was the alternative? Hatred? I was incapable of hating him – even though I wanted to, certainly it would be easier – but I couldn't, and I wasn't sure if that meant he'd won and I'd lost, or if there were no winners and losers in goodbyes, just the scar tissue to remind us something was there once, until we tore it from ourselves.

The Italians laughed at something Juliana said, and Sabrina and I made eye contact again. I sat up straighter and mirrored her empathetic smile, eager for an excuse to drag my eyes from the possibilities that now belonged to someone else. There was a sudden break in the numbness as I looked up – brief, but startling – the feeling of breathing without weight, without guilt. The feeling of letting go. Even though it was fleeting, its efficacy was enough to leave me with the knowledge it would one day be enduring.

I locked my phone, Ezra was put away, and I rose to meet the sunshine.

ACKNOWLEDGMENTS

There are so many people to thank for bringing this book to life, but no one more than my incredible editor Cushla Scanlan. Your friendship, your dedication, your creativity, and your belief in me has made this very daunting process manageable. Thank you for elevating *Delicate Friends* to its full potential with joy and humour every step of the way. I'm in awe of the delicacy and intelligence you approach creative work and the love you bestow upon every page, every paragraph, and every sentence. I feel so lucky to have caught you at the beginning of what I know is soon to be a very successful career.

Thank you to Izzy Greenslade who hand-painted the gorgeous cover image. Your talent never ceases to take my breath away, and I am so blessed by your contributions to this work, and the contributions to my life. Since the day we met, I'd have jumped at the chance to work with you in any capacity. This felt like simply the right place at the right time.

Thank you to everyone who took the time to read various drafts of *Delicate Friends*, especially those who suffered through those first iterations: Alexis, one of my longest and most cherished friendships, and whose praise and investment in this story fueled me with the drive to keep at it even when I was ready to throw in the towel; my auntie Sarah Hay, who inspires me and reminds me that writing is in our DNA; and my beta readers, Brett, Fleurette, and Alice, who I adore so much, and have all supported and cheered me on through various stages of personal and creative growth.

Thank you to my incredible proofreaders and literary soulmates: Hannah, you've become the first person I'll ask to read my writing because you understand me at such a deeply personal level, and this allows you to somehow extract the perfect note that makes everything click; Francesca, we are so similar in surprising ways, and I feel myself becoming a kinder and more grounded human the longer we spend in each other's company; and Persia, your brilliance is unmatched, and I will forever be looking to you for new things to learn. Thank you to the multi-talented Zoe for teaching me typesetting and mocking up book covers with me, and to the exuberant Josh, Max and Emma for always gassing me up and making me laugh. Our little Melbourne family is one of the brightest lights in my life, and I truly never felt more connected to my identity as a writer until I met you guys.

Thank you to my sister Serena, who knows me better than I know myself at times, and whose unwavering love empowers me and reminds me what's important in this life. When adulthood came knocking, you always did your best to let me be a little kid for that while longer. I can't imagine who I would be without you.

Thank you to my mother Lisa, who nurtured that creative child clad in *Snow White* dresses and endeavoured him to dream big and write more. We have the most sacred bond that I will be forever grateful for, and I couldn't be more proud of all the ways I take after you.

Thank you to my father Rick, who taught me the importance of work ethic between games of scrabble, and who always makes me feel loved despite the global distance between us, and to my stepmother Danielle for her infectious humour and unending support. I miss you both dearly.

Thank you to my cousin Briana for being my rock my first year in Perth, and for all our late nights looking out on the Swan River from that highrise on Adelaide Terrace. This book is, in a lot of ways, an ode to us, and to the many conversations we had about self-worth, belonging, and family.

I also want to thank everyone else I met in Perth, the friends I still keep in touch with, and the ones I haven't spoken to in a long time, because every interaction and every memory contributed to this piece in some way. It was a very formative and challenging two(ish) years, but also beautiful and rewarding. I grew up and grew down, fell in love and made mistakes, got my heart broken, travelled, and rediscovered my love for writing. I am so lucky I have a second home in Perth, a place that will always have a piece of my heart. I wish Austin could've had another chance at happiness there as I did, but resisting the urge to intertwine him and myself even more than we already are, I opted to let his path take him elsewhere.

Finally, thank you, reader. I hope you enjoyed this novel. Thank you for supporting me by buying and reading it, and I hope this is only the beginning of more to come. Self-publishing was a choice that wasn't made lightly, but I felt confident in myself and my extremely small team to capture something that would resonate with my community, whether that was young people, queer Australians, or even Perthians. Our stories expand in reach and nuance every year, and I am grateful to be just one of them. Please tell your friends and spread the word about *Delicate Friends*. It's something I am very proud of.

ABOUT THE AUTHOR

Oscar Revelins studied theatre, film, and television at the University of California, Los Angeles before pivoting to English Literature and graduating with a Bachelor of Arts at the University of Western Australia. He was born in Melbourne, spent nine years in Los Angeles, and then two in Perth, before settling back in Melbourne where he currently resides. This is his first novel.